A Common Thread

by

Iona Morrison

A Common Thread

Cover Art by *Debbie Taylor*

The Wild Rose Press, Inc.
PO Box 708
Adams Basin, NY 14410-0708
Visit us at www.thewildrosepress.com

Publishing History
First Edition, 2023
Trade Paperback ISBN 978-1-5092-5114-8
Digital ISBN 978-1-5092-5115-5

Published in the United States of America

The drums seemed far away at first but grew louder as she walked the path through the woods. Sacred chants filled the night air while the shadows of dancers moved with precision along the edge of the forest, pulling her deeper into the woods. Each song and dance seemed unique to the sound of the drums in the background. Suddenly the drumming built in intensity, the chants grew in volume, and the dancers became too numerous to count. She was mesmerized by their unexpected beauty. On they danced as the bells on their moccasins jingled, and they twirled and swayed rhythmically in step with the drumbeats. They circled around her, leading her through the maze of trees until suddenly they halted. An eerie silence filled the night as they parted enough for her to see. Hidden among the trees lay a lone figure on the ground. Facedown in the dirt, her dark black hair fanned out over her back and shoulders, but the beautiful hair didn't hide the stillness of her body.

Praise for Iona Morrison

Key to the Past. "It's a winner! Wow! Suspense to the end! I loved every word." Della Hull

Magic and Midnight Bars. "Christmas is a time for magic. If you love Christmas magic, friendships, and chocolate, this is the book for you..." Theodocia McLean

"This is another winner from Iona Morrison. It's a must read for all Blue Cove fans. A real page turner." Ruby Hill (*Beyond The Door*)

"Ms. Morrison transports you to Blue Cove and tells a story that will linger in your mind for a long time." ReNae Bowman (*The Harvest Club*)

"If you are looking for a good page turner, look no farther than Iona Morrison's Blue Cove Mystery series. Her characters have become like family to me. I was an instant fan after the first one and am anxiously awaiting the next!" Vickie Atencio

Dedication

Dedicated to the memory of K-9 Officer Radar an amazing, tracking bloodhound. Winner of the AKC Award for Caine Excellence (ACE), The American Bloodhound Club Meritorious Service Award, and Elizabeth Police Department's Safety Award. During his life of service, he located the lost, helped to solve at least twenty-four murder cases, and countless cold cases bringing closure to many families. He tracked hundreds of hours over hundreds of miles in all kinds of weather. He suffered the pain and trauma of those findings along with his human partner Frank Hurst. His loss is profoundly felt. Radar was a bighearted hero who wore a collar instead of a cape. May he rest in the peace of a job well done as his watch is now over.

Chapter One

The ringing bell above the door had barely alerted Jessie to a customer when the dark-haired woman pushed past her in a blur almost knocking her to the ground. The books Jessie carried in her arms didn't fare as well. They scattered in several directions as she steadied herself against the display table. They hit the ground with intermittent thuds, and she could only hope they weren't ruined. No one wanted to buy a new book with a scratched cover or bent edges. Between book-throwing ghosts and rude customers, her books were taking a beating. She took a deep breath and stooped to pick them up.

"Oh, I'm so sorry." The pretty woman stifled a sob as she bent to help Jessie clean up the mess she had caused but bumped heads with her instead.

"Ouch." Jessie winced and shot up rubbing her forehead.

"I can't seem to do anything right this morning," the woman muttered. "Are you okay?" She massaged the spot where their heads hit.

"I'll live," Jessie said as she reached for the woman's hand. "How about you?" Jessie glanced at her, taking in her disheveled appearance.

"Overwhelmed," she whispered swiping at the tears threatening to spill from eyes. The woman ran her fingers like a comb through her tousled hair.

Jessie placed the stack of books on the table. "I'll put these away later. Please, let's sit. You look like you need to talk." She handed her a tissue and led the weeping woman to a chair carrying the box.

"I don't know where to begin." The woman wrung her hands in her lap while her foot shook beneath the chair.

"Take your time," Jessie told her. The woman's rumpled and mismatched clothes indicated she had run out of the house in a hurry. Jessie was sure the whole look was not the norm for the attractive woman.

"Is this your store? the woman asked with a sniff.

"Yes." Jessie's eyes brightened as she glanced with pride around her store. "I'm Jessie Reynolds." She waited for the woman to continue as the silence filled the space between them.

"You're younger than I expected." She wiped her nose and shifted in the chair. "I'm not usually this rude or sloppy." The woman gestured at her mix-matched outfit. "I was in such a hurry to get here and then I practically run you over the minute I came in the door. I didn't even tell you my name. My only excuse is that I'm not thinking clearly." She sighed. "Let me begin again. My name is Marilyn Barton. I guess it's better to be late to introduce myself than not at all," she said.

"Niceties need not apply when one is feeling overwhelmed." Jessie smiled at her, not sure what to do next. "How can I help?"

"My friend told me that she read one of your articles in the paper. She thought I needed to come and talk to you." Marilyn took a deep breath. "I hope you can advise me. It's about my daughter." She broke down again.

Jessie handed her another tissue. "I might know someone who can talk to her, but I don't have any children or experience raising them. I'm not sure how much help I'd be."

"You might be the only one who can. My friend shared with me how you once had a stalker as a young girl. Is that right?"

"Yes, I did. A scary time and one I needed professional help to move past." Jessie shook her head as the recollection of Stuart Adler's face rushed into her mind. Spinning a knife in his hands, he had threatened to carve his initials on her cheek. Not one of her best memories.

"He came here once, didn't he? At least that's what my friend said she read."

"Yes, but he's in prison now, thankfully." Jessie told her the story about babysitting for his girls, a restraining order that didn't keep him away, and his thwarted attack on her at school. "He went to prison and blamed his obsession on me, though other girls also testified against him. His anger towards me festered while serving time. When he got out, he searched for me." The memory sent fresh shivers scurrying down her back. "During a confrontation right over there"— Jessie pointed at the church— "I shot the knife out of Stuart's hand. But it was Billy Sullivan, one of the local boys, that was the true hero. He hit him with a rock from his slingshot and knocked him out cold." Jessie leaned forward in the chair. "Billy saved my life."

"I want my daughter to meet you. Maybe you could tell her about your run-in with that Adler fellow. If she won't tell you what's going on I don't know what I'm going to do. I hope she'll be able to open up to someone. I'm worried sick about her."

"I'd be happy to meet her. Although, I'm not sure she'll want to talk to me."

"Please. You're my last hope. She stays in her room as much as she can. Her grades are slipping, and my once happy girl is gone. Even her one passion she lived and breathed for doesn't seem to ignite interest in her. There's nothing I can point to, but I know my daughter, and something is wrong and she's not talking." Marilyn stood. "I've taken up enough of your time and made a mess to boot. If you don't mind, I will bring her by after school before she has practice tonight. Her name is Sofia." She sniffled when she said her name. "We've always been close, but she won't talk to me. I hope she'll talk to you." She grabbed another tissue out of the box.

"I hope she will also." Jessie followed the concerned mother to the door. "Try not to worry too much." She patted Marilyn's shoulder as she walked past her.

"Stupid thing to say, Jess," she scolded herself. Of course, the woman would be worried. With teen girls, the trouble could be as simple as a breakup with a boy or as serious as someone bullying her, or worse. In her heart Jessie knew this one was serious and at some point Matt would be involved.

She grabbed the stack of books and walked toward the display table and window. After checking for damaged covers or jackets she placed each book artfully in its place. A few would have to be marked down.

Jessie wished Peyton were here, but she would be flying solo on this venture, at least for a few days. After

Jaxon and Peyton got back from their weekend in Arizona, her cousin had a message from the doctor working with her parents. He requested the sisters come at this time. He claimed it was a necessary next step for her parents' rehab and he also thought the sessions would be beneficial for the sisters too. Mr. Avery, the principal, gave Peyton the time off since the school was still closed for repairs after the shooting a few weeks before. The kids were meeting in another elementary school across town. Grams said the way things worked out, it was meant to be. Peyton, bless her heart, went reluctantly but smiling as she kissed Grams Sadie goodbye.

Her cousin privately told her she didn't want to see her dad, but she would go for Sadie's sake. Jessie couldn't blame her. The Reynolds brothers were not the easiest men to deal with. Both were strong and domineering men who always got the last word. But Peyton knew she needed to get this past her if she wanted to take her relationship with Jaxon to the next level, something Jessie often thought about herself with Matt.

While she loved her hunky cop, she wasn't sure if she was ready for marriage. Jessie held the beautiful diamond on her finger up to the light. The man could push all the right buttons. She sighed. Matt might be a bit on the overprotective side, but boy could he kiss. She'd gone weak in the knees more than once and left fanning her face. But marriage seemed to be a big decision and one she side-stepped every time he asked to set a date. She waffled between go for it and wait. Assurance was what she needed.

Her best friend Katie seemed happy enough and a

good advertisement for wedded bliss. But Jessie's parents weren't the best example of a happy marriage. They got on but something was missing. She had grown up with her dad controlling both her and her mother, and his word was final. To him, love was providing the necessities and he was good at that. She couldn't remember there being a romantic bone in his body. He never gave her mother flowers or special gifts. There were no romantic gestures, special looks, or acts of tenderness. But she did remember plenty of lectures and an occasional pat on the head for a job well done.

Thankfully, Matt was the opposite in that regard. Well maybe not in the lecture department but a true romantic. She would never forget when Matt chartered the private jet surprising her with a special date to San Diego. All because he wanted her to see the Pacific Ocean at sunset. They were in Palm Springs working a case at the time. What a man. A chauffeur-driven tour of the city, a romantic dinner, and a view of the sunset that was breathtaking were a part of their special evening. At that moment, she realized for the first time that she could fall in love with him, and she did.

The thought of marriage made her nervous, but no way did she want to lose him. At the moment, a wedding date was too much to think about with a new situation brewing. For now, she would be content to hang out for those wonderful kisses for as long as she could. He didn't seem to mind. And she didn't want to become one of those married women who whined about how quickly after marriage the romance fizzled, and the diapers began.

What she wanted was a guarantee that their love would last. She knew she would never get one, but it didn't stop her from dreaming. Her mother often called her a hopeless romantic which was her nice way of saying she was an opinionated idealist. But she liked to think of herself as a strong and independent woman with of touch of starry-eyed optimism thrown in. She smiled. She could do stubborn better than anyone she knew. Her willfulness was one of her many flaws that at times could be one of her strongest qualities. Being persistent and tenacious had often worked well and paid off for her, while being unbending had garnered her a few naughty chairs too.

Jessie busied herself as she watched the clock and the door for Sofia's arrival. At four the girl dragged in behind her mother. Sofia had dark hair pulled back into a ponytail which made her seem younger than her sixteen years. Maybe a more accurate description was vulnerable. Jessie made mental notes as she studied the girl. Her milk chocolatey brown eyes suited her pretty face and her olive complexion perfectly. But neither could compensate for the dark smudges under her eyes. This should be a happy time in her life, but her sullen expression told Jessie that happiness didn't play into her feelings at the moment.

"Sofia, this is Jessie. I'm going to leave you to talk to her," her mother told her.

"Why?" she asked. "I don't want to talk to her," she said, her tone cutting, "or anyone else. I wish you would leave me alone." She glared at her mother and pressed her lips.

What had she gotten herself into? Jessie knew the look all too well. She had utilized the same pouty, obstinate glare enough over the years.

"You won't talk to me; heaven knows I've tried.

7

But Sofia, you have to talk to someone before you explode. She'll understand. I know you don't want me around, but I'll be next door if you need me." Marilyn walked into the coffee shop.

"I won't," she called after her mom belligerently. "I don't know why she dragged me here." Sofia plopped down in a chair. "Have at it." She folded her arms across her chest.

"She's worried about you and is willing to reach out to a stranger to get you help. I would call that love." Jessie sat across from her. "That's what mothers do."

"I know." Her voice softened a tiny bit. "It's just that I don't know how to tell her. I don't want to tell anyone." With anger, she swiped at the single tear rolling down her cheek. "I hate this."

"Maybe I can help." Jessie told her the story about what happened in high school to her. "I found it hard to talk to my parents. I thought they would think what happened was my fault."

"How did you tell them?" Sofia asked sitting up straighter in the chair.

"When I begged my mom not to make me babysit his girls anymore, she asked me why. The whole story flew out of me. You can tell me what's going on, Sofia. I'm a safe place. I won't say anything to your mom unless you tell me I can." She handed Sofia a tissue as more tears filled her eyes right before the dam broke.

Once Sofia started talking, she couldn't stop all the pain stored inside of her from gushing out. Matt would need to be included in this conversation. There had to be more people involved in what happened to Sofia. Someone enabled the person or at the very least, did nothing to stop the perpetrator and helped to cover up his actions.

"Can I tell your mom?" Jessie asked her.

"Yes, but not when I'm around. Please," she begged. "I'm ashamed. It eats at me day and night."

Jessie reached for her hand. "Sofia, look at me. Remember—you didn't deserve this. It's liable to get tough over the next few months."

"It already is. There are more of us."

When her mother came back into the bookstore, Sofia told her she could talk to Jessie tomorrow. Marilyn grabbed Jessie's hand on her way out of the store mouthing the words thank you.

While going over everything Sofia had told her, the anger rose inside her. That's when Jessie noticed the young ghost observing her from outside the store. There seemed to be more to the story than even Sofia understood. The two were connected, she was sure.

Jessie went to her computer intending to search a thought that had captured her when Sofia was talking. She ended up answering her ringing phone instead. "Hey, Peyton." Jessie sat down in the nearest chair. "I was thinking about you and wishing you were here." Jessie blurted out what Sofia shared with her before she could stop herself. The abuse was something that Peyton could relate to.

"Wow. You must notify the authorities right away. In the case of a minor, there is no wiggle room. It's the law. They drummed that into my head at college and when I signed my contract at the school. I only wish I would have told a teacher or anyone when I was a kid."

"I knew you would say that. I planned on calling Matt." Jessie waved to a customer walking in the door. "When will you be home? I could use your help with this situation."

"I'll be home in a few days. Remember, I told you that you would be taking the lead on the next one. I'll cover your back, and until I'm home you can call me anytime." Peyton chuckled. "I'm going to enjoy the reprieve. Hang up and call Matt."

"Dang." Jessie heard the phone click off before she had a chance to say something smart back at her. Instead, she wrote a text to Matt asking him to call her when he had a few minutes to talk.

****

"Hey, sweetheart. I always have time for you. What's up?" Matt waved at Dylan walking past his open door.

"I heard something that you need to know about." Jessie told him about the conversation with Sofia and her mother. "I don't have a phone number or address for them, and I didn't think to ask. The mother is supposed to come back to see me tomorrow to talk. Peyton told me that I needed to tell the authorities right away. That's why I called you."

"I'll notify social services and the proper channels. You did the right thing. Assault crimes have to be reported immediately when it comes to minors. It's one more way to protect children and get criminals off the streets."

"You need to know—her parents aren't involved. They are worried about her," Jessie told him.

"I understand, but there're agencies that must get involved and investigate. With that settled, what aren't you telling me?" he asked.

"Do you mean about the ghost I saw? That probably means someone died, and the fact she showed up right after Sofia Barton left, I'm thinking the two are connected somehow. I'll tell you how when I know."

"Music to my ear. Not about the ghost but us collaborating again." He leaned back in his chair. "How about dinner and a movie tonight?"

"Sounds perfect. I'll cook, and we can watch a movie at my place," she suggested.

"Good idea. I'm fresh out of ideas of where to eat. They all taste the same after a while."

"How's it working with Jaxon staying at your place?" she asked.

"Fine. We get on. By the time Jaxon gets back to the house it's usually late. It works well for both of us. He misses Peyton this week though." Matt tilted back in his chair.

"She misses him too, but she'll be home soon. How's his house coming along?"

"It's almost done. Maybe another month is all. It'll go fast from this point. He has more people working on the place, although he wants me to do the built-in pieces and finish work. We'll work on that together. Therapy, sweet therapy, and you are too, of course."

"I remember that detail about you. You're good with your hands." She sighed. "In more ways than one."

"Why thank you very kindly, ma'am. I aim to please." He chuckled.

"Hey, I need to go. Ms. Barton just rushed through the door crying. I'll call you when I know more."

"Okay, I'll wait to hear from you." Matt turned his chair around to look out the window at the park. The days were getting longer. He was happy for more daylight. Jotting down notes from what Jessie had told him, he waited for her call. The fact that the girl's mother sought her out told him this wouldn't be an ordinary case. Add a ghost showing up a few minutes later and it kicked it up another notch. He raked his hand through his hair. Yeah, something was up. He wasn't sure how he felt about another unusual case, but he was damn glad that Jessie would be working this investigation with him.

Matt called the heads of the two agencies that needed to be notified. He also called Jaxon to check and see if the FBI had any criminal complaints against the organization that Jess told him about. Jaxon promised to call him back.

Next he made a quick call to Gary, his tech guy, and to Jeremy, Jessie's friend from New York, and got them involved in researching the background of the family and the business partners involved. He could count on them to deliver.

What was taking her so long to call back? The bookstore should be closed by now. He glanced at the clock on the wall ticking away the seconds. He tapped his pencil in rhythm with the sound. Matt's gut told him another piece was about to be added to the story. Maybe he should go to her store. He stood and reached for his jacket when Jessie came rushing through his office door.

"She's missing." Jessie rushed into his arms. "Her mother went to pick her up after practice and she was gone. No one seemed to know what had happened to Sofia. I brought Ms. Barton to talk to you. She's waiting in the hall. Is this a good time?"

"Yes. Get her." Matt loosened his hold on her. He hung his jacket back up on the hook.

"Matt, this is Marilyn Barton." The woman

followed Jessie into his office.

"Please be seated." He pushed a box of tissues toward Jessie. "You may begin when you're ready."

Ms. Barton told him about her daughter, a once thriving, happy teen who had become sullen and withdrawn the past several months. Jessie filled in what she knew from what Sofia had told her.

"She wouldn't tell me or her mother who was responsible, but she did say some of the other girls had experienced the same thing and worse."

"With no name, we have no idea who to target. We might need to interview the girls." Matt frowned.

"I wonder if they were threatened not to talk.

"Is that what happened to you?" Marilyn glanced at Jessie.

Jessie nodded. "Yes, he threatened me. I was too afraid to say anything. It took me a while to talk openly with my parents about it. I was too embarrassed and scared."

"Mrs. Barton, do you think Sofia would run away, or are you concerned she was kidnapped?" Matt asked.

"I have no idea." She stifled a sob. "I didn't encourage her to talk. I was too busy lecturing her." She shifted in her chair uncomfortably. "If only I would've paid attention to her."

"Please think over your conversations of the last several days. Did Sofia say anything that you can remember that stands out? Take your time." Out of the corner of his eye he watched Jessie reach across and squeeze Marilyn's hand for encouragement.

"Sofia didn't want to go to practice for several weeks. I told her she had to because her father worked overtime for her to have a chance at her dream, and she was being selfish. I'm not proud of what I said. If only I had stopped to hear what she was saying. She tried to tell me several times. My response was always about the money we had invested and not about her welfare. I never just listened!" Marilyn broke down and cried inconsolably.

"When did she start fighting you about going to practice?"

"She sprained her ankle on a balance beam landing and the coach and team doctor both said she needed physical therapy to rehab it. After a few more sessions, she didn't want to go anymore. I thought she didn't want to work through the pain which didn't make sense because she always had before."

"Is there anything else that stands out to you?" Matt studied her as she responded. She took a deep breath. "Something was different this time. A few months ago, Sofia moved up to the senior division, which meant a new coach and a team doctor." She wiped the tears running down her cheek. "She shared with Ms. Reynolds that someone had been touching her inappropriately, but she wouldn't say who. Just the thought of her being put through this makes me sad and angry at the same time. Who would do this?" She blew her nose.

"That's what we are going to try and find out," Matt promised her.

"He will too." Jessie nodded at him.

"I want you to understand, Sofia is a good girl. We have our arguments—she's a teenager after all. But we never argued about training and her love for the sport until recently. She enjoyed practicing with her teammates and going to meets until her injury. Sofia didn't tell me, or I would have been in that coach's face in a minute, and I would've pulled her from the program no questions asked."

"I believe you." Matt nodded. "Mrs. Barton, I want you to fill out this missing person report." He handed her the papers. "A recent photo would be helpful if you have one. We must get this information out there as soon as possible."

"Will this work?" She pulled up a picture on her phone.

"Perfect. You can send the photo to this email address, and I'll print a copy." He handed her his email address.

"What should I do next?" she asked dabbing at her nose with a tissue.

"When you're finished, I want you to go home and wait to hear from Sofia. Maybe she will try to contact you in some way. In the meantime, I will pay a visit to the training center and see what I can find out," Matt told her. "If she gets in touch or you can think of anything else that would be helpful, call me right away. Here's my number." Matt handed her his card. "Because of her age, social services will be in contact with you. Tell them what you've told me. I will inform them that we have opened an investigation on our end."

"I don't know what to do." Tears filled her eyes as she cried softly. "My husband is on his way home. He's angry and I don't know what to tell him. I'm afraid of what he might do."

"All you can both do at this point is sit tight and wait. Have him call me. Any father would feel the same way. I've already got someone checking into the business to see if there are any complaints lodged against the company or the owners. I'd be happy to tell him what we're doing to find her."

"Thank you." She took out her pen and began to fill out the report with the pertinent information.

"When you're finished you can leave the papers on my desk. I'm going to get a copy of this photo printed and forward it on the wire." Matt left his office and headed down the hall to the printer to make a copy. He took the photo to dispatch and stopped to talk to Kip and Dylan on his way back to his office.

When he walked in the door again Jessie sat alone staring out the window. He touched her shoulder. "Are you okay?"

"Yes," she said softly.

"Was Mrs. Barton all right when she left?" Matt asked.

"Not really. As you can imagine she's blaming herself. I walked her to her car. I think she is remembering conversations."

"She needs to sort through her thoughts. That's the only way she can accept what's happening." He stood beside her chair.

"We all go glibly through life not listening to someone's cries for help. It's hard to think that the people you've entrusted your child to could be endangering them. I guess it's easier to pretend that the child is exaggerating. Someday I hope we will start listening to the kids. Adults aren't always good people." Jessie covered her face with her hands.

"No, they're not. Did people always listen to you?" He leaned closer to hear her soft voice.

"No, they didn't. Stuart Adler got away with a lot before he got caught." She shuddered.

"Sometimes the system fails. I'm sorry, sweetheart." Matt massaged her tight shoulders.

"He's behind bars again. But this does stir up some bad memories." She reached for his hand on her shoulder. "I'm glad you believed me."

"Seems to me you took care of him yourself and I got there at the end." Matt clasped her hand.

"I'm a different person now." She smiled squeezing his hand.

"Yes, you are. What does your gut tell you, Jess, about this? Give me something to work with, sweetheart." He leaned his hip against the desk. "Don't hold anything back if you get something."

"Sofia is alive. I'm not sure why she is missing, but I don't believe she's in danger at the moment. She may be protecting herself. I gave her my phone number earlier. I hope she will contact me at some point when she feels that she can."

"We can't do much more tonight. How about a change of plans. Scratch the quiet dinner at your house but we can still watch a movie. I want to drive by the business and look around. We can grab a bite to eat when we're finished."

"Sounds good." Jessie stood and Matt helped her slip into her jacket.

They walked out of the station hand in hand lost in their thoughts. He pulled her tight against his side when he felt her shiver. "I like you here best of all. Are you warm enough?" he asked opening the car door.

She nodded. "I like being here too." She turned her face for the kiss that was coming.

Chapter Two

Matt lingered at the door not wanting to say goodbye to her. "Did you enjoy dinner?" He nuzzled her neck.

"Uh-huh," she said taking a breath.

"Did you like the movie?" He kissed her whispering the questions into her lips.

"Not as much as this." Jessie found herself pressed up against the door.

"My sentiment exactly. I'm glad you agree," he said before he took control of her mouth another time. Coming up for air he pushed away reluctantly from her. "You know, sweetheart, it's getting harder for me to leave."

She tugged his head down one more time and kissed him. "I know."

He pulled away. "I love you, Jess. Get some rest. I can't have my girl with dark smudges under her eyes. I'll be doing interviews tomorrow. I want to find out if there are any other victims besides Sofia."

"I'm sure there are, and the more I think about my conversation with her I'm convinced we will uncover more than we bargained for."

"I don't like the sound of that." He hugged her resting his chin on the top of her head. "But I do like you and if that's your view of things then I'm listening." The blast of chilly night air hit him when he opened the door. "See you tomorrow. Keep me posted." He went out and turned back around. "I'm glad you're on this. You have a way of making me look good." He smiled and saluted her as he strode to his car. Man, did he hate leaving every night. He had better convince her this arrangement wasn't working for either of them. Time to pull out the old charm campaign again.

****

"You've got that right, Mr. Parker. I do make you look good," she whispered. "Although, from where I'm standing you look pretty good on your own." Jessie watched him until she couldn't see him anymore. Closing the door, she locked the deadbolt. Matt had made sure the lock was added during the remodel. The man couldn't help himself; he needed to look after her. She loved the feeling and wanted to let him protect her and at the same time, she fought it. There must be a name for a person like her who couldn't make up her mind. Was it possible she could live both ways— cherished and protected—while being strong and independent? Something to think about.

Jessie went to her computer to send an email to Jeremy, her research buddy from her newspaper days. She wanted his help with a background check on the business and its owners. Sofia had shared enough with her to know there was something not kosher with the coach, trainer, and possibly another man. Sofia had danced around the subject, trying hard not to tell Jessie who the people were, but she could read between the lines. Sofia's facial expressions gave away her feelings when she talked about them. They were all guilty, including the owners on some level if they knew what was going on and didn't protect the girls.

Sofia had also revealed that the older girls on the team had suffered more. Crimes could be hidden easier with the girls eighteen or older, setting up the old deep-rooted bias of a he said, she said defense. Jessie could only imagine the threats the girls might have experienced. Her mind raced on. Finding out who the ghost was and how she died would be paramount in their investigation. Something told her that whoever the girl was, she was only the tip of the iceberg.

Jessie closed her computer, shut off the lights, and walked into her room. Happy to finally snuggle beneath the inviting warmth of the blankets, she glanced at the clock. She sent a quick text to Matt telling him goodnight. She read his return message, smiled, and turned off the bedside lamp and rolled onto her side. Comfy and warm she shut her eyes thinking about Matt but soon her thoughts drifted to the ghost that had stood outside her store. Ghosts weren't new to her but there was something that caught her heart with this one. Helpless and sad came to mind. Jessie wished she knew what her appearance had to do with Sofia Barton. "If only the ghost could talk." Sighing she burrowed under her covers and fell asleep.

The drums seemed far away at first but grew louder as she walked the path through the woods. Sacred chants filled the night air while the shadows of dancers moved with precision along the edge of the forest, pulling her deeper into the woods. Each song and dance seemed unique to the sound of the drums in the background. Suddenly the drumming built in intensity, the chants grew in volume, and the dancers became too numerous to count. She was mesmerized by their unexpected beauty. On they danced as the bells on their moccasins jingled, and they twirled and swayed rhythmically in step with the drumbeats. They circled around her, leading her through the maze of trees until suddenly they halted. An eerie silence filled the night as they parted enough for her to see. Hidden among the trees lay a lone figure on the ground. Facedown in the dirt, her dark black hair fanned out over her back and shoulders, but the beautiful hair didn't hide the stillness of her body. Dead and forgotten. Jessie gazed down on her lifeless form. Stranger still, she recognized the area where she lay.

The scene quickly altered along with the chants and drumbeats. Another body took center stage with only the landscape changing from the trees and forest to the grassy plains with the sun bright in the sky. The lone figure lay off the beaten path hidden in the tall grasses out of view. From one area to another Jessie traveled in her dream across the diversity of the country only to find another victim lying quietly and still. Not yet discovered, they were lost to those who loved them and waited anxiously for their return. The shadowy figure at the edge of her vision knew their location. Was he aware she knew too and that a common thread connected them?

Jessie awakened and reached for the lamp. She wrote down the key elements of her dreams. People were waiting to be found and a story that had been given scarcely any attention needed to be told. She would have to remedy that. How it fit in with Sofia's story she had no idea.

Jessie slipped out of bed, glancing at the clock on the way out of the bedroom door. Turning on the computer, she sat at the desk waiting for the screen to come on. She scrolled through one article after another. The statistics she read and took notes on shook her. Matt needed to see what she found. The more she read the more stunned she became. Why hadn't she seen any of these facts before? Blue Cove was making her more of an activist for women than New York ever had. After she sent a quick note to her research buddy Jeremy to fill him in on where her investigative mind was headed. She sent an email to Neil, her old boss at the newspaper, to see if he would be interested in the story when she finished it.

A hot shower was next on her agenda. The warmth felt like heaven as the pulsing droplets washed over her. She couldn't wait to tell Peyton about her dream. They were on the same page when it came to their thoughts about violence against women. The last case they had worked on had the same elements. Would it never stop? When would the laws catch up to the growing need to protect women and children not only in the world at large but here as well? She turned off the shower and admonished herself. "Stay on the story and don't get off on one of your soapboxes." She towel-dried her hair, opting to let it dry naturally because she had time this morning, along with time for a leisurely breakfast.

Enjoying her second cup of coffee, she checked through her emails. Jeremy's response brought a smile to her face. The one from Matt warmed her insides and made her stomach flutter and reminded her she needed to talk to him about the dream. How those thoughts combined in her mind made no sense. Matt could charm the socks off her, but he also served as a constant reminder of a case yet to be solved. Is that what was meant by balance? She chuckled when she saw who was calling.

"Hey, sweetheart. Did you get my text?" Matt asked.

"I did. I'm glad I was alone when I read it." She fanned her face.

"Need I ask why?" He chuckled.

"I think you already knew what my response would be. You do it on purpose," she chided him laughing as she did.

"I wanted you to know I was thinking about you."

"Seems to me you described your feelings clearly. Which reminds me—I have something to tell you. You know how my mind works."

"Damn, Jess, you're going to do it to me again. Aren't you?" he asked.

"Sorry, when it comes to you, my hunky guy, one thing leads to another. I love that about you." She flattered him and then told him about her dream.

"And you think the first body is somewhere in my jurisdiction?"

"That's exactly what I'm saying. I recognized the area if not the precise location. Matt, this is happening all over the country. Young Native American women are missing. Four out of five of them have experienced violence and one out of every two sexual violence. At least with the victims I saw in my dream there is one common thread, the murderer."

"You're hooked aren't you, sweetheart?"

"You know I am. Domestic violence among Native American women is ten times higher than the rest of the populace. I did a little research this morning. I have some writing to do," she informed him.

"You do that. I know you'll do the story justice.

Next, you're going to tell me that the case involving Sofia somehow is connected to what you're telling me. Am I right?"

"You're right as usual. I can't tell you how other than they both involve crimes against young women. If nothing else, it's the same degradation of women that makes it possible for both crimes."

"You'll get no argument from me." Matt cleared his throat. "What I can't figure out is why the agents investigating the girls' stories a year ago never moved on any of the information they gained from interviews. I need to talk to Jaxon and Tom and find out what they've found out. The FBI may have some information."

"I don't want to sound like a broken record, but men tend to believe another man over a woman. I imagine you will find a misogynistic attitude among the lead interviewers. I had to deal with it more times than I can count. That and being called little lady, and sweet thing. Sheesh, it's enough to make you sick." She slapped her hand to her forehead.

"I take it the person calling you sweet thing wasn't a boyfriend." He chuckled.

"You've got that right. They were supposed to be professionals. Not!" she shouted into the phone.

"Put that in your article too," Matt told her.

"Not that it will do any good," she told him.

"Write a book. Do whatever it takes to add your voice to the others out there. I have faith in you, Jess. Look how you're changing me. We guys can be lug-heads sometimes. We need you gals to remind us how to behave. My dad told us boys on more than one occasion he was barely civilized until he met and married mom. All that said while he called us knuckleheads, which we were. I still don't know how they managed to raise us. And the bigger miracle is that we all managed to turn out somewhat decent," he chuckled. "Although, the jury is still out on the final verdict."

"In my opinion, you're better than good. If you can get away, come by and we can have lunch together. If not, I'll see you later."

"Sounds good. I love you, sweetheart. Let me know if you hear from Sofia," he told her.

"I will. I love you too." She took the last sip of coffee in her cup. Clearing the dishes, she put them in the dishwasher. Did she dare to wonder and put the thought out into the airways about what this day would bring? Too late—she had thought it, and she couldn't take it back.

Jessie stuffed her phone in her purse. Slipping into her coat, she grabbed her keys and locked the door on her way out. She honked the horn as she passed by the inn. Her friend Sally Mansfield came to mind, and Jessie knew she needed to call her. If anyone understood violent behavior against women, it would be her. Sally lived with the hostility daily and almost died at the hands of her ex-husband. Jessie drove the rest of the way to her store with a plan taking shape in her mind.

Chapter Three

With her opening routine done, she unlocked the front door. Reba waved at her as she crossed the street from the church, a sure sign that her day would soon get more interesting.

Jessie held the door open for her. "You're out early this morning," she said as Reba whizzed past her.

"I only have a few minutes. The lady's group is meeting this morning and we are voting on new officers. You know what that means?" Reba gestured with her hand.

"I can't say that I do." Jessie followed in her wake.

"It means with any luck I can retire and someone else will be the new secretary. I've been doing the job for over five years now. Of course, I've kept an accurate record of all the ghost sightings around the church. I won't be passing that on. It's been one of the highlights of my time." Reba smiled wistfully. "It's the church politics that drives me bonkers."

"Politics?" Jessie glanced inquiringly at her.

"Oh, you know the arguments that can come up about the oddest things. It can get heated when it comes to purchases for the building or what the pastor can or can't do. Most of the time, things move along quite nicely until someone gets offended for whatever reason, and then—boom—it doesn't."

"I guess that's true whenever people group

together. It was like that where I used to work in New York. How can you prevent it?" Jessie shrugged her shoulders.

"I have no idea. As my Lawrence reminds me, people are people and on any given day your friend can become your enemy and friend again in a matter of moments."

"True." Jessie chuckled. "So, Ms. Church Secretary, have there been many ghost sightings at the church?" Jessie leaned her hip against the table.

"Yes, but I don't need to tell you." She patted Jessie's hand. "Which reminds me why I'm here. I've seen another ghost in the area and I felt sure you could tell me something about her."

"I don't have much to tell yet, only that I've seen her too."

"I know you saw her, dear. But you have more to say. I'm sure of it. Don't hold out on me. I'll be back, and you can tell me what you're not telling me now." Reba tapped her arm and rushed toward the door. "I want details." She pushed the door open. "See you soon." She waved. "Wish me luck in finding my replacement." She rushed out and headed back to the church.

Jessie nodded and smiled at her. Reba was a tad like a white tornado. The woman never failed to surprise her. Jessie would tell her about the dream. Reba would have something to say. "Another strange day," she muttered under her breath.

"Hey, Molly. I'll be in for a coffee once my grandmother gets here," Jessie said as she opened the doors to the coffee shop. "Something tells me I'll need more coffee than milk and caffeination perhaps." She laughed.

"Oh my, that sounds serious. Is everything okay? You never want anything but decaf."

"I'm not sure. Reba was here and is coming back. Between her and my strange dream, I might need something stronger. I'll probably change my mind, but I thought I should warn you up front because I don't want to shock you." Jessie laughed. "I can't have you passing out on me."

"Friend, when it comes to you, I don't think anything would surprise me. Although, caffeinated coffee might do the trick. I'm glad you told me." Molly chuckled and went to wait on a customer.

Jessie straightened the counter and turned on her computer to add a few items to her order list. She needed to keep her store stocked with the latest books. Reaching for her phone she called the city offices and entered the extension that she wanted. Her mind raced ahead to her to-do list as she waited. At least she could check this one off her list.

"Sally, this is Jessie," she said when Sally answered.

"Hey, girlfriend. What's up?" Her cheery voice came across the line.

"You want to do lunch this week? I have some questions I want to ask you," Jessie eyed some dust on the counter that she had missed and reached for the feather duster.

"Sounds good. Does tomorrow work for you? I have a clear schedule. No meetings," Sally told her.

"Perfect. How do you like your job? Is it going well?" Jessie asked.

"I love working here. This is my dream job.

Everyone, and I do mean everyone, treats me great."

"Happy to hear it." Jessie swished away the dust.

"Between you and me though Mack Everest, our illustrious town's treasurer, is a little on the tense side. He reminds me of my ex—all tied up in knots. Probably only because he works too hard. Anyway, I'll see you tomorrow and we can catch up. I have a department planning meeting to get to. I have to keep pushing the town to tourists as you know. But it's not hard to do because this place almost sells itself."

"Is Java Joe's at noon okay with you? That way I can keep an eye on my store in case Grams needs my help."

"Works for me. How is Sadie by the way?" Sally asked.

"She's doing well. You'll be able to see her tomorrow. I know she'll be happy to see you."

"I'll be there. Love you, friend." Sally disconnected the call.

Jessie smiled. Sally sounded much better than she had in years. Chad Bennett might be one of the reasons, and her new job didn't hurt either. Moving to the cove had worked its magic on her with a bit of help from Elida, known lovingly as their local fairy. Sally deserved a break, and Jessie couldn't be happier for her friend. The bell above the door signaled that the time had come for her to work. Jessie almost laughed aloud. Books and people—she had the best job ever.

****

Matt found his fascination with Jessie darn amazing. His desire to be with her hadn't diminished at all. The more bizarre twists life threw at them the more intrigued he became by her. She was a mystery to him and one that he wanted to investigate for the rest of his life. Matt grinned. He couldn't help himself.

"Hey, Parker, what has you smiling this morning?" Dylan stood in the open doorway.

"Thinking."

"Let me guess. A blue-eyed, blonde has you grinning." Dylan chuckled.

"Could be. How's married life?" Matt asked.

"No complaints. Katie keeps me on my toes. Honestly, Matt, she's a handful." Dylan's eyes lit up. "But marriage has its perks."

"You knew Katie was a strong woman before you married her." Matt leaned back in his chair.

"I did, and I wouldn't change anything about her. She's feisty, and I like it." Dylan walked into the office. "What's on the agenda for today?"

Matt brought him up to speed on Sofia Barton's story. "She's gone missing, and we need to investigate the business that's involved. I figure we should go there this morning and ask a few questions. I have a list of other girls involved in the program that we'll need to interview. Something tells me Sofia is the tip of the iceberg."

"I'm with you. I'll grab my coat and meet you in the lunchroom." Dylan walked out of his office.

Matt slipped on his jacket. He reached for his phone and sent a text to Jessie.

—*I'll see you at lunch. Checking out the business this morning. Let me know if you hear anything more about Sofia*—

—*Will do. See you.*— Her text came back with a smile emoji.

Matt and Dylan walked out the door together.

Dylan investigating a case with him seemed like old times. They had been through a lot together, including the whole mess with Chief Anderson, the repercussions of which still impacted the Blue Cove police department.

"What are we looking at?" Dylan latched his seatbelt.

"Right now, we only have Sofia's story. According to her, a few of the girls talked to an agent from the FBI and the police. I have Maxwell and Kincaid looking into that side of the story for me. If it proves true, someone slipped up big time." Matt pulled out of the station parking lot. "Besides those involved in the investigation, there are several others who could be culpable."

"Is the business legit? Does it have any complaints against it?" Dylan asked.

"You know, basic complaints up until a year ago. But more have been lodged against the owners in the past few months. We need to talk to parents as well as the kids involved." Matt turned into the parking lot of the studio.

"What kind of grievances are we looking at?" Dylan glanced at him.

"Beyond price, several parents issued concerns about the trainer and her husband. Several were angry that their oppositions had not been adequately addressed and they pulled their daughters from the program."

"Sounds fishy, doesn't it?" Dylan opened the door and stepped out of the car.

"You can say that again."

Matt and Dylan questioned the owner and the

coach. They were tight-lipped. Matt did his best to read between the lines and not get angry with them. Anderson, the chief of police before him, had signed off on the investigation and cleared the studio of any wrongdoing. Knowing what he now knew, Anderson probably was paid off to stop the investigation. He had lost his way toward the end of his career and took a few others along with him. The anger still surfaced close to the boiling point, when Matt thought about how close he came to losing Jessie because he couldn't believe Anderson might be guilty. The chief had trained him and was like a father figure to him besides being a good friend. Matt's respect for the man clouded his judgment. He couldn't see all the warnings at the time but looking back now he could see several. *Damn.* Matt pushed the door open.

"What do you think?" Dylan asked as they left the building.

"When she said they were cleared of all wrongdoing by Anderson my skin crawled. You know better than most how dirty he got toward the end. Looks to me like we need to open another investigation. All I need is the name of the lead FBI agent that interviewed the girls at that time and then I'll know for sure. If his name happens to be Zach Johnson—" he paused "—you get my drift."

"Yep. I thought you might be leaning that way. I wonder how many other cases we might need to revisit where Anderson was involved? What a mess he left behind," Dylan said.

"I still find it hard to believe he could do what he did. He overlooked the crimes of the Harvest Club. Nothing should surprise me, but it still does. You're right; we will be cleaning up the mess for a while as more of Anderson's corruption surfaces." Matt frowned and unlocked the car.

"We're talking kids here." Dylan's hand fisted at his side. "Damn, that guy turned out to be a real jerk." Dylan scowled. "And that's putting it nicely. Katie is working on me to clean up my language. No easy task, but I'm working at it." He chuckled. "Especially, in her presence. Otherwise, I have to put money in a jar and endure one of her reminders."

"Knowing you, that jar is filling up." Matt latched his seat belt.

"Hell, yes. This marriage business is a total mystery to me but I'm learning as I enjoy the ride."

"Marriage. Hell, women are a mystery. But they're one mystery I don't mind investigating." Matt started the car.

"Especially, your curly-haired sweetheart. I get it." Dylan smiled. "But now what are we going to do about those folks?" He pointed at the dance studio and attached gym.

"We're going to figure out what they're covering up and shut down their business." He pulled out of the parking lot. "I'm sure they are guilty, and now all we have to do is prove it."

****

The morning had rushed by. Between a second visit with Reba and customers, Jessie wanted a breather. At least Reba was happy and still flying high. She was officially retired from her secretary post in the women's group. She had great hopes for her replacement whom she approved of in every way. She smiled, glancing at Sadie and Reba when they laughed. The two were still talking about Reba's retirement and their ideas concerning her dream and the ghost. Jessie didn't want to think about the details anymore, much less talk about them.

Seeing all those young women still shook her more than she cared to analyze. She could hold out hope that it was only a dream and not real, but in her heart of hearts, she knew better. Plus, she had this nagging suspicion in the back of her mind that someone was aware that she knew. How was that even possible? As Peyton liked to say, she would have to think outside the box on this one. Her cousin was better at that skill than she was. Jessie loved her plans; they made her feel in control of a situation. There didn't seem to be a way to scheme her way out of this investigation.

****

He had a perfect view of her store. Adjusting the binoculars brought the inside of the store closer to him. The two old women sitting at the table, and the customers who came and went all became clear objects in his line of vision. She had bested him way too many times and now it was his turn to get even. Always the most popular girl wherever she went, and damn he had landed at the same company with her.

She perplexed him, mesmerized him, and left him tongue-tied every time she spoke to him. Nice enough, but she never gave his ideas the time of day. Soon she would have to. He was a master strategist; she would never see him coming. For now, he would toy with her playing a game until he could reel her in.

His pulse quickened as he watched her move around the store talking to people. Her smile could light up a room. He would give her that. He had waited for this moment for a long time. Being the bad guy might be fun for once. Good old Dexter always playing by the rules and there when you need him to be. Too bad that when promotion time came around no one ever thought of him. Enough. He'd had enough.

Could she sense him watching her? He slipped behind the bush, concealing himself. Not possible, but it added to the high of the moment. Maybe she would make the game more challenging. Licking his lips, he liked the idea of her knowing. That's when the idea popped into his head. He moved the thoughts around in his mind like chess pieces, arranging them in the order of each move he would make. Damn, he liked how his brain worked when it grabbed hold of an idea. *Ready or not, here I come.* He sat back and enjoyed the show.

Memorizing each of her movements and gestures, he sorted them in his head. Details were important; she had taught him that. He only had a short window of time to learn as much as he could. He liked to think of this time as stalking his prey.

Interesting. What do we have here? He focused on the police car that pulled into the open space in front of her store upping the ante a bit more. He rubbed his hands together and watched in delight. The officer walked into the store and stopped to talk to the older women giving one of them a kiss on the cheek. *Cute, but weird.* Dexter shook his head and adjusted the glasses. "Ah, so that's how it is. Jessie's boyfriend is a cop." *Game's on. Dexter gets to play keep-away from the police.*

Not exactly sure how he'd go about fulfilling his fantasy, he would figure out his next move. The reality was at his fingertips, and he planned to enjoy every minute and get paid to boot.

Chapter Four

"Hey, sweetheart." Matt kissed Jessie's cheek. "You ready to eat? These two sweet ladies said they'd watch the store." He patted Reba and Sadie on their shoulders and whispered something in Reba's ear. "Your store couldn't be in better hands."

"I couldn't agree more." She hugged her grandmother. "If it gets crazy, I'm right next store."

"Go on, dear. We'll be fine." Sadie gave her a playful push.

"Behave yourselves, ladies," Matt told them with a grin on his face.

"Now I ask you, what fun would that be? Move along, you two. It will be dinner time before you get started." Reba chuckled. "Nothing to see here."

"I don't think they want us around." He put his hand on Jessie's back and maneuvered her toward the open doors.

"You might be right. Those two are trouble with a capital T." Jessie laughed. "I wonder how my Grandpa Max handled Grams, or Lawrence does Reba."

"Probably the same way Katie handles Dylan." Once they ordered he told her about his conversation with Dylan and the swear jar.

"That sounds like Katie. Do you think Dylan is happy?" She glanced at him as she asked.

"Yes, I do. He loves his wife." Matt reached for her

hand. "Did you hear from Mrs. Barton or Sofia?"

"No. How did it go at the training center?" She took a sip of her water.

"They wouldn't talk. I did learn one fascinating piece of information though. When they were under investigation before, guess who cleared them of all wrongdoing?"

"I have no idea. Who?" They thanked Molly when she placed their lunch in front of them.

"Anderson," Matt informed her taking a bite of his sandwich.

"I guess it makes sense. He was the police chief at the time." Jessie placed the napkin on her lap.

"He was taking kickbacks from the Harvest Club at the time. Doesn't it make you wonder if they paid him to make their troubles go away?" Matt sipped his iced tea.

"I never thought about that. I wonder what they had to pay him and if Zach Johnson interviewed any of the girls. Those two had quite the operation going."

"I knew you'd understand. I have Kincaid and Maxwell at the FBI looking into the Johnson side of things. Dylan and I are going to revisit some of Anderson's cases. I have a sinking feeling he may have left us with a few problems." Matt shook his head and leaned back in the chair.

"Wow. I never thought he could have been paid to look the other way on more cases, but anything is possible, I guess." Jessie frowned.

"It does make me contemplate what else we might find. The guy was corrupt, no doubt about it. The only question I need to answer is for how long. Which would then bring up how many other cases we might be looking at."

"For now, let's concentrate on this one." Jessie sipped her tea and took a bite of her salad.

"That's my girl. I can see your mind working as we speak."

"I've been thinking about Sofia and my dream most of the morning. I knew there was more to the story. The ghost tells me that much, and there's something else but I'm not sure what it means yet. Someone is watching my store," she told him, leaving out a few details.

"Be clear, what do you mean." Matt scrutinized her as she talked.

"He—yes, I'm sure it's him—and he's observing the comings and goings. Why, is not clear to me at this point, but I have a feeling he'll let me know when he's ready."

"Are you worried about him?" Matt asked.

"Not at the moment. I'll tell you if we should be." She touched his clenched hand.

"Great, I thought we dealt with all your enemies." Matt shook his head in disgust again.

"How would I ever know? Do you know how many articles I've written in the past several years? I'm sure I can find out, but who I made mad—that's a different story altogether." She pursed her lips and reached for her iced tea. "How many people have you made angry over the past several years?"

"I imagine a few would like a shot at me. But I don't want to traipse through that minefield. Contemplating Anderson's cases that he screwed up is more than enough for me." He leaned near to her. "It still rattles me when I think about how close I came to losing you. The question I want answered is how long was he dirty, and did we miss anyone who might have worked alongside him?"

"I never thought about that possibility. I was just happy to take him out of circulation. We know Fred did his bidding, and of course Zach, but whether there is anyone else—that's an unknown." She stroked his hand. "Was it hard for you to shoot Anderson? I know he was important to you, and he was your mentor."

"Not once I saw you on the table and what he was about to do with the scalpel in his hand. Hearing his maniacal detailed description made my decision an easy one. He wasn't the man I knew. By that point in time, he was frantic and couldn't be stopped any other way." Matt stared over her head lost in his memory.

"What makes someone like him turn?" Taking her napkin, she wiped her mouth. "He seemed like such a nice man. I don't get it. Don't get me wrong. I understand the money but not the logic."

"You and me both. People with greater minds than mine have studied the answer to that question. I'm sure there are hundreds of papers and articles. No one answer fits every criminal mind. But at the end of the day power, money, and fear are big drawing cards."

"I'm sure you're right. Still, it would be interesting to interview a person like Zach to figure out what motivated him to turn to the wrong side of the law."

"Don't even think about that scenario. No way would I let you near that man." Matt leaned across the table getting near her face.

"Settle down." She patted his hand. "I didn't say I wanted to—but if did—you couldn't stop me and probably would get me the appointment at the prison."

She flashed him a smile. "You'd grumble and bristle but there's not much you wouldn't do for me."

He raked his hand through his hair. "Sweetheart, that's not nice. You should at least let me keep the illusion. I like to believe I can control you even if I know better."

"That's one of the many reasons why I love you. You get me." She patted his cheek. "I should get back to work.

"I love you too." He stood and waited for her to stand. "What I don't get, you'll tell me."

"You've got that right." She smiled. "We make a good team."

"Heck yeah." He placed his hand possessively on her back. "I'll see you later, sweetheart. You can count on it." He kissed her cheek under Sadie's and Reba's watchful eyes. "More to come later," he whispered in her ear.

"Promises, always promises." She grinned at him.

"Ladies." He smiled and nodded as he walked by them on his way out of the door.

****

Jessie followed his movement until he drove away. Wow, she loved that man.

"You know, Jessie dear, that is one handsome man. He reminds me of your grandpa when I first met him. He was such a charmer and when he held me in his arms, I would go weak in the knees." Sadie sighed. "Someday remind me to tell you our story."

"Love does that to you." Reba exhaled. "My Lawrence still does that to me."

"Okay, you two. Enough with the swooning." She chuckled. "What's on your mind?" Jessie sat at the table across from them.

"Well, besides the fact we think you should hold on tight to Matt because he's a keeper. We've also talked about our earlier conversation, and we agree. Why don't you tell her Sadie."

"This case may be a bit trickier than it looks on the surface. You will be dealing with three fronts. One is rooted in hatred. Another has its footing in corruption that goes deeper than it appears, and the third is a personal vendetta started by jealousy, but all are connected by a common thread." Sadie patted her hand. "Of course, that's mostly Reba's analysis but I concur with her."

"Okay, you two, lay it on me." Jessie shook her head.

"You understand how this works, Jessie. We only say what we hear. Most crime develops over time. Some, of course, happen in the heat of passion. All crimes make little sense to the observer until you dig beneath the surface. Think back over your cases with Matt and you'll see what we mean." Reba glanced at Sadie.

"What she means is the light will turn on when you need it." Sadie shrugged her shoulders. "That seems to be the way of it."

"I know the clues come when we need them, but sometimes I wish a case could be simple with no weird twists to it."

"Crimes don't happen in neat tidy packages," Reba said. "People have been found guilty with circumstantial evidence only to be freed later when new evidence surfaces. A rush to judgment is often wrong. Search for the evidence and let the story speak to you.

The facts will let you know."

"Yes." Thankfully with that declaration, their conversation ended, and Jessie was rescued by several customers who came into the store. The serious conversation was over, and she enjoyed chatting with one of the teachers who stopped in to order a book for a friend.

Her bookstore allowed her to meet the community. She couldn't imagine a job she could love any more. She waved at Reba and Sadie as they left. Taking a deep breath, she planned on enjoying the rest of her afternoon. Well, almost. The nagging thought of someone watching her didn't help, along with the ghost who remained out front. At some point the ghost would come in. They all did. Even Jessie's conversation with Peyton didn't yield any answers. She sighed. "Let the story speak to you." She closed her eyes willing herself to hear what it said.

Chapter Five

Sometimes life hands you a gift, and yesterday had brought one his way. While he chilled, he learned. The old ladies were one of her weak spots. He tucked that knowledge away for future use. The cop was her boyfriend. A tough guy who seemed on the protective side when it came to her. He might need to do some fancy maneuvering to get past him. His approach to her had to be when the cop wasn't nearby. A challenge, but one he was up for. Still, it could be fun to best a cop. He might need to find out more about the man. The thought gave him a rush. As for a ghost—he didn't believe in any of the junk and had no idea how their conversation had turned so silly. He turned the earpiece over in his hand. The small listening device had worked wonders just like the salesman had said.

A good day's work as far as he was concerned. The next part of his plan was to get to know his subject by listening and observing her. Of course, he already knew Jessie from their days in New York, but time had changed things a bit. He had to be prepared for any eventuality. One fact about her that remained true, she was a strong woman. He didn't want to kill her unless she forced him to. He would be glad to oblige her, but prison wasn't an option. His plan was simple. He wanted to crush her and climb over her to get to the top. What he also wanted to do was to take her down a peg or two and embarrass the hell out of her. He chuckled and tipped his head to the woman scurrying by.

Women were the problem with the ills of the world. Why couldn't they be happy to stay home where they belonged? No, they wanted more. Even his mother wasn't content with all she had. Nope, she left him with his maniac of a father to go out and live. He searched for years for the tramp and never found her. Until he met Jessie, and he was sure he had discovered her clone.

****

Matt spent the day going through a few of the old files regarding the training center. There appeared to be a lot of details left out of the final report. Basic questions were unanswered in the interview notes. There was enough info in the file to make the investigation appear normal at first glance but none of it connected as he dug deeper. Anderson signed off on an inept report which infuriated him. This was shoddy police work at best and a cover-up, and not a good one, at worst.

"Matt, Jaxon is line one," Joe told him when he answered his phone.

"Okay, thanks." Matt pushed line one. "Hey, Jaxon, I hope you have something for me."

"Tom is in a meeting, but he wanted me to call you right away. We got this piece of information this morning. It seems whoever interviewed the girls put their own spin on the stories in the final report. Tom said to tell you it was Zach Johnson who initialed and signed the final reports. He said you would understand."

"Damn." Matt tapped his pen on the open file.

"We're looking at a coverup. I wonder how much they got paid to overlook the crime."

"What's the skinny on Johnson? I read an FBI report on him," Jaxon asked.

Matt told him about Zach's part in the Harvest Club. "He teamed with Chief Anderson to cover the club's criminal activity. He continued to promote corruption from prison while recruiting, pushing illegal weapons sales in the Collector's Club from the inside. As you know, I shot Anderson, so he's no longer a threat."

"Could Zach still be active?" Jaxon asked.

"Anything is possible. It's hard to keep track of what they're doing from the inside. We face enough problems on the outside. Still, it would be nice to know what our boy might be up to, and if anyone is playing along." Matt leaned back in his chair.

"If he knows his way around a computer and has time on his hands, believe me, he can do a lot of damage. Cybercrime is on the rise. Almost every group does their recruiting online. There are a lot of shadow organizations and hate groups on the dark web. It's the downside to the tech age and almost impossible to monitor day and night. But we have people who are doing that twenty-four seven."

"See what you can dig up for me in your spare time," Matt told him. "Do you have any of that?"

"Not enough," Jaxon informed him. "At least my house is coming along now that I can hire some of it out. The kitchen should be finished this week. I can't wait to have Peyton see it. I won't have to take up your guest room much longer."

"No worries there. How's it going with Peyton and

her parents?" Matt asked.

"They're talking, but as she said, it will take a whole lot more than words. She's heard her fair share of empty promises and apologies over the years. As for me, I'm ready for her to be home."

"I bet." Matt doodled on his notepad. "Any conversation with her parents is a start, I guess. From what Jess told me Peyton had a rough childhood." Matt glanced out the window at a man who seemed out of place standing there. "Let me know if there's any evidence that Zach is at it again."

"Tom or I will get back to you as soon as possible," Jaxon told him.

"Hey, are you ready to leave the agency yet? We dress casually over here at Blue Cove Police Department. No ties and jackets. That alone makes working with me worth it." Matt chuckled. "See you later. I'm going to miss seeing you drag through the door from my recliner with my feet up." Matt disconnected the call.

He wouldn't mind having Jaxon on his team. He was there often enough. Tom Maxwell had razzed him about stealing Jaxon out from under his nose. It wasn't true, of course. Jaxon had moved back to the area from Arizona because of the job with the FBI. Still, Matt wouldn't mind recruiting him away from the Agency.

For the rest of the day, Matt spent time in records pulling old files. Most of Anderson's cases hadn't made it into the computer yet. He had hired Janet Olson and a couple others to input files into the new program the department had purchased. Jaxon had recommended the program on his first visit to the cove. Matt had sent Gary and Janet to New York to train. The first files to make it into the database were all their latest cases and investigations still in progress. It would be a while before any of Anderson's old reports made it into the database. Which meant time for him in the records room going through boxes of reports and evidence. The old way. He lifted another box off the shelf labeled "Training Center." Matt carried the box to the table in the center of the room and began to go through the files. The first file he opened had several odd entries. The more he read through the notations several red flags popped up.

Damn, it was just like he had thought. His fist clenched at his side. He wondered how many other cases had been tampered with. He needed to get a team to go through all the back cases starting with this one. Matt had no idea what he was looking at, only that there were several idiosyncrasies visible on his first pass through the file. What would a deep dive into the info of the page turn up? He carried the box to his office. The coverup would take keen, fresh eyes to spot the irregularities in the report. "Damn, Anderson, what were you thinking? If you were thinking at all." Matt frowned. Could his one-time idol fall any farther in his estimation? He would soon find out.

****

"Sofia, where are you?" Jessie mused. "Call me, sweetie." Jessie straightened the store while working through her closing routine. All day yesterday, she had the strangest feeling that someone was watching the store. She was smart enough not to dismiss the feeling. All her experiences of the past year had taught her enough to know that if she could sense it, she'd better listen. It was a man, but she had no idea who. One thing she did know for certain, he seemed quite angry with her. Who wasn't these days?

"Get in line, buddy. You aren't the first, and you won't be the last. But I'm no pushover, so you'd better be prepared for a fight." She walked to the front of the store. "I know you are out there. It's time to show your hand. You might be surprised." Jessie stood motionless watching the church across the street.

That church, such a beautiful and unassuming place with its lovely steeple and stained-glass windows, was where it all began for her. Life had gone all the way from quiet to strange from the moment she went to work in that building. Her first day in town, on the sidewalk in front of the church, a woman stared at her tapping her foot impatiently. Later during a tour of the church Jessie saw the woman's picture hanging in the foyer and learned she was one of their pastors. She had been murdered and her body was found outside the church. Jessie's first ghost sighting had shaken her but everyone at the church seemed to take it in stride. They had even told her about their church ghost. Her interest piqued, she had to find out Pastor Gina's story, which led her to Matt and eventually to the Harvest Club. During her days working at the church, she had seen Gina's ghost many times and Reba who kept track of all the sightings became her friend.

She had loved working there. The staff had welcomed her to town and were still counted among her good friends. At least now, she wasn't alone in her bizarre life of ghosts and crime-solving. Her cousin Peyton was in the same boat and seemed to take the weirdness to a whole new level. What had they gotten themselves into?

Lunch today with Sally had been fun and valuable. Their talk had been an eye-opening experience. Jessie asked her about domestic abuse, control, and a few other subjects that had come to mind. Her pen rarely stopped the whole time Sally talked. They agreed to meet again because Jessie knew in her heart that this information would be useful in their current case.

What made every day tolerable and exciting was Matt. She smiled thinking about him. He surprised her with his thoughtfulness. Why she was dragging her feet on setting a date she had no idea. She analyzed every word, action, and scenario to death. She was tired of it and couldn't imagine how he must feel. Matt didn't complain but hinted often enough. He wanted a wedding date, but she wasn't ready. His kisses could make her forget every question and throw caution to the wind. But as soon as he walked out the door, she would be back to second-guessing herself again. "Jessie, my girl, you need therapy." She straightened the books on the table.

An angry someone yesterday had spied on her, and she wrestled with whether to tell Matt more details. She mentioned the man but not the whole story. She wasn't ready for a Parker intervention. Locking the door, she turned the sign on the door to closed. She didn't need to make the decision at the moment. She had a few days to sort it all out. "Sofia, call. I need to know that you're okay."

Chapter Six

Matt separated a stack of files to take with him to study later. He wanted Jaxon to look over them too. Maybe between the two of them they could find a smoking gun. His gut told him that someone at the training center should have been prosecuted years ago. Some of the students studied ballet and dance while others were in gymnastic classes. The business was a renowned training center and families paid handsomely to send their sons and daughters there. Some of the kids competed at the national and international levels. A big boon for the studio, which wouldn't want bad publicity. How much did the owner have to pay to keep a brewing scandal out of the news? If he remembered correctly, his mom talked about a rumor circulating in town about the center a few years back. He didn't pay much attention then but now he needed to call and talk to her. Hopefully, she would remember a few more details than he could.

Tomorrow Dylan and Kip were starting interviews with several families who had filed complaints against the studio recently. Matt wanted to take Jessie along to talk to some of the young women that were interviewed at the time of the first reports. Jessie's presence might make it easier for them to talk. He sent her a quick text.

—Jess, can you go with me tomorrow to interview a couple of girls? I'm setting up times now for the

afternoon.—

—*Sounds great. I will see if Sadie or Audrey can work for me. What time?*—

—*I'll send you the times once I know them.*— Matt's fingers typed out the words.

—*Thank you.*—

Matt called her. "Hey sweetheart, I gave up texting. I want to hear your voice," he said when she answered.

"That's nice. What's up?"

"I'll pick you up at your place around six for dinner. Does that work for you? We can talk about the interviews then." He leaned back in his chair. Hearing her voice made him happy as he twirled a pen between his fingers. "Thank you."

"Of course, and you're welcome. May I ask what for?" she asked.

"For being you. As much as I like to hear your voice, I love to see your beautiful face even more. Truth is, I like everything about you. I'm addicted to you. What can I say?" He smiled glancing out the window.

"Well, when you put it that way, you're very welcome. Although, you might want to see a therapist about your addiction issue." She laughed.

"Not to worry, sweetheart. I can live with it."

"If you can, I can too. I'll see you at six," she told him.

"Perfect. See you soon." He slipped on his glasses to look over another file.

Matt had spent most of the afternoon returning calls. He set up appointments and gave the night crew their assignments. At five he grabbed the files off his desk and stopped by Dylan's office on his way out. Matt knocked on the open door.

"Hey, Chief, what's up?" Dylan asked.

"I know your schedule is full tomorrow with interviews. Be sure to let me know how they go, will you?" Matt told him.

Dylan nodded. "I'll fill you in as soon as I get back. If I think you need to know sooner, I'll text you."

"That would be great. I have interviews scheduled myself. I gave you the most recent complaints lodged against the studio by the newer families. Jessie and I are talking with the girls who were interviewed when Zach was the lead investigator. Something tells me it didn't go well. It may take a bit to get them to talk. I wouldn't blame them if they never trusted law enforcement again." Matt leaned his shoulder against the door jam.

"Do you think Zach and Anderson were taking payoffs that far back?" Dylan stood and reached for his coat.

"Yeah, I do. What I want to know is what crime they were making go away, and who still may be playing the same game in the department now. I think it's still going on."

"Damn." Dylan grimaced, puckering his brow. "If you're on your way out I'll walk with you. Katie has dinner ready, and I like to help her serve the guests when I can."

"Let's go." Matt pushed away from the door. "I'll fill you in on what I know at this point."

****

Jessie walked in the door after pulling her key out of the lock. She reached her hand into her purse in search of her ringing phone. "Hey, cousin, you're just the person who I wanted to talk to. Other than Sofia that is." Jessie dropped down on the nearest chair.

"I take it you haven't heard from her," Peyton stated.

"Nope, not a word today, which has me wondering. But there's something else I wanted to run by you." Jessie stretched her legs out. "I'm trying to figure out where to begin."

"Start at the beginning, cous. I'm listening."

"A couple of weeks ago I went with Katie to shop in the city. I had the strangest sensation that someone was following us. The anger I sensed in whoever it was seemed extremely intense. I have no idea who it could be, or why he's angry with me, but I swear I felt something like this once before in one of our other cases."

"Have you told Matt?" Peyton asked.

"Not everything. You know how protective he can be. I wanted to wait until I was sure. The thing is yesterday it went up a notch." Jessie explained what happened at work. "I know he saw Matt. I'm waiting for him to play his hand before I give Matt the extra details. It may be nothing more than a disgruntled person from my past and right now Matt has enough to deal with."

"I hope you're not making a mistake. I think you should tell him. Although, I probably wouldn't." Peyton muttered.

"At least you're being honest." Jessie yanked the pillow out from behind her and tossed it on the couch. "I'll wait for a bit but if this guy shows his hand, then I'll have to tell him. Of course, I'll get the standard lecture on why I should have told him." Jessie sighed. "You want to hear something crazy?" Jessie asked.

"Sure I do, especially if it's funny."

"I've learned to love his little talks. He gives them with such caring." Jessie smiled to herself. "He gets all worked up and I find it kind of sexy. I'm hopeless." She placed her hand dramatically on her forehead.

"Nothing you say usually surprises me, but this comes close," Peyton told her.

"I know. I can hardly believe it myself, but if you tell anyone I'll deny it vehemently." Jessie sat forward in the chair. "That man of mine turns my insides into mush whenever he looks me in the eyes. I rarely hear what he says in those moments."

"There was a time I would have laughed at that statement and said you were exaggerating. But I get it now. Jaxon has the same effect on me. I guess that's what love does to you."

"You think? Not that I don't love Matt, but in those moments, I'm not thinking sweet, loving thoughts. Don't ask me to go into more details. I wouldn't want to ruin my stellar good girl reputation." Jessie walked over to the couch and pitched the pillow back to the chair.

"No details are necessary. I understand. I'm plagued with the same thoughts, I bet. We should compare notes. We are like sisters after all. I get how your imaginative mind works. Mine is right there with yours."

"Pastor John might use another word to describe our thoughts." Jessie laughed fanning her face playfully.

"Does it make you think any more about getting married?" Peyton asked.

"Yes, and no. Yes, because the thought of living with my hunky cop sends shivers of the best kind running through me. But the no comes as a red flashing light when I try to imagine what everyday life might look like. I want to see a few good examples of happy marriages before I set a date. I'm closer than I was but I'm not there yet. I need reassurance that people can be married and still be in love. I don't want that all-consuming spark to fizzle out."

"Maybe it doesn't fizzle as much as become more manageable. It would be hard to be consumed every day." Peyton chuckled. "I'm no expert on the subject but Jaxon's parents still seem to sizzle around each other. They touch each other constantly, and the looks they give each other make me want to leave the room. I can see why Jaxon is romantic with them as his example."

"Nice to know. Our parents, on the other hand, leave a lot to be desired. You could freeze a side of beef with the warmth between them." Jessie paced around the living. "Enough of all this marriage talk. It's not helping. Although I am intrigued about comparing notes about our wayward thoughts. We must get together when you get home and do just that. Love you, cousin. See you in a few days."

"Love you too. I'll give you the advice you once gave me. Tell Matt everything; he needs to know."

"I'll think about it. Bye." Jessie disconnected the call before Peyton could say anything else. She smiled at the quiet phone and stuffed it into her purse. Matt would be here in a few minutes. She rushed into the bedroom to run a brush through her hair.

Peyton got her. Jessie's childhood had been a piece of cake compared to her cousin's. Darn those Reynolds brothers. How could they have been raised by someone like Sadie and Max and turned out the way they did? It made her want to yank her hair out and think twice about most men. Until Matt. He had broken through every barrier she had erected. He rushed in and stole her heart before she could come up with a plan to stop him. Now she didn't want to.

****

Matt talked with Dylan on his way out of the station and then followed him to the inn pulling in the space beside Jessie's car. Hopefully, she found someone to work for her tomorrow so she could do interviews with him. Matt knew this path to her cottage by heart. He had walked it often enough. He smiled. If he had to walk it backward or blindfolded, he would find a way to get there. Knowing she was there waiting was reward enough.

He knocked and walked in the unlocked door, the words already formulating in his mind about his next lecture. He stopped when he saw her raised hand.

"Before you say anything," she said waving her hand at him. "I saw you pull in the parking space, and I unlocked the door as you were walking down the path. I thought I should stop you from making a big mistake and needing to apologize."

"You could be wrong. I might not have said anything," he grumbled.

"How can you say that with a straight face? You're nothing if not predictable. You were itching to lecture me." She shook her head. "I helped you out before you got in trouble. You owe me big time."

He pulled her into his arms. "Is that right?" He kissed her. "How am I doing?"

"Not bad. You might have to work harder at

convincing me, though."

"Sweetheart, you know how I love a good challenge. Convincing is like a second language to me." He tightened his hold on her.

"Convince away."

"Darlin', it's an art form and can't be rushed. I might have to spread it out over the next several weeks. But convince you, I will." He rubbed his lips across her ear.

"You can start by buying this girl dinner. I'm starving." Jessie pulled out of his hold and reached for her coat.

He held her jacket while she slipped her arms in. "That's easy enough to do. But you know how I like a good challenge. This isn't over by a longshot."

"That's good." She stopped to kiss him as she sauntered out the door. "I like surprises."

Chapter Seven

Jessie slipped between the covers, propping her pillows behind her back. She always learned a lot listening to Matt talk about a case. How his mind worked to put facts together continued to amaze her. He shared what he had seen in the files and how someone had doctored several of Anderson's old cases, which made their interviews tomorrow even more important. Sadie and Audrey would watch the store so she could go with Matt. It felt like old times to be working with him on a new investigation. He was entertaining at dinner and charming as always. She should have told him her concerns, but he had enough on his plate, and she didn't want to worry him tonight. She pursed her lips and frowned. "You should have told him, girl, and you know it. Reverting to your old stubborn ways could get you killed," she muttered into the darkness.

Where was the magic when she needed it? She rolled onto her side tucking the covers under her chin. No fairies in this case, which was probably good. The last case had Matt doubting his sanity. This investigation had a different feel to it. What were the hidden surprises yet to come? There were bound to be more than a few. One part of her was excited and the other simply wanted to hide away in some unknown place until the case was solved. Never one to run from a challenge, she would meet it head-on. With that settled in her mind, she went to sleep.

****

Matt glanced at Jaxon, who was reading over the file he had handed him. "Does anything stand out to you?"

"Out of the gate, I see a few red flags. I'll put notations next to the areas. Will that work?" Jaxon reached for his pen.

"Perfect. What's your first impression?" Matt tapped his fingers on the arm of his recliner.

"My first take is that someone's attempt at a coverup isn't a great one. I guess you can be thankful for that. The question is who did it and why? They probably felt the files would be buried in the records department and never looked at again." Jaxon flipped to the back of the page.

"That's what I thought too. I'm doing interviews tomorrow, and I hope Jessie's presence will help the young women open up. After the last group of agents took their testimonies and did nothing with them, I wouldn't blame the women if they didn't trust any of us."

"She'll make it easier for them." Jaxon glanced at the file page again. "Tell me, Parker, do you feel good about everyone working in your department now?

"One of the department officers with access to records was arrested along with a few others from Anderson's time, but something tells me there's still someone we need to find."

"What makes you think that?" Jaxon asked.

"To start with the case file wasn't in the right location. Some of the lines have recently been redacted and the changed notations have no signature of authorization. Anytime a file is updated or changed the person must sign off on it after I do. As you can see my signature isn't on any of the changes and no one has initialed the changes either."

"Looks like you have an internal investigation to open up." Jaxon handed him back the file. "We have someone on the inside at the prison checking out Johnson. If he's active, we'll know shortly. Tom said he'll get you the info as soon as he hears back." Jaxon leaned his head back against the sofa. "Just so you know our inside guy is good."

Matt laughed. "Spoken like an official agent. You're a real team player. Talking about your guy the way you did, there's no hope to rescue you now. You're trapped in the long hours and heavy caseloads working for the man. I tried to recruit you to a simple small-town police force, but you're lost to us." Matt did a facepalm.

"You know how it is. You have to talk the talk. But hey, the jury is still out on whether I'm in the agency for good. This is my trial period. They may not want me."

"Yeah right. Top in your class, years of experience as a homicide detective, and you have one of the Reynolds girls working with you. Tom has been itching to get at Jessie. With you he gets Peyton. You're a shoo-in. I'd say you don't have to worry about job security."

"How long did you work for the agency?" Jaxon asked.

"Two of the longest years of my life." Matt chuckled. "You'll be there for years. There's no way Tom will let you leave and take Peyton."

"Peyton seals the deal." Jaxon smiled. "In more ways than one."

"I know the feeling, man." Matt leaned back in his chair and tossed him another file. "Keep reading and tell me every impression you get. I want to get this mess straightened out even if I have to go back through all of Anderson's cases. I'm finding out he was a real slug. He turned his eyes on crimes while he got paid under the table." Matt frowned. "Nothing worse than a dirty cop. I haven't known many, and it still shocks me that Anderson went that way. I don't believe he always was. But my goal is to find out when and why."

"It's more of a shock when it's someone you admire." Jaxon tossed Matt the remote. "I'll go over this before I go to sleep. Right now, I want to see the scores. Turn it on, will you?"

"I thought you'd never ask." Matt clicked on the station to watch the sports scores. He settled back in his chair putting up his legs. "Man, you've got to get one of these chairs. Call it a business expense. Nothing destresses me like my chair and sports. Except possibly Jessie sometimes."

"Sometimes?" Jaxon's brows rose.

"There are times my girl adds to my stress level. If you know what I mean. I want to set a wedding date and she avoids the subject. I'm not sure why. Another subject I want answers to."

"It must be tough when you finally make up your mind and get put on hold."

"You could say that. I spend a lot more time in the chair when date nights leave me feeling on edge. I'm determined to get a date on the calendar before the summer. I want something to hold on to."

"No need to worry about Jessie. She's totally into you." Jaxon leaned his head back against the sofa.

"I'm not worried about that. I want her around all the time. This coming home to an empty house does nothing for me anymore. It's strange when you wake up one day and you don't want to be a bachelor any longer."

"I hear you. It's a bit of a shock when it happens." Jaxon grinned. "Before you know it you care about colors and dish patterns. Speaking of your chair, Peyton noticed your chair because she is sending me ads about recliners. I might have to go and try one on for size. She's helping me decorate the new place. In the process, I'm hoping she can see herself living there. When it's cold out the garage is a good selling point." Jaxon chuckled. "She mentioned it more than once."

"That's a good idea. Get her invested in the place and she'll want to live there." Matt stroked his chin. "Keep talking. You're giving me some good ideas. I'm looking for ways to charm my girl into setting a date for our wedding. She's a challenge but there's nothing that stirs me more than a good challenge."

"About the case, you're investigating. Is there anything strange happening?" Jaxon ran his fingers along the edge of the file.

"Strange how?" Matt asked.

"Oh, you know—your average time travel, hanging out in two dimensions, with a few ghosts thrown in."

"So far, it's been fairly tame. A dream, a ghost, but I don't believe for a minute that is the extent of what's going on. I have a nagging suspicion that Jessie isn't telling me something. She doesn't like her life disrupted, which she knows I will do in a heartbeat if I think she's in the crosshairs. I'm biding my time until she comes clean. If she doesn't soon, I'll be having a chat with her. There's not much she won't do to avoid one of my lectures." Matt grinned and glanced back at the TV. "She keeps me on my toes. No wonder I love her. There's nothing predictable about her other than her stubborn streak."

****

The dream began like the others, but the scene began to change rapidly. Walking alone on a dirt road, she didn't see a landmark that she recognized. Homes were scattered few and far between. The sky filled with numerous stars that on any other night would amaze her. Tonight, they barely gave enough light for her to see her hand in front of her face, much less see if he was following her. The lights in the distance and the sound of a pickup as it rattled down the road caused a wave of fear to wash over her. Jessie's heart raced, along with the faceless woman as she ran mindlessly off the main road through the sagebrush and sandy dirt. She stumbled, fell, and got up to run again. The nearer the lights came the more panic rose inside her. Was it the girl's fear she felt or her own? He was looking for her and he wouldn't give up until he found her. Jessie tossed and turned as the dream continued. The truck stopped and a spotlight from the top of the truck began to scan the area as the door opened. She dropped to the ground scrambling on her hands and knees over the rough terrain. Her hands were scratched every time she hit some unknown object on the land or held onto a stubby bush to stabilize herself. All the while she could hear the sounds of his cursing as he searched for her. Breathing raggedly her hand reached out for something to hold onto, when the earth gave way beneath her. She landed hard knocking the wind out of her. How far had she fallen? Finally, Jessie could see the girl's face. She awakened with a start. Her own face stared back at her.

Jessie sat up, plumping her pillows behind her. Turning on the light, she took deep breaths. Maybe she needed to talk to Matt after all. Either that or she had to get her imagination under control. Now she knew how Scrooge felt when he saw his name on the headstone after his visit from the ghost. How she loved that story. She would see that scene through a new lens from now on. Was this what was going to happen or was it a warning of someone's intent? She had no idea. Maybe someone didn't like her getting too close to the truth. She shut off the light, and the room seemed darker than before. What she needed was a nightlight like Peyton's fairy light. Something to remind her of the good magic that was still possible.

Chapter Eight

Jessie turned the light back on, sat up, and reached for her phone. *—If you're awake give me a call.* — She texted Peyton and leaned back against the headboard. The padded headboard had been expensive but at this moment a worthwhile investment. Trying to sort through the images in her mind from her dream she reached for her notepad and pencil on the nightstand. Her brow furrowed as she wrote down the memories. What had she got herself into now? Someone was not only angry but seemed to want her dead or at least injured. "Come on, Peyton, I need you to call."

"Jess, what's up?" Peyton said when Jessie answered moments later.

Jessie told her about the dream. "What made it different this time when I saw the victim's face…" Jessie gulped shaking her head at the image in her mind.

"What? Don't leave me hanging?" Peyton told her.

"I was looking at me." Her voice sounded strained even to her.

"Call Matt. Do it now, or I will!" Peyton yelled.

"Don't go nuclear on me. I'll tell him tomorrow. It's too late to call him now. Besides, I'm still trying to make sense of what I saw."

"What's there to think about? Just so you know, I'm telling Jaxon," Peyton promised.

"Go ahead. You can threaten all you want. I'll tell Matt when I'm ready to."

"You're too stubborn for your own good. I mean it, Jess. I'm telling Jaxon, and you'll be hearing from Matt whether you like it or not."

"Whatever." Jessie rolled her eyes, even though her cousin couldn't see it. "How does it feel to be dating a millionaire?"

"I know what you're doing, and it isn't going to work. Changing the subject is a juvenile tactic. I should know. I've used it often enough when I don't want to face the music." Peyton laughed. "Jaxon is still the same, amazing man. He's only just signed the papers and the money will be transferred sometime in the next week." Peyton paused and silence filled the line.

"Are you still there or did you hang up?" Jessie asked.

"I want you to be careful. Premonitions are nothing to ignore. I tried to in Arizona and almost died. I'm scared for you, cousin. We've been at this long enough to know this is no game. What's going on in your head? Tell me. You wanted me to call."

For the next thirty minutes, Jessie talked in circles, going through one scenario after another until she could see the last few days more clearly. "Don't worry. I'll call him. I know he needs to know. You can tell Jaxon if you want. I won't get mad. I know Matt loves me. I needed to tell someone. It's how I work things out. It makes more sense to me now." Jessie placed her notebook back on the nightstand. "You know me. I have to have a plan. I can't stand to feel out of control. After the dream, I panicked. Simply talking to you has helped."

"Who do you think is after you?" Peyton asked.

"I have no idea, but he'll tip his hand and I'll be ready when he does. If you see or hear anything, don't leave me hanging. I helped you last time." Jessie stacked her hands behind her head.

"Yes, you did, and you know I will too. We think alike. But I want Matt to watch over you."

"You won't have to worry about that. Once he knows he'll be stuck to me like glue. I'm not sure it'll help anyway. I believe my stalker and I are destined to meet whether I like it or not."

"Bummer. I wished you wouldn't have told me that. I understand, even though I don't want to. Promise me you'll be careful. I'll be home tomorrow night late. Only for Grams would I have made this trip at all. I didn't want to, but I guess it was good."

"Sorry, I didn't even ask how it was going. You can tell me all about it when you get home. Is Madison still with you?"

"No, she left a couple of days ago. I've been hanging with Destiny and her mom helping them pack, but I'm ready to be home. Jaxon is calling me. I'll see you tomorrow. Goodnight, cousin."

Talking with Peyton had helped. She was right; no way could Jessie ignore a premonition. She would be dumb to ignore the warning and she couldn't unsee what she had seen even if she wanted to. Lord knew she wanted to. Shutting off the light, she laid her head back on the pillow with her phone in her hand. Matt would be calling her as soon as Jaxon told him what was up. Going over how she wanted to respond to him, she made it to her fourth point before her phone rang. She let it ring several times before she answered simply to be ornery. "Hello," she said feigning the sound of waking out of sleep.

****

"Hi, sweetheart. Did I wake you, my stubborn angel?" Matt chuckled.

"Not really." She shook her head. "Busted," she mumbled under her breath.

"I didn't think you could fall asleep that fast knowing that I would be calling you. If I know you at all, I'd say you've been thinking of ways to defend your actions. I can't wait to hear what you've come up with. Give it to me."

"I was the one who told Peyton she was free to tell Jaxon. That should count for something."

"One brownie point for permission." He paused to get control. "The question I have is why didn't you tell me? I am the man in your life, aren't I? Shouldn't I have a little warning if someone is after you?" His fist clenched at his side.

"Of course, but all I have now is a feeling and a dream. That's not much to go on."

"I beg your pardon; I can't believe you just said that. Your feelings have been too accurate to ever discount. I'm not a total idiot, Jess. I can be dense, but even I respect what you see and hear. Start at the beginning and tell me what you know so far." He tapped his fingers on the bed. "Don't leave anything out.

"The first time I sensed something was off is when Katie and I went into the city." Jessie told him about the incident. She went on to explain about the day at work and her recent dream leaving out the ending. "I'm not sure your knowledge will change anything. I'm convinced we are going to meet one way or another."

"What does that mean? You don't think I can protect you from this thug?" Matt ground out between clenched teeth.

"Don't go all caveman on me. It's not that. Call it a premonition. We have met in the past, and we will meet again. That's all."

"We'll see about that. By the way, Jess, I know you left out the ending of your dream. Don't spare me. Like you, I need to know the details so I can plan. I know how you love your plans."

"There's not much to add. Are you mad at me?" she asked.

"Not mad, only disappointed. I thought by now you trusted me enough to tell me anything. You know, Jess, I've worked on my need to lecture you, and I've even let you have your way when instinct told me not to, but it hasn't seemed to move the needle when it comes to your trust issues with me. Sweet dreams. We'll talk tomorrow." He hung up smiling.

His girl was something. Damn, he loved her. Hopefully, she would figure it out soon enough and learn to tell him everything. Okay, he had a few things he needed to learn too. Women! Was there a man alive who could understand how their minds worked? Disappointed, hell yes; deterred, no way. She was worth every moment of this strange dance they were having.

****

Jessie swiped at the tears in her eyes. He was right, of course. A lecture would have been easier to swallow than feeling his disappointment. Matt should have been the first person she talked to. The problem was that she couldn't seem to separate the man and the authoritative figure he exuded. She owed her skittish nature to all things strong in a man to her father. Matt wasn't like him at all except for the professional side. The question was could she get past it? Was love enough? She had some thinking to do. It was unfair of her to hold him hostage to her hangups.

Laying her head back on the pillow, Jessie let the tears roll. *Dad, it's time for me and you to have a reckoning of our relationship.* "Darn you, Reynolds men." After planning her next steps, and a few glances at the clock, she closed her eyes and dreamed of Matt.

Chapter Nine

The bookstore was hopping. Jessie barely had time
to stop and think. She loved days like this. The store
was filled with people clustered together in small
groups chatting and drinking coffee. Books and
magazines were being bought and read in the store and
going out the door in bags. The whole scene was the
way she had always envisioned it when she dreamed of
owning a store. Except for the ghost hanging around
most of the day weaving in and out of her customers.
She could honestly say that was something that had
never been on her radar. She couldn't wait for her
cousin to get home tonight. Peyton had a way of putting
things into perspective for her. Which was what she
needed after her conversation with her dad earlier.
Confused and mystified described her feelings best at
the moment.

Her dad had spent time with his brother and his
eyes were opened. The evidence of what his brother had
put his two girls through not only disgusted him but
made him take a long look at himself. His attitude on
everything they talked about seemed to have softened
and he had even apologized to Jessie. Their
conversation took the wind right out of her sails. She
had called to do battle and instead turned into a
weeping mess—even more tears than her usual amount.
For her, tears seemed to help her view life more clearly

once they passed. What could she say? Tears were therapeutic.

When her dad told her that everything he had done had been because he loved her, she about lost it. Then he quickly added he could see how she might not see it that way and that he was sorry for being tough on her and her mom. Jessie wanted to know what had changed him. Peyton would know, and maybe Sadie would too. Although, her dad said he needed to apologize to his mom and even choked up when he said he wished he could tell his dad, something he would regret for the rest of his life. The morning had been emotional in more ways than she could count. Darn. She swiped at the tears forming in her eyes simply thinking about their talk. Maybe there was something to that whole curse thing on their ancestors being broken in the last case. Both the Reynolds men seemed to be going through some kind of transformation.

"You're preoccupied, dear girl." Reba stood in front of the counter. "You didn't even see me come through the doors from Joe's."

"Let's say, I've had an eventful morning." Jessie glanced at her friend. "I have interviews later on today with Matt. I have a full day."

"Yes, dear, and it has nothing to with all the folks in the store, living or otherwise, does it?" She patted Jessie's hand. "This is your moment for growth and change. Life often affords us the opportunity. Grab it with both of your hands and hold on. Things you will hear in the next few days are filled with truths that will help you solve the investigation looming before you."

"Reba, you're something." She smiled at her friend. "How do you know these things?"

"The same way you do, only I've had more years to practice. I like to think of it this way. Life moves along until something happens suddenly to open our eyes to see our real image as others see us. We often see ourselves through rose-tinted glasses. A taste of reality happens when we see the truth about ourselves. I think this has happened to your dad. Am I right?"

"Yes, you could say that. I'm still in shock."

"What you need is a good cup of tea. Molly is bringing one for you. I'll save the space at the end of the table for us." Reba went to the center table, placed her coat on a chair, and sat on the other one.

"I'll join you in a minute." Jessie checked out a customer and went to help another. It never failed to amaze her how Reba always showed up at the right time. The moment things began to heat up in her life Reba appeared like clockwork. The woman was a mystery to her.

Jessie joined Reba for conversation and a small reprieve. "Your right—tea makes things better." She took another sip.

"Of course, it does. Now let's get down to business. Why's the ghost hanging out in your store?"

"I was hoping you could tell me." Jessie rubbed her forehead and pushed a wayward curl out of her eye.

"Looks like we'll have to put our great minds together to figure it out." Reba patted Jessie's hand and reached for her lemon bar. "Would you like one?"

"No, I'm good." She shook her head. "Did I tell you that I had lunch with Sally Mansfield the other day?

"I remember you told me you were going to. How did it go?" Reba took a bite of her lemon bar.

"I asked her everything I could think of about abusive relationships. I wish I would have thought to ask you to join us. We agreed to go again. I think you should come along."

"Hmm. That sounds good. Until you go with Matt later, we have some sleuthing to do." Reba wiped her mouth daintily on the corner of her napkin. They learned their heads close to each other and plotted.

****

Dylan's interviews were going well according to the text Matt received from him. Matt began a new file. Something told him this investigation would have too many changes that needed to be added. All the parents they had talked to so far had heard rumors about the business in recent days. Some even went as far as to say they had seen the changes in the daughter or son but had no idea why. Several parents were angry about the lack of transparency from the staff. The owners never addressed their questions and concerns. Several opted to pull their kids out of class after receiving no answers.

Matt's conversation last night with his mother had proven beneficial. She repeated a lot of the rumors that were going around when they were still living in the area. She reminded him to look in the newspaper archives. They had carried several stories about the ongoing investigation at the time. It had been front-page news for several weeks and then one day the paper ran an article saying the studio had been exonerated. The journalist covering the story had asked a lot of questions in her last article that went unanswered. After that, his mother said she didn't hear anything else. That story died and was replaced with some other newsworthy one that came along. Her advice had been good. The archives were proving to be full of valuable info. His mom was right about the unanswered questions. They were a great starting point. He wrote them on his notepad.

Glancing at his watch, Matt noted he needed to pick Jessie up in a while and he could use some food. His favorite spot was near his favorite girl. He reached for his jacket and walked out of his office. He notified Kenny where he could be reached on his way out.

From the moment he got behind the wheel he went over his conversation with Jessie last night. He was more determined than ever to enjoy these exhilarating moments of the chase. She brought out his caveman tendencies. He wanted to pick her up, throw her over his shoulder, and take her to his hideaway to cherish for the rest of their lives. She kept him on edge. He smiled. She enticed him and exasperated him, often at the same time. Man, he loved her. The question was, what was he going to do about her? His parents and brothers keep asking when the wedding was, and his answer remained the same: I'll let you know as soon as the date is reserved.

He parked a few stores down from Jessie's in the first open space. Before Joe's, he went first to the place that called to his heart. He paused before opening the door. Jessie's head was bent close to Reba's, lost in conversation. Her store had several customers milling about. The first words that came to his mind were, this is the calm before the storm. With that he pushed the door open, the bell rang above the door, and Jessie jumped into action.

"Hi, sweetheart." He bent his head and kissed her cheek. "How's my girl?" He glanced at Reba when he asked it.

"She's good." Reba smiled at him.

"Aren't you early?" Jessie asked.

"I wanted food and to see you, of course." He took her hand in his. "You're busy. Will you be able to leave?"

"Audrey is taking over for me. She can handle it. She's my most experienced worker. I'm thinking of hiring Peyton for the summer to help out too. It's getting busier. All good news as far as I'm concerned. Enjoy your lunch. I'll be ready when you are." She gave him a nudge toward the door.

"I'll do that." He couldn't help but wonder what she was up to now. Her formality made him smile. Some day he wished he could get a peek inside her mind to understand what went on in there. Between premonitions, ghosts, and Reba it was bound to be one busy place.

After ordering, Matt sat at a table where he could keep an eye on Jessie at work. If there was someone after her who hadn't shown his hand, he had to keep his eyes open. He didn't want to aggravate her, but he wasn't about to be lax either. If the past year had taught him anything, it was that Jess was stubborn but could be persuaded if he approached the subject right. Because I said so, didn't work with her. Sadie told him once that was always what her father said after he demanded she did something his way. He got it. Keeping an eye on her was one of his favorite pastimes anyways.

****

He got a kick out of watching the cop. The guy had it bad. He still remembered the first time she walked into the police station on assignment in New York. It felt like all the air had sucked out of him. It didn't last long. She had walked by him like he didn't exist. The desk sergeant tripped all over himself to answer her questions after he had been sitting there for what seemed like hours. The man wouldn't give him the time of day. The next day he read what should have been his story online. She had scooped the article right out from under him. He almost felt sorry for the cop.

Jessie needed to see him; it was part of his plan. The fact that she didn't know what he looked like made it more fun. There were many ways to change appearances. Hair dye, several colored contacts, and a nip here and tuck there, and we're talking about a brand-new man. *Let's try out my theory.* He stood leaving a tip on the table and nodded and smiled when he passed her cop on his way into the store.

Once inside, he stopped to look at the display of books near the front window. With a book in his hand, he positioned himself so he could see her move around the store. The old lady seemed to be mighty important to her. He feigned reading the cover because Jessie was headed his way. The contest was about to begin.

"May I help you." She smiled sweetly at him.

"I'm just looking, but thanks." He placed the book back on the table and picked up another one.

"Let me know if I can help you find something." She turned to walk away.

"I'll do that." He watched her move to another customer. The way she had scrutinized his face made him wonder. Maybe he should leave before she recognized something about him. Slipping the envelope out of his pocket, he placed it on the bookshelf near the door. "You have a nice store here. I'm sure I'll be back." He saw her wave, but the troubled expression on her face told a different story. Something about the encounter felt off.

Chapter Ten

"Hello." Matt squeezed Jessie's shoulders. "Where are you? You didn't hear me walk up behind you."

"Sorry." She turned in his arms. "Have you ever looked at someone and sworn you knew them from somewhere? There's something familiar about them but they look so different you think it can't possibly be the same person."

"I suppose that might have happened at some point. Why?" Matt stroked her cheek with the back of his hand.

"It just happened to me. I can't place where, but I know that I've met the man before."

"Man, what man? Is he still in the store?" Matt asked. He followed her to the front of the store.

"He stood there looking at the books and then left." She pointed at the display table. "I got close when I asked if he needed any help. He left soon afterward." Her eyes automatically followed the path he took. She noticed the envelope propped against one of the books. "What have we got here?" Her hand reached out to grab it.

"Wait. Let's do this by the rules just in case." Matt retreated into the coffee shop and came back carrying a pair of gloves and a bag, He carefully opened the envelope and unfolded the paper inside."

My, my, it's been a long time. I thought I'd never

see you again but that didn't stop me from trying to find you. Then like a gift from heaven you showed up in New York one day and I followed you home. How does that make you feel? Unsettled, I hope. Afraid, dare I hope. Let's just say you should be.

"Damn, Jess." Matt raked his hand through his hair. "He knows you even if you don't recognize him." He took out his notepad. "Tell me every detail you can remember about his appearance while it's still fresh in your mind. Hair color?"

"Brown," she replied.

"Eyes?" he asked.

"Blueish-green. I remember thinking they looked fake somehow." She scrunched her face.

"Colored contacts, possibly?" Matt glanced at her.

"Could be," she said.

"Tell me what else you can remember." Matt tapped his pen against the notepad.

Jessie described his height, the clothes he was wearing, and a scar she remembered seeing on his chin. "I remember the scar because it had an odd design. It reminded me of a signet ring. Do you remember my friend, I use that term lightly, who had all those disguises?" she asked.

"You mean the serial killer who showed up at Katie's class reunion party? How could I ever forget you flying out of the tree to knock the gun he had pointed at me out of his hands. In one moment, I felt love, fear, and relief when I saw you shooting out of the tree. You're something, you know it?" He reached for her hand. "This can't be the same guy. He's locked away in prison for life. Tell me who this one is."

"I have no idea." She frowned, shaking her head.

"Let's change the subject for now. Okay?"

"Sure. Have you heard from Sophia?" he asked squeezing her shoulder reassuringly.

"Not yet. Reba and I were talking about her. I'm beginning to wonder what's going on. I thought she would have called before now. I hope she's okay. I sense that she is but sometimes I wonder if I know anything at all."

"What brought that on? You've got a great track record. Confidence has never been an issue with you before." His brows rose.

"I'll tell you later. I had a conversation with my dad earlier, and now I seem to be second-guessing everything. Something happened to my dad, and I'm trying to figure out what." Jessie waved at Audrey when she walked in the door.

"Are you ready to leave?" he asked her.

"I will be in a minute." Jessie gave a few directions to Audrey about a new group meeting in the afternoon. She walked over to the table where Reba sat drinking her tea. "Grams will be here in a few minutes. I'll talk to you later." She hugged Reba.

"I'm going to hang around for a while. I want to see Sadie and check out the next book in the series that I'm reading." She patted Jessie's hand. "Go along, sweet girl. You're keeping Mr. Parker waiting. Don't leave him cooling his heels too long." Reba chuckled. "Besides, I want to have another cup of tea and read. I have nowhere to be. I can help Audrey if she needs me."

"That had a double meaning, didn't it?" Jessie smiled at her. Reba was a sly one. Motioning at Matt, she said, "I'm ready." She grabbed her purse and slipped her arms into the sleeves while Matt held her jacket.

After they were in the car and driving down the road, Matt glanced at her. "What's going on with your dad?"

Jessie explained her strange conversation with her father earlier. "I know certain events can impact a person's life and cause changes. His attitude change seems too abrupt. It felt almost like I was having whiplash. He even told me that he couldn't promise that he wouldn't fall back into the old pattern of doing things, but he would try hard not to."

"That's a good thing, isn't it?" Matt moved into the turn lane.

"I guess. Still, it was somewhat unsettling." She glanced out the passenger window.

"Why did it upset you?" he asked.

"I planned on telling him how he had made me feel over the years. I finally got up the nerve and he stopped me in my tracks with his apology. I guess it unnerved me. I spent most of the conversation in tears." She searched in her purse for a tissue.

"No offense, but tears come easily to you." He smiled at her.

"Yes, they do. They're my therapy." She wiped at the moisture in her eyes.

"Whatever helps. Look, sweetheart, things have a way of working." He glanced at her. "This will too."

"I know," she said softly. "I never thought I would hear my dad say some of the things he said. I've waited many years to hear them. It's all good." She placed her hand on his arm.

"If you're happy, then I'm happy." He squeezed

her hand and then signaled a turn. "I have several interviews set up at a secure location for today. I didn't want anyone getting wind of us visiting the girls at their homes."

"Were their parents in agreement?" Jessie asked.

"Most of these girls are no longer minors but were at the time. Some said their parents would be with them and others wanted to be on their own. The thing is they don't trust the authorities. They feel like the system failed them. That is where you come in."

"You do know the system does often fail women. They are made to feel guilty no matter what. From what they wear to how they act, they are often the ones that get blamed for the crimes committed against them. The victim is frequently victimized again in court. It used to make me wonder when I covered some of the stories if men were considered responsible for any of their actions."

"You'll get no argument from me. And these girls need you in their corner. I'm sure there'll be others who do too." Matt turned into the parking lot of the community center. "Let's see where this takes us." He opened the car door for her.

"That's a loaded statement," Jessie muttered under her breath.

****

The five young women sitting in front of them listened to Jessie tell her story of how the system had failed her. One by one they opened up and told their stories about repeated abuse at the hands of a doctor and the people who lied to cover up what he did. They were all underage at the time and trusted the agent who dismissed their testimonies in a misogynistic way.

"Nothing was ever done. But we are no longer underage, and we are working with a lawyer. We are bringing a civil case against the owners and the doctor, and we're turning a light on the authorities that failed us. More families are signing on to the suit all the time," the oldest of the five girls explained. "Since they did nothing, they enabled the doctor to assault more kids. He probably still is."

"We are investigating the center right now concerning a missing girl. I'd like to work with your lawyer on the timing of the lawsuit. We don't want to be working against each other." Matt handed the girl his card. "Have him call me, please."

"I have one question if you don't mind." Jessie touched the girl's hand. "Did anyone in your group die recently?"

"Yes, how did you know?" one of the girls asked.

"Call it a hunch."

"Marcia simply couldn't live with what happened and she committed suicide. We are still coming to terms with her death." The girl dabbed at her eyes with the tissue Jessie handed her.

"I promise you, this guy here"—she touched Matt's arm—"will do everything he can to change that. He's the best."

"I hope so. I won't hold my breath, though." She frowned at Matt. "I don't mean to be rude, but I find it hard to believe after all these years that anyone cares."

"As much as I hate talking about it, I will. This man needs to be stopped," the youngest of the girls said. "Marcia was a good friend, a beautiful gymnast, and a kind soul. She looked after me when I made the team. She never let me go to the doctor's office alone.

He destroyed her." For the next ten minutes, she told them about her friend Marcia and the abuse she endured, mentioning several people who she thought were guilty. "I don't believe he was ever investigated."

They talked for a few more minutes before everyone left. The details that the girls shared brought memories flooding back to Jessie. *The same account repeats itself over and over again with the same story.* She frowned. *Only different faces and locations.* Would it ever stop? The statistics regarding the Native America women told a similar narrative. She wanted to help Matt take the guilty parties in this case out of circulation. Maybe getting them wouldn't change the world but it might save another young girl following her dream from this predator. One could hope. She gathered her belongings from the table and followed Matt to the door.

"You're quiet." He reached for her hand lacing his finger through hers.

"I'm mad." She squeezed his hand in hers. "I've heard the same description in countless reports I've read. It's frustrating that nothing ever changes."

"I hear you. What can I say? Change comes slowly." They walked out the door together.

"Yeah, well, I'm tired of making excuses for it. I want to fight back." Jessie leaned her head back against the headrest. "One criminal at a time. I can see why you love your job." She closed her eyes and took a deep breath. "Something tells me, Matt, you need to call Frank. Radar's nose will be needed to find the body and maybe a killer in the process."

"We'll talk about this more later, but I'm sure you're right. I want to know how you came to that conclusion. I'm sure it will be a fascinating conversation." Matt glanced at her. The smile on her face brought one to his.

Chapter Eleven

"Sweetheart, we're here." Matt gently shook Jessie awake. "I'll pick you up at home at six. You deserve dinner after what you heard today." He leaned over and kissed her. "I love working with you."

"The feeling is mutual." She touched his cheek. "You have to nail those guys."

"We will. Wait. I want to open your door," he said when she reached for the door handle.

"I've got it. I'll see you later." She got out of the car.

He watched her until she was in the store. Signaling, he pulled away from the curb. Matt could understand her aggravation. The system was run by people, and people weren't perfect. Damn, it annoyed him. For every thug he took off the street another one took their place. He had always thought of Blue Cove differently, but they had a crime ring operating right under their noses led by the chief of police before him. Nothing was ever as it seems. He was more determined to clean up the mess of his predecessor. He had no idea how deep the corruption ran or how many cases were impacted. Who were the other people in town that were involved or knew what was going on? It might take him years, but he would find out. Cleaning up the town to match its projected image was his new pet project.

Once back at the station he went directly to

Dylan's office. After they discussed how the interviews went, Matt stood and closed the door.

"What's on your mind?" Dylan asked. "You never close the door. This must be important."

"I don't want anyone else to hear our conversation." Matt sat in the chair in front of Dylan's desk. He put on his glasses and took out his notepad and pen.

"You look like you're on some kind of mission, and I want to know what it is." Dylan's forehead furrowed.

"And you know this how?" Matt asked.

"Your serious expression and glasses are a giveaway."

"You came to work here before I did, and I'd like to ask you a few questions about that time." Matt leaned forward. "What was Anderson like when you first hired on?"

"He seemed like a decent enough guy. I was never close to him like you were." Dylan crossed his arms over his chest. "The thing is, he was going through some personal things at home. You never knew which guy would show up. Somedays he was great to be around and other days he seemed angry at anyone that got near him. He never confided in me what was going on but there were rumors."

"What kind of rumors?" Matt asked.

"You know, the usual—money troubles and marriage problems." Dylan stroked his chin. "I remember seeing some strange characters hanging around the station in those days. Anderson always had an excuse for why they were there. None of it seemed to jive at the time."

"You must have had a theory." Matt twirled the pen in his hand.

"I did. I never told my ideas to anyone, though. I mean, who could I tell? He was the chief." Dylan ran his hand through his hair.

"I get that. I believed he could do no wrong." Matt shook his head. "I'm only beginning to understand how corrupt he was, and I want to know why."

"I thought at the time—and still do—that there was something unsavory going on." Dylan paused. "Now when I look back after knowing about Anderson's involvement in the Harvest Club, I can see there was a crime syndicate operating in town. A few of the officers were operating in tandem with members of the city council. Money was passed under the table for the department to look the other way. When we learned about the money Anderson had at the time of his death, I know he didn't come by it legally. His wife never knew he had it."

"Agreed. I have a sinking feeling that there are a lot of investigations that we'll be cleaning up in the next few years. For now, this case is priority number one. That and a murder that Jessie dreamed about. Before you ask, there isn't a body or any other details yet." Matt explained about Jessie's dreams. "One of the victims is somewhere in our area. The first thing I need to do is look in our missing person reports."

"Maybe you should have Jessie look through them," Dylan suggested.

"Good idea." Matt leaned back in the chair. They kicked around ideas until it was time to leave.

"Do you think anyone is still working here that shouldn't be?" Dylan asked.

"I guess we're about to find out." Matt stood. "Let me know if anything else comes to mind."

****

Jessie looked around the store after the last customer left. This was her first moment to take a breather since getting back earlier. Audrey and Reba were in a chatty mood and the bookstore stayed busy until well past closing time. She would never complain about business being brisk. Even an occasional ghost couldn't deter her. She loved her life.

If only Sofia would call, she could breathe a lot easier. At least, Peyton would be home tonight, and Jessie could bounce things off her. Matt didn't always get what she was saying, although he tried hard. The more she thought about those girls today the more upset she became. The way the system worked didn't make it easy on the victim. In every court case she reported on including her own, the defense often shredded the character of the victim. That's exactly what the investigating agents did to those girls. It was time for society to quit excusing a man's bad behavior by trying to blame the victim for his abuse. Being in the news industry she understood that there were times the situation was reversed, and a man was accused of something he didn't do, but those times were few and far between in comparison.

Jessie went through her closing routine and left the store knowing that her stalker was close by watching her movement. Another thing to add to her anger. "Don't skulk in the shadows. Show yourself, jerk," she muttered under her breath. Starting her car, she drove home.

"Hey, cousin, where are you?" Peyton asked when

Jessie answered her phone.

"I just got home. Where are you?" Jessie took her keys out of the ignition.

"The plane landed, and I'll be starting my trek home as soon as I claim my bag."

"How was your flight?" Jessie asked.

"Good. It's the drive I'm dreading. I'm ready to be home. I'm trying to figure out how I feel about the past several days. I think Madison is too. No matter how much my dad apologized it's hard to believe this time will be any different. We've heard it all before."

"I understand. Believe me, I do. I have a lot I want to talk to you about too. I'm going to dinner with Matt but if you get bored on your drive home give me a call. Promise you'll call me when you get home. No matter what time. I'll worry until you do," Jessie told her.

"I will. I've missed you, Jess. I can't wait to sleep in my own bed tonight. Besides missing Jaxon, I'm eager to be home. Talk to you soon."

Jessie rushed to get ready. Running the brush through her hair, she reached for her lip gloss. Matt knocked and this time she had remembered to lock it. She wouldn't have to endure another one of his super-sweet lectures on staying safe. She was growing to appreciate those moments more than she wanted to acknowledge. A tidbit she jotted down on her pros and cons list titled, "Should I set a date or wait." She smiled at the man of her dreams when she opened the door.

He smiled back. "You look happy. Do you mind telling me why?" He blocked her from heading out the door.

"I'm glad to see you." She winked at him.

"Now I'm intrigued. Tell me more." He pulled her

into his arms.

"I talked to Peyton and she's on her way home. Oh, and I'm in the middle of a very delicate plan that I'm working on." She fluttered her lashes at him flirtatiously.

"Fill me in on this plan that has you smiling like you're delighted to see me." Matt nibbled on her ear.

"I am happy to see you. As far as the plan goes, I only have one entry so far. When it's finished, you'll be the first to know." She lifted her face to the kiss that she could see in his eyes. He didn't disappoint her.

"Fair enough." He smiled at the bemused look on her face. "I like this side of you, sweetheart."

"I'm glad you like me." Jessie peeked up at him.

"My feelings go way beyond like, Jess." He kissed her again. "Are you ready for dinner?"

She nodded and handed him her heavy sweater while she reached for her purse. "Yes, please." She slipped her arms in and strolled out the door in front of him.

To her way of thinking the evening had been almost perfect. Matt managed to make their investigation interesting not only because of the case itself but because he was beyond charming and attentive. Dinner was good but Matt—she smiled tapping her fingers on her temple—let's just say he was great. How she loved the man. She thought about how he tiptoed around telling her what she had to do. Cute in an endearing sort of way. Twice he almost broke into a sweat to keep from lecturing her. What a man. She chuckled recalling the grimace on his face and his uplifted chin stiff like granite when she explained how she told her stalker to come and get her. Never once did he tell her, but he did ask her through clenched teeth to please be careful not to become the damn man's target. His statement didn't equate since she already was his target and Matt knew it.

They ended up laughing at the absurdity of their conversation. Any normal person listening to their casual talk about ghosts, dreams of dead women, and a body that had yet to be found might think they were more than a little strange. Poor Matt. Since she came into his life all the craziness was now simply a dinner conversation. She needed to be nicer to him. As hard as all this had been for her, it must leave him scratching his head all the time.

Jessie got ready for bed and waited for Peyton's call. She slipped beneath the soft warm blankets with a sigh. Reaching for the book on her nightstand, she opened to the spot where she had left off. Reading her favorite author these days reminded her how much she missed her late-night chats with Katie about their favorite books.

Chapter Twelve

Caught up in a riveting story, Jessie wanted to put the book down but couldn't, even though the words were starting to blur together on the page. Her ringing phone came as a relief. She placed the bookmark on the page and closed the book.

"I almost didn't call because it's so late," Peyton said when Jessie answered.

"Oh, I'm glad you did. I got into a book. I was caught in that I need to read one more chapter trap." Jessie laughed. "I had started to beg for someone to stop me. Thank you."

"I'm happy to be of service, cousin." Peyton chuckled. "I got home later than I anticipated. I stopped several times on the way for coffee and to shake the cobwebs out of my brain. I'm not great at long drives by myself. I don't know how Jaxon did it every week."

"Our long drives were always together when we left New York. Oh, those were the days when we were off on some crazy adventures." Jessie sighed.

"We still have some strange trips now, only of a different variety, eh, cous?"

"True. Speaking of strange, let me fill you in on what's been going on since you left. I need you to think about it and we can talk more tomorrow." Jessie began with her dreams, progressed through the note left in her bookstore, and ended with seeing her face as the victim.

"Add to those, my dad's actions are messing with my head. I think you can see where I'm going with this."

"How long have I been gone? At least you told Matt, and I'm proud of you."

"I'm proud of myself too. I'm even more proud of Matt," Jessie told her about her evening with Matt. "He constantly surprises me. Thanks for calling me. Besides wanting to know you got home safe, I put the book down and now I can go to sleep."

"In that case, my job is finished here. I'll talk to you tomorrow. I need to let Jaxon know I'm here safe and sound."

"I'm not sure about the whole sound part." Jessie chuckled.

"Ha, ha, aren't you funny. Truthfully, I'm glad to be home and away from the drama. My bed is calling to me. Goodnight, cousin, sweet dreams only."

"Yes, please. I can live with that. Goodnight." Jessie shut off her light, snuggled under her covers, and tried to go to sleep while rewriting the last chapter she had read in her mind more to her liking. Something else popped into her head and she sat up turning on the light again.

****

Matt had dropped Jessie off at home and made it home without yelling at her once. Oh, he had wanted to, but she would have only yelled back. He may have lectured her on his way home in his head, but she never heard him utter one word. He grinned and he felt better for it. She was a handful, but never mind.

He reached for the remote as soon as he sat in his chair. Putting his feet up, he searched through the channels until he found what he wanted. What was he going to do about a stalker? He needed to get Jeremy involved. Maybe he could get a lead on a possible suspect. Texting a message, he sent it to his friend. The stalker had to be someone from her days in New York. Matt was sure of that one detail. Other than that, he had nothing to go on. From what Matt gathered, the stalker saw her when she was in the city with Katie and followed her.

Dang, this day had been a long one. All he wanted to do at the moment was zone out with a game, and he had found the perfect one to watch. He didn't care who won which meant he wouldn't get bent out of shape if his team lost. Never a good thing if you're trying to chill.

"Hey. Finally, home from the trenches I see." Matt muted the sound on the TV when Jaxon came through the door.

"This day was an overly long one. I spent more time in the car than anywhere else. I'm glad to be sitting on something that doesn't move." Jaxon sat back on the sofa leaning his head against the back.

"Those days are killers. I remember them well." Matt unmuted the sound. "What you need is some mindless TV."

"Sounds good to me. Something to eat wouldn't hurt either." Jaxon stood and walked into the kitchen. "Can I get you anything while I'm up?"

"I'm right behind you. There's a commercial on." Matt opened the cupboard and pulled out a couple of plates. "There's some turkey in the tray," he said when Jaxon opened the fridge. "Pull out the lettuce, tomatoes, and mayonnaise too while you're in there." He reached for the bag of chips and the bread in the pantry.

Jaxon grabbed a beer. "Do you want one?" He took out another when Matt nodded.

"The perfect drink to wash it all down." Matt began to build his sandwich, a sloppy work of art that he couldn't wait to sink his teeth into. How he could eat again so soon after dinner left him wondering about himself. The truth was he could eat almost anytime.

With full plates, they walked back into the living room. "I have no idea why I'm eating again. I went to dinner with Jess earlier." Matt positioned the plate on the table next to his chair within reach while he got comfortable.

"Do I detect a bit of stress? Mindless TV and food—that sounds like a stress reliever to me." Jaxon chuckled. "Don't tell me; let me guess. Jessie is challenging you again."

"Always, but at least my life never gets boring with her." Matt took a bite of his sandwich and went on to explain their conversation at dinner. "I feel like she's holding back something from me. I have no idea what but that's a discussion for another day."

"They are way out of our league. You know that, don't you? We are along for the ride, but they are light years ahead of us." Jaxon took a sip of his beer.

"I get it but that doesn't stop me from wanting to be prepared for the next surprise."

"Well, that's an oxymoron. How can you be both prepared and surprised? Surprise means unexpected does it not?" Jaxon laughed. "Good luck being prepared for the unexpected. I feel your pain, man. I'm right there with you."

"At least I'm not alone." Matt reached for his sandwich and took another bite. Mayonnaise and tomato squirted down his chin. "Man, this is sloppy. Just the way I like it." He never took his eyes off the TV while wiping his chin with a napkin. "How come yours isn't dripping?" Matt glanced at Jaxon.

"I didn't put half the ingredients on mine that you have on yours. This is how I make a sandwich after years and years of my mom telling me what constitutes a great sandwich and leave enough for your brothers." Jaxon laughed at Matt's expression. "Peyton's home. I think I'll give her a call." Jaxon picked up his plate and unfinished beer and walked past Matt toward the hall.

Matt lifted his messy sandwich as he passed. "Bro, this is a classic. Your mom will never know. I promise I won't tell. You're free, man," he called after Jaxon with laughter in his voice. "Tell Peyton hi from me. Maybe she'll tell you what Jessie's not telling me." Damn, he wished he knew.

****

She was going over her rewrite one more time when her phone rang. Bummer. She had forgotten to put it on silent mode. She reached for it as she sat up. "Hello." Her voice sounded groggy even to her.

"Hey, Jess, I'm sorry if awakened you," a feminine voice said.

"Katie, is that you?"

"In the flesh." Katie giggled.

"You're the last person I expected to hear from at this time of night. I thought you'd be with your new husband doing other things." Jessie chuckled.

"Right you are there, but he's the one who told me to call you."

"Why?" Jessie asked.

"We had this strange guy stop by the inn for

dinner. He started asking questions about the cottages and who lived there. He wanted to know if I knew a Jessica Reynolds."

"What did you tell him?" Jessie turned on the light, and Katie had her attention.

"I didn't give him much. I mostly stared at him. Thank goodness Dylan came up and talked to him. Dylan got information out of him lickety-split. The man told us he had already rented a room somewhere else, or he would have rented a room. I told him we were full anyway. I lied, of course." Katie exhaled into the phone. "Dylan was concerned enough to put a tail on him when he left here."

"I bet he's the same guy that came into my store earlier. Did anything stand out to you about his looks?"

"Something didn't seem right about him. His eye color seemed too intense," Katie said.

"Colored contacts, perhaps," Jessie mused. "I know I've seen him somewhere before, but then again, I'm not sure I have."

"Yes, with you anything is possible. Anyways, Dylan thought you should know. The guy was an odd bird and Dylan is talking to Matt about him right this minute." Katie cleared her throat. "Jessie, he was creepy. There was something almost maniacal about him. Honestly, I thought he would laugh bizarrely at any moment. Once again, as your best friend, I'm afraid for you. How do you attract these people?"

"I have no idea. I don't try to, that's for sure. I'd rather not have to worry about any of them. I don't want you to worry either."

"After meeting him that's easier said than done. I told you before, Jessica Lynn, quit searching for trouble. All the ghost junk and stories you chase bring these nuts out of the woodwork. You're asking for trouble when you try to find answers. Leave things alone. And now Peyton is following in your footsteps. But I still love you both, even if you are weird."

"That's kind of you." Jessie rolled her eyes.

"Did you just roll your eyes at me? You did, I know it."

"I'm not denying it. I know you don't believe this, Katie. I don't try to see these things. This only started happening to me when I moved here to be by you. I could say you're to blame for all this strangeness, but I won't because you're my friend. But you can stop with your lectures that don't apply. I can't stop something I have no control over, and neither can my cousin." Jessie swiped at the tears threatening to spill out of her eyes. "You should go be with your husband. I'll talk to you tomorrow." Jessie hung up before Katie could argue.

She loved her friend and knew Katie didn't understand. Neither did she, but she was learning to live with it. Who was the man? *Think, Jessie.* Turning her phone to silent mode, she laid her head back against the pillow. No way did she want to talk to Matt right now.

Chapter Thirteen

Sitting alone in his hotel room, he shook his head at his stupidity. Maybe he had been too cocky going to the inn. That woman's husband had turned the tables on him. He thought he could get the woman to talk but she stared at him strangely and gave him nothing. But when her husband joined her, they learned plenty from him. The guy's questions were direct and each one unnerved him. Damn, he would need to lie low for a while. Added to his dilemma, he noticed there was a car tailing him on the way back to his room. The occupant wasn't trying to hide what he was doing. Another element to unsettle him. Why? Were they on to him? He needed to do some heavy thinking about what his next step should be. If his instinct was right, that man was running a check on him right now. The guy had to be a cop. A damn cop. How could he be so stupid? He slammed his fist against the table.

****

"I'm telling you, Matt, this guy could be a problem. I had him followed. He's staying at a motel outside of town. He freaked Katie out," Dylan told him. "I got a close enough look at his face that I can check out some wanted bulletins or mug shots and see if our boy is among them. In the meantime, our tail will keep him under surveillance and notify me if he leaves his room or heads back this way."

"Great. Thanks, Dylan. What are we looking at?" Matt asked.

"He was definitely interested in Jessie. Katie didn't give him anything because she was creeped out," he explained. "At least, that's what she told me. I was able to get more out of him than I think he realized." Dylan went on to tell Matt what he had learned. "I'm working on a profile for you now and will have it on your desk tomorrow morning."

"Sounds good. I would call Jessie tonight to see if she has any ideas about who he might be, but I have a feeling she won't want to talk. Especially, if Katie told her you were calling me."

"She did," Dylan said.

"I figured as much. Tomorrow will be soon enough. Since he's being shadowed, Jessie should be safe enough tonight. But if he feels cornered, that might not bode well in the long run. We'll talk more tomorrow." Matt lifted his glasses to the top of his head.

"Okay."

Matt shut off the TV and headed to bed. He wanted to call Jessie, but he didn't. His next best choice was to send her a text. He couldn't hear her bristle that way. "You're a coward, my friend." He stretched out on his bed. "You're damn right about that. I don't like disappointing my girl," he said to himself as he pushed send.

—*Sleep well and have sweet dreams, my love. Someone is watching over you.*—

Matt could sleep better knowing he had sent an officer to watch over her cottage with a promise to call him if anyone came near it.

****

The sun pouring through the small opening in her curtain was the first sign that morning had arrived. As Jessie stretched, the conversation with Katie last night rushed into her mind. She reached for her phone and smiled when she read the text. Matt hadn't tried to call with a lecture. He was growing, and she was too. The endearment stood out in her mind. She liked him calling her, my love. With a sigh, she swung her legs out from under the covers and sat on the edge of the bed. She was sure this wouldn't be the extent of the conversation, but this was a good indication they could manage to discuss it like two grown adults without ripping apart their relationship.

One could hope her last thought wasn't wishful thinking. Jessie rushed through her morning routine and was ready for work. She waved at Peyton who was walking out the door at the same time. "Where are you off to? I thought you would be sleeping in this morning," Jessie called out.

"I'm meeting Jaxon at Joe's for coffee. Then I thought I would help you in the store if you wanted me."

"Of course, I want you. I thought you'd be back at the school today." Jessie started walking toward Peyton on the path.

"I go back to work on Monday. I can't wait to see my kids again. I'm not sure about being crowded in the other school, but the work isn't finished on our building yet."

"Reminders of a scary time. At least, we can catch up today. I want to hear about your trip." Jessie grabbed her arm as they walked the path to their cars. "I missed you."

"I missed you too. I can't wait to hear what's been happening in our, not so much, quiet little peaceful community," Peyton said as she got into her car.

Jessie waved as she backed out of the parking space. Of course, she had to do her traditional honk as she drove by the inn hoping her friend could hear. Katie's comments last night reminded her of how much she loved having Peyton who understood this strange new world in which she found herself. Life before ghosts and strange cases seemed lost in the past. Katie didn't understand her anymore. This new reality for her came with a lot of questions. At least she had someone who understood what she felt. Peyton stood right beside her in the ghost department. Matt tried to understand. One of the many reasons she loved him.

Understanding her dreams and what she was supposed to do about them was number one on her list. Obviously, the murder victims she had seen wanted closure along with their families. What was her part in that? The girls who they interviewed were searching for answers. How could she help? Sofia needed to be found, and waiting to hear from her was getting troublesome. *Why hasn't she called? And who desired her dead and why? Would he be successful?* Her dream left her wondering. Was it her fate or a warning?

When Jessie opened the doors to the coffee shop, she waved at Jaxon and Peyton. They made a striking couple. As soon as she unlocked the front door the first person to walk in was Marilyn Barton.

"Have you heard from Sofia?" Jessie asked her.

"No." She shook her head. "I was hoping you had. But I think she's all right. I would know if she wasn't, wouldn't I?" Marilyn looked at her with questioning eyes. "I mean a mother should know if her child is dead. Unless I am foolishly holding onto hope and refusing to believe what's in front of me. It's been days." She reached for the tissue in the box on the counter.

"Sofia will call when she can." Jessie crossed her fingers behind her back. "Why don't you sit down in one of my comfy chairs and I'll bring you a cup of tea or coffee, whichever you prefer." She walked with her to the chair.

"Coffee would be nice." She reached for the magazine on the table beside her and began to flip through the pages absently. "Cream, please," she said as Jessie walked away.

"Coffee it is." Jessie returned with the cup and one of Molly's wonderful blueberry scones. When Marilyn reached for her purse Jessie told her, "This is on me. Try to relax if you can. Maybe Sofia will call while you're here." Again, Jessie crossed her fingers behind her back.

Sofia didn't call when her mother was there. Jessie wished she had. But enough was going on in the store to keep her and Peyton busy with little time to talk. First Reba came in on her way to the church and delivered one of her cryptic messages on the run. She warned them about an odd-looking man with a patch covering his eye and a limp. Peyton proved to be no help at all. She dissolved into laughter every time she looked at Jessie.

"Are we to be visited by Blackbeard's ghost?" Jessie couldn't help herself.

Peyton giggled. "Arr, with his peg leg and a

pirate's patch upon his eye."

"Could you be serious for a moment?" Jessie tried not to smile but to no avail.

"I'm trying but you have to admit that is one of the strangest things she has ever said to us, and there have been a few of them."

"I wonder what she could mean. I hope she comes back to tell us." Jessie pushed her hair behind her ears.

"I'm not sure I want to know. What if she meant it literally?" Peyton frowned.

As Jessie recounted to Matt later, "That was the sanest part of the day. It went downhill from there. Besides the ghosts moving in and out of my customers hypnotically, I kid you not, the atmosphere in the store seemed charged." She patted Matt's hand and took note of his perplexed expression. She had no idea men rolled their eyes like that. "And if that wasn't enough, a man came into the store wearing a patch over his eye. His limp caught my attention. He told Peyton he had slipped on the ice."

"You're kidding me." Matt shook his head. "None of this is real. Right?"

"No. Even I couldn't make something this crazy up. The man kept skulking around the edges of the store asking the oddest questions. When Reba came back after her meeting, she turned white as a ghost. She came up and whispered in my ear that he was the one she saw. She told me he wasn't who he seemed to be. At that point, I almost laughed in her face." Jessie smiled thinking about her reaction. "I was still trying to figure out who he was trying to be. If he didn't want to draw attention to himself, he was doing a poor job at it."

"Did you say ghosts?" he asked.

"Yes, I did. And don't ask why there were more than one because I have no idea." She shrugged her shoulders.

"What happened next?" Matt leaned back in his chair.

"Well, one of the ghosts didn't like the man, or at least that's my take on it because she began to circle him like a whirling dervish. I could see the man's anxiety rising with each of her spins around him. He suddenly lifted the patch off his eye as if he were trying to see what was bothering him. He had a nasty shiner. Next, his noticeable limp seemed to magically disappear when he ran out the door with the ghost in hot pursuit." She got a case of the giggles and couldn't continue.

"Jess, sweetheart, get a hold of yourself." Matt smiled at her. "I want to know what your gut tells you?"

"Excuse me… My gut doesn't talk. Peyton and I do though." She went on to explain her theory of it all for the next thirty minutes.

"Something to think about. Could you make it concise? You lost me when you circled the theory for the third time." Matt lifted her chin to make her look at him. "Concentrate, please."

"I thought I was. Bottom line, he was in disguise, and I'm sure I've seen him working somewhere around town, or maybe it was the police station. I'm not sure which one."

"Finally, a piece of information I can work with. If you remember, tell me, please."

She nodded. "I thought my first version was better. You have to admit my store is a happening place."

"You could say it that way if you'd like. I was

thinking something different though." He laced his fingers through hers.

"Dare I ask what?" She chuckled when he shook his head.

Their conversation turned "normal" after that. Jessie smiled later when she thought of all the times Matt looked at her oddly all through dinner and during the movie. She kept count. Twenty-five times to be exact. No doubt she had shaken up his well-ordered life, but he liked it, and she knew he loved her. She could only imagine what their life together would look like. It couldn't get much stranger. Nope, she had better not utter those words in the airwaves. It might present a challenge to the powers that be to prove her wrong.

Chapter Fourteen

Between the odd man coming into her store and the strange dream she had the night before Jessie found herself chasing a rabbit trail researching the pirate Blackbeard. It wasn't that she thought the pirate had in some way come into her store but something about the patch had intrigued her. She had dreamed of pirates and swashbuckling adventures all night. A dream that had all the makings of a great romance novel. Jessie laughed. Maybe she would write if she found the time. There were relatively few known facts about the man whose real name was Edward Teach. Born in England, he turned to piracy after serving in the queen's navy. The effects of war, perhaps? Teach chose a frightening name and appearance to help with his persona, not much different than other criminals in history. His changes were made to minimize resistance to his plunder. Who would be afraid of a man named Edward? But Blackbeard was another thing altogether. Hmm. She tapped her fingers on the desk. The legends surrounding the pirate were scarier than the man. Those who crossed paths with him said he looked like the devil himself in battle. With his long unruly beard, dressed in all black from head to toe, and with several guns strapped across his chest, most of his victims surrendered their cargo rather than fight. He promised to slaughter anyone who resisted in horrible ways with no mercy while those who didn't resist were left alive. Their stories helped to romanticize him long after his death.

Jessie's mind took off. She wondered if his ghost still roamed the seas. That image of evil would be enough to spur fear. There was more to the odd man who came into her store and their silly conversation about Blackbeard. No, the man didn't cause fear, but he did start a conversation. Now all she had to do was figure it out. Maybe the fear factor was reversed when it came to the man in her store. He looked normal but looks often were deceiving. She couldn't help wondering who gave him that black eye.

She shut her computer down. If she didn't hurry, she would be late. She shook her head. Her mind was a strange place some days. It wasn't about the pirate but more about his escapades. Were they looking at something similar in a suspect today?

In what part of the case did he belong or have a role? Was he simply there to get her thinking outside the box? She couldn't wait to talk to Peyton and see if she had any ideas. Jess poured her coffee into her to-go mug. She slipped into her jacket, grabbed her purse, and locked the door on her way out. The weird thing about that man yesterday was that he seemed familiar. That made two for two, and she had no idea how she knew either of them.

As she drove to work, she went over her conversation with Matt last night. The thought hit her that maybe the man yesterday was trying to bring attention to himself and not hide it. But why would he want to? More questions than answers, and she needed to think about the book order that had to go out this morning. The book order got her thinking of Evan Foster who delivered her books and the investigation that took her to Palm Springs to find his wife Adriana. Because of that case she had a sweet baby girl named after her. Nothing happened by chance. At least, not lately, and her store seemed to have more than its share of the unusual.

The first time she saw Evan, her store was still in process, and if truth be told, he made her nervous. He was shocked to see the same woman he had dreamed about several times too. The bookstore had been the center of many strange happenings, and yesterday seemed no different. Her life took noteworthy to a whole new level.

Jessie went about her morning routine to open her store. Peyton promised to help later on if she needed her. Turning the open sign around she unlocked the front door. Her phone in her pocket started to buzz at the same time the bell above the door rang. Looking at her phone, she knew she needed to take the call. "I'll be right with you," she told the woman as she looked around.

"Hello, this is Jessie," she answered her phone.

"Hi, I'm Sofia's friend. She asked me to call you because she's afraid that someone is tracking her phone."

"Is she okay?" Jessie asked.

"She's scared. They told her if she talked they would hurt her family, and that's why she went into hiding. Could you tell her mom that she's good?"

"Of course. Where is she and who said they would hurt her family?" Jessie asked.

"I can't answer either of those questions because I

don't know. She wouldn't tell me. All I know is Sofia called and asked me to contact you. She said you would understand."

"What's your name, so I can tell her mother?" Jessie watched the customer walk around the store and stop at the table with discounted books.

"My name is Jenna Simpson. Her mom knows me well," the girl said.

"Thank you, Jenna. If you hear from Sofia don't hesitate to call me anytime." Jessie turned off her phone and walked over to help her customer.

As soon as the woman paid for her purchases, Jessie called and left a message for Matt about Sofia. Next on her list was Marilyn Barton to let her know that Jenna Simpson had called. Marilyn was both relieved and angry. She wanted her daughter home and not to have to hide out because of some threat. Nothing Jessie said calmed her. Marilyn was ready to go to battle over her daughter.

Matt's diplomacy might be needed. If Marilyn went into the gym in her present state, she would tip them off to the ongoing investigation and her daughter's involvement. She could put the girl in danger. Jessie straightened the book table hoping some great idea would make its way into her head. Where were the answers when you needed them most? Matt would be talking to Jenna Simpson for sure probably a few times.

****

Matt listened to Jessie's message again on his way back into town. A body had been found by a tourist doing some backcountry hiking. Matt spent the morning at the site with his team collecting evidence for forensics. He had left when the coroner took the body away. The young woman was found just as Jessie had seen in her dream.

His car knew where he needed to go first. Parking in front of her store, Matt smiled at the image he could see through the window. The sunlight glistened off her curls, as she stood motionless at the display table. Lost in thoughts she didn't even see him watching her. What was his girl thinking about now?

Matt walked in the door and watched her turn when the bell rang. "Hi, sweetheart."

"Oh, I didn't see you drive up." She smiled sheepishly as she walked toward him.

"I noticed. I was beginning to wonder where you were." He hugged her, resting his chin on the top of her head.

"Thinking is all," she replied absentmindedly.

"I figured as much. About what?" He squeezed her tighter.

"Too many things to count. You know how my mind works." She pushed back to glance at his face.

"I'm about to add another one." He led her to the table and pulled out a chair for her.

"Is that why you're here? I thought maybe you had come because of the phone call." She leaned back in the chair when he sat next to her.

"I'm here about your message, and I have one of my own." Reaching for her hand he began to explain about finding the body. "It was like how you described her. She was found by someone walking in the woods not far from the reservation but hidden off the main paths."

"Do you know who she is?"

"Not yet. Lewis should help with that. I'll check through missing persons when I get back to the station."

"I'm sorry, but I'm not surprised." She stroked his hand. "The dream had been too real not to be true." She rubbed her forehead.

"Are you hungry?" he asked.

"I could eat something."

"I'll go buy us lunch, and then I want you to tell me about Jenna's call and what your instincts are telling you." He stood and walked into the coffee shop. He returned a few minutes later with their lunch. "Your store is quiet. Has it been like this all morning?"

"I've had only one customer this morning. I have no idea why. I guess every day can't be a busy one." She took a bite of the chicken salad sandwich and smiled. "You know me and what I like."

"I should by now. I pay attention, and I'm a quick learner." He grinned. "Tell me about the call."

"It was pretty cut and dry." She explained to him about what Jenna told her. "I was more concerned about Marilyn's reaction to it. Although, I would feel the same way, I'm sure. She promised me she would wait until you called her."

"I'll take care of it." He pushed her hair back that had fallen over her cheek. "Promise me you'll stop worrying. At least, you have one less thing to worry about. I don't like seeing these creases on your forehead." His finger traced the line.

Jessie wrapped up the rest of her sandwich and stood when two ladies walked into the store. "I need to talk to you about something else, but not now. We can talk later." She leaned close to him so only he could hear.

Matt finished his sandwich and watched her at work. Something was bothering her. Maybe she had finally decided to tell him. The question was, was he ready to hear it? He cleaned up his trash and waved at her as he walked toward the front door.

"Matt, wait up a minute." Jessie rushed in his direction. "Thank you for stopping to tell me. I knew what I saw was real. Sometimes I don't know how to interpret my dreams but this one had been self-explanatory."

"You seem troubled, Jess. What's going on?" He leaned close and lowered his voice.

"I'll talk to you tonight. I'll make something for dinner." She turned to check on her customer.

"I'll be there but I'll bring dinner. I don't want you to have to work. See you." He gave her a quick kiss and left. Yep, something was bothering her, and if it concerned her, it would probably trouble him. Not knowing was disquieting. He stood for a moment by his car door and watched her talking to her customer. She affected him in too many ways to count. Love was a risky business. It seemed that as euphoric as the emotion could feel at times, it could also leave him vulnerable and worried more often than not.

Chapter Fifteen

Jessie watched Matt drive away. He could sense her mood even though she had tried hard not to let him see how troubled she felt. Her mother always told her that she couldn't hide her emotions—they were always written on her face. Adulthood hadn't improved her ability. At least she hadn't broken down into tears, her usual practice. Poor Matt didn't know what to do when her waterworks started. He tried. She smiled. At least now he simply held her and didn't pound her back trying to comfort her. The man didn't know his own strength.

How would he take the news when she told him about the dream that had her fretting? She wasn't sure how she felt about the nightmare. How could she even begin to imagine how he would feel? If the situation were reversed and a premonition was about him, she would be freaked out. The ringing bell above the door brought reinforcements and the two people she wanted to see most.

"Hello, dear girl. I met Peyton on my way in. We are here because you need us to be." Reba removed her coat and placed it over the chair. "It's time to talk."

"I'm glad you're here."

"Of course, you are." Reba sat at the table and patted the chair next to her. "Peyton is going to get our tea and treats. We need to put our heads together and come up with a plan."

"I swear you have a second sense about these things." Jessie sat beside Reba.

"Your cousin was worried after you told her about the last dream. It shook me at first too but then I thought of several questions that I have. Details make a big difference in the meaning of dreams and premonitions. As soon as Peyton returns, we need to go over my questions." Reba crossed her legs at the ankles and made herself comfortable. "There's our girl now."

Peyton placed the three cups of tea on the table. Molly followed with a plate of mini scones and lemon bars. "Enjoy, ladies." Molly smiled when Reba pressed a few bills into her hands. "Thank you."

"You work hard, Molly. You deserve this and much more. Your young man is good to you. The happiness is written on your face. Young love is wonderful." Reba sighed as Molly retreated back into the coffee shop. "Looks to me like Molly has a new addition on the way. I might be wrong, but I seldom am."

"I guess she'll tell us when she's ready." Jessie turned to look at Molly through the doors. "It would be awesome if she was."

"Or when she knows. She may not know it yet," Reba added. "Okay, tell me about your dream."

Jessie explained her unsettling dream. "When I saw the victim had my face, it shook me."

"When she told me that piece of news, I admit I freaked a bit." Peyton sipped her tea. She reached across the table and squeezed her cousin's hand.

"The first question I have is, were your eyes open or closed?" Reba waited for her answer and then proceeded to ask her several other questions.

"The area wasn't familiar to me. I don't remember seeing any area around the cove, like the landscape I could see. Although, it was dark." Jessie reached for one of the mini scones. "My eyes were open."

"This is my take on it. I don't want you to be afraid but to be prepared. Plus, you will need to make that handsome man of yours feel at ease." Reba spent the next several minutes telling Jessie what she thought. "Someone is going to try to abduct you, but you can outsmart them. But that has nothing to do with your dream. You will be invested in that scene somehow. Do you remember the strange man who came into your store?"

"Yes, we laughed about him." Jessie smiled at Peyton.

"Don't forget things aren't always as they seem. But you, my girl, are up to the task." Reba reached for a lemon bar.

"Because of that man, I researched a pirate. What seemed strange to me at the time makes a whole lot more sense now. Our conversation today is similar to my thoughts yesterday. I need to think about all this for a while." Jessie jumped up when the bell rang. She had to get back to work but not before she popped the last bite of scone into her mouth and sipped the last of her tea. As she started to walk away, she overheard Reba talking to Peyton.

"She'll be all right. I know it in my heart." Those few words did more to assure Jessie than anything anyone else could say. Reba always knew. It didn't mean she wouldn't have to face down an angry man. It simply met she would live to tell the story. Music to her ears, a small kernel of hope to latch onto, that's what those words gave her in the face of a dream that still overwhelmed her to think about. The angst that came with the dream still unsettled her.

Plus, she still had to find a way to tell Matt. Jessie could only imagine his reaction. There had to be a way to make her dream easier for him to process without causing undue concern. *But tell him I must, because even I know that I'll require his help at some point.*

"Hey, cousin, are you okay?" Peyton hugged her.

"Yes and no. You know the feeling."

"Sure do. I wanted you to know that I have the same impression as Reba regarding your dream," Peyton said. "Ultimately, you will be fine. But I think we may be looking at someone who doesn't think conventionally, which might present a challenge. We'll work through this together. I'm here like you were there for me."

"Have you noticed that the same theme keeps popping up? Unconventional is one way of describing him but another thought came to my mind. Patchy or erratic, which is harder to plan for. It also means he may not be as clever and careful as he thinks."

"Less than careful means our suspect can mess up along the way and hand you a lifeline," Peyton said. "Patchy is a perfect description considering the strange guy yesterday. We can't forget our sense of humor." Peyton chuckled.

"How can we ever forget him? I tell you, Peyton, the strangest people come into this store. I can't for the life of me figure out why." Jessie smiled at the next customer walking in the door. "We had better get to work. You help that lady, and I'll wait on her." Jessie pointed at a woman standing near one of the bookshelves.

"Hopefully, they're both normal," Peyton whispered as she crossed her fingers.

"May I help you?" Jessie asked the attractive woman.

"Yes, I'm here to see you." The woman pointed at her.

Another mother of one of the girls told her their story. Jessie understood their pain. What could she do but put a bandage on a gaping wound? At least she was kept busy most of the afternoon but now the closer her talk got with Matt the more nervous she became.

Once at home, she paced from the window back to the couch. Her mind raced through ways she could explain to Matt not only her dream but the fact she would be fine on her own. The knock came on the door precisely at the moment an ingenious idea came into her mind.

Taking her time to open the door she formulated the conversation in her mind. "Hi," she said as she opened the door.

"Hi, yourself." He grinned. The bag in his hand that contained their dinner smelled yummy as he walked past her.

The grumbling from her stomach was her timely response. "What's for dinner?" she asked. "It smells good."

"Patterson's had a comfort food special, and I couldn't help myself. Calorie packed I'm sure, but what's not to like about fried chicken and baked mac and cheese?" He pulled the food out of the bag. "I did get you a dinner salad for your healthy eating pleasure."

He reached into the second bag. "Of course, there's no way I could pass up Patterson's famous lemon meringue pie. I hope you like lemon." He pulled her into his arms and gave her a quick kiss.

"I'm sure I can force it down." She smiled at him as she pulled out of his arms. Jessie set the table while Matt watched her.

"How did your day go?" Matt asked. "Or should I wait to ask that until after we are through with dinner?"

"It doesn't matter." Jessie took a chicken breast, a spoonful of macaroni, and some salad and placed her napkin on her lap. As she ate, she told him about her day while leaving out a few details. She told him about the woman who came to see her. They had talked to her daughter during the interviews. "I felt bad for her. She's angry and devastated. I get her frustration. I know the feeling all too well."

Jessie loved moments like this. She glanced at Matt often. He was easy to look at and listening to him talk about his day over dinner gave her a sense of continuity. He had his glasses on which meant he'd been reading files and his eyes were tired. Is this what a relationship was supposed to be? Steady, comfortable, and with a sense of connection. She could learn to love these times. Matt did everything he could to include her and make her feel special. Was it a pipe dream to believe these moments could last? She wanted to believe that no matter what life threw at them their love would endure. She sighed.

****

His girl had been thoughtful through dinner, which often confused him. What was she thinking about? He had caught her watching him several times, followed by a few sighs.

"Jess, do you want some decaf to go with your pie?" He stood clearing their plates from the table. "I'll have to tell Patterson next time I see him what a great meal that was. He told me tonight's special was a winner and he was right."

"Coffee sounds good." Jessie opened the dishwasher and loaded their dishes.

"Are you okay? You seem preoccupied tonight." He handed her the silverware.

"I'm fine. I liked listening to you share about your day." She grabbed two cups out of the cupboard and poured in the hot liquid "Let's eat our dessert in the living room. We may as well be comfortable."

"This is what I'm talking about." He took a big bite of the pie. "Best lemon pie ever."

She wiped a bit of meringue off his lip. "I couldn't help myself." She pulled her hand back. "I love these on you." She touched the rim of his glasses.

"I don't mind, sweetheart. I like when you touch me." He reached for her hand and held her fingers to his lips. "Do you have the same feeling that I do?" He kissed each one. "We're good together."

"Yes," she said softly.

That simple word was music to Matt's ears. Not wanting to spoil the moment he would let her off the hook tonight. No serious conversation, he opted for casual conversation, words of love punctuated with kisses, and some TV show playing in the background which he paid little attention to. He could sense as the night moved on that she relaxed in his arms. The evening was perfect.

"Jess, I know you need to tell me something? What

if I call you when I get home and you can tell me then?" He stood and pulled her into his hug when she stood. "Tonight needed to be about us being together." He kissed her. "I love you, sweetheart. We'll talk in a few."

"Thank you." She framed his face with her hands. "You knew exactly what I needed." She glanced at the beautiful ring on her finger. "I love you too."

Something important happened tonight but Matt couldn't find the words to describe the strange sensation. He had to be careful not to blow this new special connection between them. Trust wasn't easy to regain once lost. "Remain steady, old man," he said his breath rising from his lips in the cold car.

Matt pulled into the garage when he arrived home. He clicked the remote and whistled on his way into the house. He took his glasses off and slipped them into his pocket. He forgot that he still had them on until Jessie reminded him.

"Long day?" Jaxon asked.

"Nope, I was hanging out with Jessie. How about you?" Matt sat in his favorite chair.

"I got home in time for dinner with Peyton. Anytime I get to spend with her is great."

"Seems like you two are getting serious." Matt reached for his phone to send a text to Jessie.

—I'll call you in half-hour.—

She replied with a smiley face.

"You could say that. I can't see myself with anyone else. Just when I think I need to take our relationship slower she surprises me and I'm ready to buy a ring."

"I know a good jeweler when you're ready." Matt

grinned at him. "Those two gals can mess with your head in a good way."

****

Jessie had thirty minutes to come up with the best way to tell Matt. For some reason, she was calm about it. He would understand. Walking over to her computer, she checked her emails before heading to her room. The one she read first was from Jeremy. He had been looking into several areas for her. How he managed to get into employee files she didn't know and wouldn't dare ask. He compiled a shortlist of people who might have a grudge against her. She didn't like the thought of her actions making someone angry at her. He also had a lengthy list of missing Native American girls from all across the country. She printed the information. There was enough info to start a search for answers.

She wished Jeremy would move here. Katie was taken but she was sure there was a girl out there for him. She would love to help him find her. Wishful thinking on her part. Jeremy was a good friend and he deserved only the best. *And I know the perfect girl.* Jessie smiled, closed down her computer, and got ready for a phone call.

She stretched her legs out on her bed plumping pillows behind her back and waited. She studied the list of male counterparts who had issues with her. The sad thing was she couldn't remember who a couple of them were. Two of them had been a constant thorn in her side with their misogynistic attitudes. Constantly calling her little lady, they told her it was time to go home and that the newsroom was for the big boys. She held her own, which infuriated them. Could that make one of them angry enough to come after her? To track her down and

125

threaten her? Anything was possible. Except both of those men were a nuisance but family men. She couldn't see either of them being her stalker. It had to be one of the other names on the list and she couldn't remember who they were. Jessie reached for her ringing phone.

"Were you sitting on your phone?" He chuckled.

"I was waiting for your call. You did say thirty minutes."

"Yes, I did. I'm nothing if not punctual." He cleared his throat. "I got an email from Jeremy. He said he sent one to you too."

"Yes, I've been reading through the information he sent." Jessie shuffled the pages in her hand.

"Does anyone stand out to you?" he asked.

"Not really," Jessie said as she went on to explain what she knew about the two men who she remembered. "The other two I have no idea who they are."

"Jeremy suggested it could be someone obsessed with you who felt jilted by your lack of response to him. There's a fine line between love and hate. You never know what will push someone over the line."

"I doubt that theory. I have no clue who those two men are, or if I ever saw them." Jessie scrunched her face.

"Sweetheart, no sense prolonging the misery. Tell me what's going on."

Jessie had rehearsed the dream and Reba's words over in her mind many times and the whole explanation blurted out of her in a short amount of time. From the man with the patch, to what she learned about the pirate, she left nothing out. Not even seeing herself as the victim in her dream. "Reba's words softened what I had seen in my dream. Honestly, the dream had me freaked."

"Damn, Jess. I wasn't expecting that. You've been carrying this all by yourself. Sweetheart, you have to learn to trust me. I'm working hard not to overreact and you're going to have to do the same."

"Okay," she said softly.

"I'm not saying that I don't want to hide you away because I do. But I've come to recognize your many strengths and that you're a different woman than you were a year ago when we first met. The past year has changed you. You're much stronger."

"Thank you." She smiled to herself. His words were like a warm blanket around her heart.

"I will do all I can to keep you out of harm's way, but I promise I will try not to smother you if I can help myself. But when it comes to an open investigation, I have to have the last word."

"I can live with that," she told him.

"With that settled, let's go over all of this again."

Jessie began to go over all her dreams, the ghosts, and the weird guy with the patch. "We can't forget the guy who I think I recognized that left that strange note. He's a definite suspect."

"You've given me a lot to go over. I'll run the info by Jaxon too. This investigation seems to be getting bigger by the minute. I have Frank coming with his dog to go over the crime site. I might have him see if he can track Sofie."

"Sounds perfect." Jessie yawned. "I have an early morning tomorrow."

"Sweet dreams." Matt disconnected the call.

Matt, you're a prince among men. She sighed, pulled up the covers, and snuggled under them. Fingers were crossed for sweet dreams of her handsome man.

Chapter Sixteen

Her prince was agitated but quite proud of himself for keeping his cool. Jessie would have someone to keep an eye on her whether she knew or not. He didn't know why, but instinct told him that Jessie was headed into uncharted waters with him following in her wake. He hated being taken by surprise. The investigation seemed fairly routine up to this point, which should be a good place to be. But normal when it came to Jessie was what three boys making plans were to their parents hearing their whispers—a wake-up call.

What is normal anymore? Investigations with a ghost are par for the course since Jess. It had almost become routine, but he had a gnawing feeling there was more to come, a lot more. Jessie would be in the center of any trouble, he had no doubt. For now, he'd talk over what he knew with Jaxon and Dylan tomorrow. *How do you prepare for the unknown?* He had no idea, but he would do his damnedest.

"Matt are you awake?" Jaxon knocked on his door.

"Yep. What's up?"

"Our snitch on the inside that I told you about says Zach Johnson is involved in some kind of operation from prison. As of now, we don't know what the operation is, but our guy is working his way into the circle to find out."

"I figured Zach had his hands in it somewhere.

129

He's dirty. Johnson operated the Collectors Club online from prison and I want to know what he's been up to since we busted him for that." Matt frowned. "He must be getting better at hiding his tracks to have gone under the radar this long." He raked his fingers through his hair.

"I read about that group. They had some grand ideas and a lot of illegal weapons." Jaxon shook his head.

"They did, and thankfully we were able to shut them down before they enacted those plans." Matt frowned. "Something bothers me about this case though."

"Oh, what's that?" Jaxon leaned his hip against the door frame.

"Before you knocked, I was thinking about what we have to this point. It's been too tidy."

"Isn't that a good thing?" Jaxon asked.

"You tell me. In light of our last few cases involving the Reynolds, this is not normal."

"I see your point. I wonder if Peyton has anything. I'll ask her."

"Thanks. I know I should be happy, but I'm worried." Matt sat on the edge of the bed. "Apprehensive isn't a term used often to describe me. If anything, I'm overconfident before I'm knocked upside the head. I have to wonder why I'm bothered now. Let me know if you get anything. I might be having withdrawals from the weird." Matt chuckled.

"I get it. When it comes to us, ordinary might be disconcerting. I've been thinking outside the box so much that I have no idea what a normal investigation looks like anymore." Jaxon folded his arms across his chest. "Maybe that's your problem too."

"One can hope. Hey, thanks for the info on Zach. I hope your guy can get us more details. Meanwhile Jeremy and Gary are searching for unusual recruiting websites online."

Jaxon pushed away from the frame. "Don't think too much." He closed the door. "Good luck with that."

"I heard that, Jaxon," Matt snapped. He stretched out on the bed prepared for a long night lost in thought.

****

"Hi." Jessie waved at her cousin as she walked out the door the next day. "Are you working at the other school?"

"Yes." Peyton met her in the middle of the path.

"I'll bet it'll be hard the first day back at your school," Jessie told her.

"I'm dreading it and at the same time looking forward to going back. I think in some regards it will be therapeutic," she said as she opened her car door. "Have a good day. I'll stop by the store later and you can catch me up on what's going on."

"Sounds good." Jessie got in her car. She honked the horn as she drove by the inn.

The sky was blue, the sun shining, and the temps were supposed to be warmer today. All good news in her book. Spring was here and soon her summer hours would come along with the tourists. First on her agenda for the day was a job interview for an open position in the store. She didn't want to work a twelve-hour day.

Her store still made her happy every time she walked through the doors. Idle Time Books was one of the better decisions she had made. Even her dad couldn't find fault with her sound business choices. Her dad was a whole other subject. He seemed like a different man. Even her mom said the same several times in conversations lately. Maybe there was something to that whole family curse thing that Elida and Mila had told them about. No idea, but something had happened to alter the man. Her dad's transformation reminded her of Matt's words, change comes slowly.

She would take it warily as a gift. Hopefully, it would be permanent. The same seemed true with Peyton's dad. Peyton had a lot more to overcome when it came to her dad. The abuse Jessie's cousins had endured would take years for the trust to be rebuilt. For now, they were both in a wait-and-see mode. Curse or no curse, both men had made the choices for their lives that they had to live with and compensate for.

She waved at Molly as she opened the doors. Joe's was hopping. Kenny and Molly had turned their business into a prosperous enterprise. The coffee shop had a great atmosphere, friendly service, and some of the best food around. Joe's was one of the best spots in town for a quick bite to eat, and the big plus was that it opened to her bookstore. What's not to love—coffee and books or, in Reba's case, tea. People wandered into her store with coffee in their hands or went from her store into Joe's for something to drink with their book. A true win, win for both of their businesses. Molly welcomed Jessie on her first day in town and they had been good friends ever since.

"As soon as it slows down, I'll be in with your favorite," Molly called to her. "I have something to tell you."

"Sounds good, especially if by my favorite you

mean one of your blueberry scones." Jessie smiled at her and walked to the front of the store to open. She tried to guess what Molly wanted to tell her. Her game ended when her first customer walked in the door.

"Can I help you?" Jessie asked the woman.

"I've come to see the woman who has filled my dreams the last several nights. You are unique, I've been told, and will help to solve a great mystery or at least part of it," the woman told her as she walked closer to her.

"I'm not sure what you're talking about." Jessie studied the beautiful woman. There was a mysterious aura around her. And how did she come to be in the woman's dreams?

She flung her long dark hair over her shoulder. "No, I'm sure you don't." Her deep brown eyes stared thoughtfully at Jessie. "Before I leave, you will." She motioned to the chairs. "Sit. I don't have much time, and there is much you need to know."

Jessie sat, though she had no idea what to expect. "I'm listening."

"You don't know me, but I know you. My name is not important, but my message is." She reached for Jessie's hand. "You're being watched. He knows you've seen him."

Heat shot through Jessie's arm and down her back at the point of the woman's contact. She was tempted to push her hand away and stand, but she didn't move. "I think names are important. Mine is Jessie."

"I already know yours." She shook her head stopping Jessie's question. "You have been in my dreams, as I've told you. I was led to this place to find you. I've traveled a great distance to contact you. Your heart toward the hurting is well known, and I've been directed to give you a message." The woman's piercing eyes stared at her in an almost mesmerizing fashion.

"Still, I would like to know your name," Jessie told her. "It seems important to me to know the name of the person giving me a message."

Her lips turned up at the corners. "You're astute, for one new to this world."

"Let's just say, I learn quickly." Jessie leaned back against the chair feeling more at ease.

"My name is Kimama." The woman paused long enough for her name to sink in.

"Oh, my. No wonder you didn't want to tell me. How is any of this possible?" Jessie was dumbfounded as the full understanding of who the woman was hit her. Jessie had read about Kimama in a diary from the 1800s. In it, Cara had described her friend Kimama as beautiful, and Jessie agreed. If anything, Cara didn't do her justice.

"You've heard of me. I was certain you had. I've traveled beyond the door to reach you at this time and place." She reached for Jessie's hand. "You're about to embark on an improbable journey." She put her hand up. "I don't want to be interrupted." She went on to explain for the next ten minutes what she wanted Jessie to understand. "I don't want for you only to see the tears but to feel them. You can tell your cousin for she will understand. Yes, I know of her too. She found the book and my son. I'm resting peacefully now in my world. But you must not tell anybody else until your work is done." Kimama stood. "You've seen the girls who others have not, and now you will feel the sorrow of their stolen dreams." She walked out of the store without looking back.

Jessie was sure her mouth was hanging open. How would she ever make it without telling Matt? Did what had just happened, happen at all? She was finding it hard to believe. Kimama seemed to know things about her including her dreams. Wow, did she need to talk to Peyton. Like Cara, Kimama mentioned the world beyond the door.

"I've been trying to bring you your scone and coffee for at least the last ten minutes. Every time I started to bring it to you something came up to stop me," Molly told her placing both on the table. "Are you okay? You've been sitting there alone in the same place for at least ten minutes."

"I'm fine. Daydreaming is all." Jessie's mind started to race ahead. Molly hadn't seen the woman. Was she even real? She sure seemed to be.

"I wanted to tell you my good news." Molly's voice pulled Jessie back into the moment.

"I can't wait to hear. I can always use good news." Jessie smiled at her.

"I'm pregnant." Molly beamed. "Kenny couldn't be more pleased and I'm over the moon happy. Of course, I'll have to figure it all out with the business and hire a bit more help, but I'm sure I can do both."

"That's wonderful, Molly. I'm excited for you. Looks like we will be planning a baby shower." Jessie clasped her hand.

"A baby shower is exactly what we need to plan," Reba said as she walked in the door. "How exciting for you, my dear." She squeezed Molly's shoulder and then pulled her into a big motherly hug. "Lawrence and I always wanted children, but it wasn't meant to be. But now, dear girl, I can love on yours."

"Yes. A baby can never have too much love." Molly smiled at Reba. "Can I interest you in a cup of tea and a lemon bar?"

"Nothing for me today, dear. I have an early lunch." Reba removed her jacket and sat across from Jessie. "I know you can't tell me details, but I know you've had a visitor," she said as soon as Molly left them.

"How?" Jessie asked shaking her head.

"People who know this world, know. It's as simple as that." Reba smoothed her hair into place with her hand.

The two chatted in between Jessie waiting on customers. Her mind still was reeling from the strange visit she had. She was grateful for Reba's company and wanted badly to tell her everything. Although her presence helped to make things seem a bit more normal, they were far from that. A frown seemed permanently etched on her face.

"No frowning, dear. Remember the wrinkles. I know you are worried about keeping her visit from Matt. He wouldn't understand yet. When he needs to know he will. Plus, she did say that you could tell Peyton. I'm sure that will be helpful," Reba told her.

"Lady. sometimes you shock me with what you understand." She patted Reba's hand. "One of these days we need to have a long talk about how."

"We will, but I doubt it's necessary. You come from a long line who had the same gift in varying degrees. You have yet to understand the full potential of it." Reba stood reaching for her jacket. "I need to leave because I'm meeting my handsome man for lunch. I believe it will all work out, dear." Reba slipped her jacket on.

"You and me both." Jessie smiled at her. She put her arm around Reba's shoulders and walked with her to the door.

"I can't wait to hear the details in due time." Reba waved as she left.

Jessie found herself anxious for Peyton to get there. She needed to tell someone about the strange visitor. Where did she begin? She tried to sort through her thoughts and put them in order. Peyton would understand. Her experiences had been stranger than any Jessie had been involved in. Besides a few ghosts and a quick jaunt through the mirror into another dimension, Jessie's experiences seemed simple in comparison to Peyton's. Her happenings were far out of the normal realm, at least to Jessie's way of thinking. The odd thing was that this investigation had been fairly routine up to this point.

In all the strangeness, she couldn't forget the man who was mad at her. How could she have made so many unknown enemies in such a short time on this earth? Jessie shook her head. She always thought of herself as a nice person. Maybe she needed a reality check.

Chapter Seventeen

The empty store was inviting. This was the perfect time to get at her as she sat alone. She had not moved an inch for at least ten minutes. Her mouth moved as if she talked with someone, but no one was near her. As hard as he tried, he couldn't get into her store from any door. Was she a witch? Did she sense him nearby? Something he needed to think about before he enacted his plans against her. He might have to adjust and make some changes to his original ideas. Today added a strange twist to his campaign against her.

He wandered back to where he parked his car. The motel where he was staying wasn't that nice. Maybe he would move to the next town over. He knew he was under surveillance and often he had a tail when driving away from the motel. It was time to step away for a few days and take the heat off. A different car, a better place to stay, and a change in his looks might help too. He would leave a message for her on his way out of town. He didn't want her to think he had forgotten about her.

****

Matt's day had started with Kenny's great news. He liked to see his officers happy in their home lives. Good marriages made for better job performance and better camaraderie on the force. Matt had laughed when Joe told Kenny to be prepared not to sleep for months. He remembered after Joe's first baby arrived. Joe looked like the walking dead for a few months. Kenny took the razzing all in stride. The guys did a good job of teasing one another all in good fun. Joe took some taunting himself since he was now in the same place as Kenny with his wife expecting a second child.

Matt enjoyed observing the guys together; for the most part, they all got on great. He had noticed a couple of standouts who steered clear of the teasing and friendships. Matt wanted to know why? Were they introverts or hiding something? All of them were possible suspects until he found out who had changed those reports recently. And he would find out.

Matt remembered the night Jessie met Joe's little girl. She held her most of the evening. After returning the little one to her mother, Jessie stepped away and that's when the sniper bullet hit her. Thankfully, he had made her wear a vest or she might have been dead. Instinct saved her and him on more than one occasion. She fought him every step of the way during their early days together. He grinned. At least now, he knew she loved him. He was hooked the first time he saw her even though he tried to push her away. His stubborn girl took longer to convince.

Dylan knocked on his open door. "Do you have a minute?"

"Come in." Matt waved him in.

"Here's a copy of all the notes from the interviews you asked for." He placed the folder on the corner of Matt's desk and sat in the chair. "Is there any news on the missing girl?"

"Nothing new since her friend called Jessie. Frank is coming to town tomorrow. You know the routine. Sofia's mother is bringing one of her favorite stuffed animals by later for a scent item. Frank said we could try tracking her from the studio. He's also going to go over the murder site."

"Do you want me to go along?" Dylan asked.

"Sure do. I'll read over these." Matt picked up the file. "Come back in thirty minutes and tell me what your instinct says about all this."

"I'll give you time to digest my notes. My feelings should come through loud and clear." Dylan stood. "I can tell you upfront, there's something dirty going on."

Matt nodded. "I agree. Jaxon told me that Zach Johnson is leading something from prison. They have an insider trying to find out what."

"Johnson, what a waste. He seemed like a nice guy once upon a time." Dylan walked to the door.

"Hey, why don't you and Katie join us for dinner tomorrow night with Frank. I'm sure Jessie and Peyton would love to spend time with her. The three of them can chat while we talk shop."

"Sounds good. Katie would love it."

Matt studied Dylan's notes and understood his thoughts on the subject after he was done. Dylan's notes were extensive and insightful. Matt still wanted to hear Dylan's observations on the subject. He stretched his arms over his head and stood.

He spent the next forty minutes in Dylan's office as they went through each of the girls one by one. Dylan confirmed what Matt's gut had already told him. The business was hiding some bad actors and had been for a while. They were still paying someone to look the other way. Not on his watch, not this time.

****

Jessie glanced at the clock and rushed to the door

holding it open for Peyton. "Boy am I glad that you're finally here. You won't believe what happened to me today. Well, maybe you will believe it, but I think even you will be amazed by what I tell you." Jessie rambled tugging her on her hand. "I've been waiting to tell you for what seems like hours. I feel like I'm going to bust."

"Hold on there; you're talking too fast." Peyton followed her cousin inside. "Sit." She pulled out a chair. "Gather your thoughts or as I tell my students use your words. I'll go get us a treat while you collect yourself." Peyton walked into Joe's and came back in a short time later placing two cups of tea and mini scones in front of her cousin. "Okay, cous, I'm listening."

"You'll never guess what happened to me today." Jessie started to jump up.

Peyton yanked her back down. "I can't guess, and I don't want to. Tell me. The suspense is killing me." Peyton laughed.

"She told me I couldn't tell anyone but you. She knew you. Isn't that crazy? It's all too weird."

"Whoa, Jess, you're not making a lick of sense. Start at the beginning and go slower." Peyton placed her hand over Jessie's tapping fingers to stop them.

"Okay." She took a deep breath. "Let me start again. This beautiful woman came into my store. Nobody could see her but me. I didn't know that at the time, but I figured it out later from Molly's comments."

"You're rambling again." Peyton placed her hand over Jessie's mouth.

"I don't know an easy way to say this." Jessie blew out her breath. "Kimama came to see me today."

"Are you kidding me?" Peyton asked.

"Nope, she sat right there." Jessie pointed at the

chair. "Cara described her perfectly. Her presence commanded attention." Jessie's eyes sparkled with excitement. "Peyton, she was grateful for our help in finding her son. Isn't that awesome?"

"Pretty cool, but what has rattled you? I don't think I've seen you like this before." Peyton grabbed her hand to stop Jessie's tapping fingers.

"Ask Matt and Jaxon what I was like when you went through the book." Jessie shrugged her shoulder. "Truthfully, it's all the other things she said that has me worried." Jessie proceeded to tell her cousin about what Kimama had told her.

"Wow. Are you sure you can't tell Matt or Reba?" Peyton asked.

"Yes. But she did say that you could when the time is right."

"And when would that be?" Peyton frowned.

"When I'm gone. He'll need assurance that I'm coming back." Jessie scrunched her face. "I know how this sounds. Kimama called it an improbable journey, and I'm sure she's right."

"How, and when? Do you have any more details at all?" Peyton asked.

"I guess it's like when you found the journal. It will happen the way it's supposed to."

"What should we do?" Peyton glanced at her cousin.

"We live with the secret until it happens, if it even happens." Jessie squeezed Peyton's hand. "Who would have thought that journal you found would lead to what happened today? I'm both scared and excited."

"I know the feeling." Peyton sipped her tea.

"Before I forget to tell you, Matt texted me earlier

and said we're having dinner tomorrow night with Frank. You and Jaxon are supposed to come. I know he'll tell Jaxon, but I wanted to give you a heads up. Sometimes the guys aren't always timely with their information."

"Thanks for letting me know." Peyton turned when the bell above the door began ringing. "I guess it's time to get to work."

"Here we go again." Jessie jumped up. No one was there, as the bell kept ringing. They had an unseen visitor. There was nothing to do except wait until they showed themselves. Jessie went to the front door and reached her hand toward the bell to silence it. The minute her hand touched the bell a strange energy shot through her hand down her arm. "That wasn't nice," she said. The bell stopped, but a book flew through the air toward Peyton. "Watch out."

Peyton's hand reached out and nabbed the book mid-air before it smacked her in the face. "Enough is enough. Show yourself." Peyton turned around in a circle viewing the whole store.

"I have no idea." Jessie shrugged her shoulders. "We've never had this happen before. Odd as it may sound, we've seen the ghost along with their actions."

"What if we aren't looking at a ghost? There may be other possibilities."

"Like what?" Jessie spoke softly to Peyton.

"I don't know, but there has to be. Listen." Peyton put her hands to her lips. "Someone was laughing as the books randomly flew off the bottom shelves."

"Great." Jessie palmed her forehead. "Another attack on my books. What's next?"

"That would be your bookmarks." Peyton pointed

143

at the basket on the counter as it flipped upside down.

"Stop!" Jessie yelled as she saw the little creature run across the counter clearing it as he ran. He tipped his hat and laughed with a wink at her as he slid to the ground. "Oh my gosh, somebody must have left the door in the woods open because I swear I saw a leprechaun run across my counter. How can that be?" The door opened, and the bell rang, followed by another bout of laughter.

"Good day to you, ladies. Greetings from the other side of the door." The little man tipped his hat and was gone.

"Are you kidding me? Who turned him loose?" Jessie looked at the mess that was left behind. "Why?"

"I have no answer for this one. Mischief maybe. Or maybe he came through with Kimama."

"Once again, we're left to clean up the mess." Jessie started collecting bookmarks that were strewn about.

"Wouldn't you know he would pick the bottom shelves?" Peyton got down on her hands and knees to return books to their spot.

"We live a charmed and lucky life. I'm grateful that no one came in the store during that weird episode." Jessie started to laugh with Peyton soon joining in. This was another secret she wouldn't tell Matt. What could she tell him? She had no idea if what she saw even happened or why. "Our secret." She glanced at Peyton.

"Yes." She nodded. "Who would believe us anyway?"

Chapter Eighteen

Jessie drove home thinking about her strange day. Kimama's visit she understood on some level. Jessie had a mission to fulfill if what she heard was real. The rest of the day didn't fit into the whole scenario at all. Nothing about that bizarre imp made any sense. He intended mischief and that's what he did. His greeting had her assessing what he meant, or was there any reasoning behind his nonsense.

Matt accepted much about her crazy life but today strange rose to a whole new level. No way would he get this. He often looked at her oddly some days when she tried to explain another event in her life or at the bookstore. At least those looks happened less now than at the beginning of their relationship. She smiled remembering how she walked into his office a little over a year ago. She had spent the weekend trying to figure out the perfect outfit to wear. Not wanting to appear desperate but she also wanted to portray confidence. He shot her down and told her to stay out of his case. She got in his face and told him she was already in it. Their relationship had been passionate from the beginning but not always in a good way.

The year brought a lot of changes and growth to both of them. Matt was a keeper. He must love her, or he wouldn't put up with all the baggage that came with her. When she pulled into her space Katie was standing on the path in front of her waving at her.

"I've been watching for you. You're late and so is Peyton." Katie tapped her foot waving an envelope at her.

"We had to shelve some books after the store closed. Besides, we aren't that late. Peyton should be right behind me."

"Here's your mail." Katie handed her a big envelope will several pieces of mail in it. "While you're at it you can take Peyton's too. I don't know how to change the system. The cottages are considered a part of the inn."

"I keep forgetting to come to the desk to get my mail. I get most of mine at the store, but I still get mail here too."

"It's no big deal. I forget to give it to you until the letters start to build up. I miss hanging out with you. I'm looking forward to dinner with you all tomorrow. Matt asked us to come along. It should be fun."

"It seems like forever since we had time to chill, chat, or read our favorite book together." Jessie reached for the envelope in Katie's hand. "Another reason among many for why I don't want to get married," Jessie said under her breath.

"I'll call you later with several great reasons why marriage is great. Hint: it involves waking up next to the man you love and sleeping in each other's arms." Katie held up her hand. "I know what you're going to say—people can do that without marriage but not this good little Irish girl."

"Oh, please. You, who made goo goo eyes at Pastor Kevin and every other good-looking guy in town when you thought Dylan wasn't interested."

"Of course, I did, but not anymore. A girl has to keep her options open." Katie laughed. "I'll talk to you later. My hunky husband is waiting for me."

"If you don't call because you're preoccupied, let's say, I'll talk to you tomorrow." Jessie smiled and made her way down the path to her cottage. Unlocking the door, she took off her coat and placed the envelope on her desk to check later.

Matt had to work late and told her that he might stop by later. She was looking forward to watching her favorite mystery on TV. After she made a turkey sandwich, she reached for her glass of iced tea and headed into the living room to veg with one of her favorite shows.

Following the day she had, this was the perfect way to spend her evening. She didn't want to think about murders, odd visitors from the past, or the little man running through the store tossing the books off the lower shelves. Poor Matt. He didn't stand a chance. She gave up telling Katie about most things anymore. She would freak out if she knew about all the happenings now. Thank heavens for Peyton. At least, they understood each other. Peyton never questioned that she saw Kimama only how and when her journey would begin. The one detail that Kimama left out.

During a commercial, Jessie remembered her mail and went to her desk to get the big envelope. She sorted through the contents, separating the important from the junk mail. The last piece she pulled out was a white envelope addressed to her. The minute she touched the envelope she knew this was no ordinary piece of mail.

She knew the routine. In the kitchen, she kept a pair of rubber gloves for such an occasion. What did that say about her? Her parents wouldn't recognize this side of her life. She hardly did.

She opened the envelope with care and began to read the words on the page. "Well aren't you just the sweetest thing," she muttered as she read the words again.

Jessie, sweet Jessie. I've been watching you and your cop boyfriend. It seems you like him a lot and might be hurt if anything happened to him or those two dear old ladies. And now I can add another pretty lady to the mix of those you care about. Any one of them might be fun to toy with on my way to you. I'm not gone, only watching from a distance. I'll be here to get you when you least expect it. We have some unfinished business.

"Well, get in line, mister." Jessie dropped the envelope on the end table. The knock at the door came at the perfect time. She would let Matt deal with it.

"I see you didn't lock the door again," he said as he walked in.

"Oops, I forgot." She stood and walked into his arms. "In my defense, I was carrying something when I came in the door, and I simply forgot. I hope you'll go easy on me." She glanced up at his face.

"A little misdirection. What's up?" he asked.

She took his hand leading him over to the couch and once he was seated she handed him her gloves and the letter. "I'm sure you'll want to read this nice letter."

"Damn, Jess, this is the second time. This guy means business. Who is he? Any ideas?" Matt put the note in the bag she handed him along with the envelope.

"No idea. He's a mystery to me. Pretty much this

whole year has been a walk-through of uncharted waters for us all. Here I thought I was a likable person. But a serial killer who was mad because I wouldn't date him in high school, a stalker, and an angry sociopath from my days working in the newsroom have told me a different story. I might need a gut check, as they say."

"You're too damn sweet if you ask me. When you put it like that, you've had a tough year." He draped his arm around her.

"You think." She turned to look at him. "Are you hungry? I can make you a turkey sandwich."

"I'd like that. It's been a long day." He followed her into the kitchen.

"Mustard or mayo?" she asked taking the turkey out of the fridge.

"Mayo," Matt told her.

"Lettuce and tomato?"

"Yes to both. Do you have chips and beer?" He opened the fridge to look.

"I do. There's a great craft beer in there. You need to try it." She cut his sandwich and placed it on a plate with a handful of chips.

"Thanks, babe, this looks good. I'll try the beer. I'm willing to try anything once."

They sat on the couch side by side. "How is your sandwich?" she asked.

"Just what I needed. I didn't realize how hungry I was." He took a swig of his beer. "This isn't bad either." He looked at the label again. "Now, with my hunger satisfied, what are we going to do about this guy? We've had him under surveillance. One of my officers followed him out of town. He's staying a few towns over. Do you want to bet that he rents a different car? The car he's driving is a rental. Kip already checked it out. We know the name of the man who rented the car but I'm guessing he used a fake ID. He seems to be covering his tracks. My guy is notifying the car rental agencies in the town where he's staying and asked them to notify us. The bad guys always forget some detail that will trip them up eventually. We are running his ID and I will let you know what we find out."

"I'd appreciate it. Maybe his name will ring a bell."

****

Matt hadn't told Jessie everything he knew about the guy at the moment. There was no need to worry her at this point. They did a sweep of his motel room after their suspect had checked out. His team found prints on several surfaces along with a partial glass of water they could extract his DNA from. He was in the system and Matt had a name. But before he worried her with the details, he wanted to figure out what the man's game was. Dylan was running down some leads and Jeremy was going over employee files at the newsroom. They would have a lot better picture of their man soon. Jessie would get the profile of her stalker as soon as they could put all the pieces together. Hopefully, his name and face would ring a bell with her.

Meanwhile more girls were coming forward to tell their stories. The case against the gym and studio was gaining momentum. On the surface, everything seemed to be moving forward but Matt had a nagging suspicion that he was missing something major. He would have to continue to go over every detail until a fact jumped out at him or at least gave him a direction to start looking. He knew Johnson was up to no good from prison and that was bad enough. But he had a strong impression that Jessie would need his help. She rarely wanted his or anyone's help, much less needed it, but he felt sure this time might be an exception. The idea wasn't sitting well with him. He had to keep his heart out of it and his eyes and ears in the game.

Chapter Nineteen

Jessie finished her morning routine and breakfast. Reaching for her phone she called her cousin on her way out the door. Peyton must have already left because her car was gone. "Hi, cousin," Jessie said when Peyton answered the phone. "Can you talk for a minute?"

"Yes, I'm in the school parking lot finishing my coffee before I go in. I'm getting ready to confront a room full of little people. What's up?" Peyton asked.

"I admire you. Your teaching job is not easy." Jessie stuck the key in the ignition and the engine purred.

"I love working with the kids, but I can't go into the classroom unprepared, or they would eat me alive. I don't mean that literally, of course. But those kiddos seem to know if I'm off my game and will challenge me all morning." Peyton chuckled.

"Will you be stopping by the store later?" Jessie asked.

"I planned on it. Why?"

"No particular reason. I was wondering is all. I wanted to see if you had any advice to give me after our conversation yesterday. Be thinking about it, okay. I have to admit I'm a bit nervous about what Kimama told me."

"I will. I'll be there around two, which is later than

normal. I'm helping the art teacher for a couple of hours. Those double class sizes can be murder for a teacher on their own. Art projects need all hands on deck, especially with first graders." She finished her last drop of coffee. "There are plenty of messes to go around."

"We should exercise together tomorrow." Jessie changed the subject. "I found a great new place to run not far from town. It's a beautiful path through the trees with views of the ocean along the way. The weather is supposed to be near perfect for the next few days I think we should go tomorrow. It will be a welcome break from the gym." Jessie could see the path in her mind as she described it to Peyton. "You'll love it."

"Sounds good to me. Being outside will be nice for a change. It's been a while. I'll see you at two," Peyton told her.

"I hope you have some good advice for me. When I went through the mirror, it happened with no one coming to tell me ahead of time. I'm not sure I like knowing in advance something is going to take place. Especially when I have no idea when or how. I'm not fond of being taken by surprise unless it comes as a total surprise in a good way. It's all the speculating that gets me, and not being able to talk it over with Matt is tough too."

"I'm sorry your conversation yesterday left you feeling on edge. I would be too." Peyton sighed. "I felt the same way in Arizona. The premonition that told me I could be a victim was unsettling. Anticipating when or where was the hard part. Of course, the real event of being shot wasn't that fun either."

"No, I'm sure it wasn't. I knew you'd understand.

We'll talk more later." Jessie shut off her phone. She'd better get to the store.

Boy, oh boy, would she like to get Matt's opinion on the subject. Dinner tonight with Frank and her friends would be good. Katie was always good for a laugh. Maybe between Peyton and Katie she could think about something else for a while. Her concern for Sofia, the threatening notes, and a promise of some kind of strange trip didn't leave much room in her head.

It would be good to see Frank again. The last time he was in town he told her that he was working with a new bloodhound puppy named Carlene and showed her several pictures. What a little cutie. Radar would soon retire and was earning his free time helping him train his sweet replacement. She couldn't imagine Frank without Radar by his side. But the new puppy was catching on and becoming quite good at what she was bred to do.

Frank had shared about the wide range of emotions that a working K-9 and his handler go through together. Jessie had to admit she hadn't thought much about how finding a murder victim impacted them both. They were connected on so many levels. The memory of their conversation that night came back to her along with some of the emotions she had felt.

"A K-9 officer is more than a partner. He is a friend. My dog's eyes speak volumes to me along with his unconditional love," Frank told her. "There's nothing like coming home and hearing him bay and watching him running toward me."

Jessie remembered how teary-eyed she got when Frank talked about Radar. The bond between them was a strong one. He was proud of the many great awards the dog had received for his awesome service. But most of all he loved the way his best buddy sensed his mood as they did a track and then sat at his feet in the evening when their work was done. Radar would soon be able to retire with honor for a job well done. He might not have to work as hard, but he would always travel with Frank, if not physically, in his heart.

All Jessie knew about the subject was that Radar had done an amazing job on all the cases he worked with them. From finding Abigail in the old shack before she succumbed to the cold, to finding murder victims seen only in dreams, their investigations would have taken a lot longer to solve without Radar's help. He found the mass gravesites at the boarding school, and she loved seeing him work. She would treasure each time she could see Radar in action until Carlene took his place when she was ready. She would have her larger-than-life personality and ways of solving cases soon enough. But Radar would always have a special place in Jessie's heart because he was the first bloodhound she had ever seen track.

Jessie went through her morning opening routine at the store her mind racing from one thought to another. Waving at the smiling but extremely pale Molly when she opened the doors to the coffee shop, she went in to get a cup of coffee. "Are you feeling okay?"

"I'm fine but I have a touch of morning sickness. Working with all this food isn't helping. Some smells are worse than others. It's usually better after nine-thirty and several soda crackers. I'm downing my sixth right now." Molly smiled and nibbled. "No one tells you that you might feel like puking every morning and sometimes evening when you tell them you're pregnant."

"I can wait. Thank you very much." Jessie laughed.

"I'm not complaining." Molly paused. "That's not true. I'm complaining but I don't want to be. I'm happy about our coming attraction." Molly patted her flat stomach. "It's hard to believe this little peanut growing inside me could make me feel like vomiting. How can that be?"

"I hope that's a rhetorical question because you're asking the wrong person otherwise. I know nothing about this subject. Ghosts I get, babies not so much." Jessie touched her friend's hand. "I do understand enough to know that babies and kids, in general, make for lots of work as far as I can see but must bring a lot of happiness with them because people keep having them." Jessie chuckled. "I'm not much help, am I?"

Molly shook her head. "But you tried, and that counts for something. At least you were honest about the work part. Most people say, a baby, oh how wonderful, and proceed to tell me their horror stories of childbirth. Honestly, Jessie, it makes me wonder how I got myself into this. Not literally, I know the how but I'm not sure about the why. I'll give you an answer in about seven months give or take a week or two." Molly nibbled on another soda cracker and sighed.

"Molly, you'll be a great mother, and there's no doubt in my mind you'll love your little one more than life itself."

"I know I will. I'm feeling sorry for myself, that's all. At least Kenny has been extra sweet to me. He almost makes me forget this sick feeling. Thankfully, it doesn't last all day and he waits on me in the evening if I start feeling a bit off. And I do love how he massages my feet."

"Not lasting should put some color back in those beautiful cheeks or a touch of blush might do the trick as Reba would say. You know where to find me if you need a break." Jessie pointed into her store. "You can use me as an excuse to sit and relax for a few minutes."

"I might take you up on your offer." Molly smiled and waited on the next person in line.

Note to Jessie, you need to put morning sickness on your list of cons. It doesn't sound like fun at all. Jessie went to the front of the store, turned the sign around to open, and noticed her ghost was back again. "Enjoy your day," she whispered.

****

Later, after the group met for dinner, Matt went over the conversations from the evening. Jaxon had told him that they were closing in on Johnson's activities and he should have answers for him in the next day or two. Their snitch had overheard someone bragging about the money he had made on an investment that Johnson had let him in on. He wasn't talking about stocks.

Jessie seemed preoccupied. Even Katie couldn't bring her out of her strange mood. He didn't want to antagonize her, but he wanted to know what was up. She was more stubborn than him. Damn, he was getting soft when it came to her, although he liked to think he was growing.

Frank and Radar were asleep for the night, and Jaxon had gone over to Peyton's after dinner. Jessie told him she was tired and left before he could stop her. He stretched out his legs on the bed propping the pillows behind his back. Reaching for his phone he called her.

"Hi, sweetheart, you were gone before I could give you a proper goodbye. What's going on?"

"I was tired," she answered softly.

"That's not good enough, Jess. You're not telling me something. You don't hide your emotions well." He frowned.

"I always tell you, eventually," she said.

"Why not now? I'm listening." Matt raked his hand through his hair.

"If I could explain you know I would. Matt, you have to trust me on this one. Some things have no explanations. I've been wrestling with it for a couple of days."

"Maybe I can help, babe. We've worked through some strange things together, haven't we?" he asked.

"Yes. And believe me, as soon as I figure out how to tell you, you'll be the first person we talk to."

"We?" he asked.

"I've been talking to Peyton and we're trying to determine how to clarify the facts as we know them at the moment," she told him.

"Fair enough. As long as I have your word you won't do anything rash without notifying me first." Matt crossed his arms holding his breath until she answered.

"You have my promise I won't do anything on my own."

"I'll hold you that." He smiled.

"You're free to. I'm sorry I didn't stick around long enough for my goodbye kiss. There are too many things crowding my mind."

"I could tell. When even Katie couldn't bait you, I

realized something was wrong."

"Did I miss something?" she asked.

"You could say that. Katie tried several times to engage you in conversation, along with Frank. You weren't responding in your normal manner."

"Again, I'm sorry. I'm sure I'll work through this and be back to my normal self before you know it. All these strange events are too hard to explain. Hopefully, it will become easier with time."

"Damn, Jess, I have no idea how you do it, but you handle all of the interruptions to your normal fairly well. I know I couldn't manage as well as you have. You make me a better cop."

"Thank you." She sniffed.

They talked for a while longer. He wasn't completely satisfied with her answers, but he understood she was doing the best she could to handle all that randomly popped up in her life. What he didn't tell her was that seeing one ghost when he rescued her from Anderson was enough to last him a lifetime.

Chapter Twenty

Matt's team along with Frank and Radar were out early at the murder site. Matt pointed out where they had found the body and handed Frank a scent item from the victim's body. Frank let the dog smell the item in the bag. Radar went to work. He worked his way through the area back and forth until he seemed to pick something up. He tracked through the wooded area past several small houses coming to one about five miles from where the body was found.

"Dylan, you need to get Judge Sanders on the phone. He told me last night he would issue a search warrant based on the track and scan it to us and the tribe. I'll call the tribal police. As soon as we have their consent, we'll question the folks who live here and search the premise." Matt reached in his pocket for his phone. "Let me know as soon as the judge sends the warrant." Matt stepped away from the group to talk to the tribal police chief for several minutes. Thankfully they had already received a faxed copy of the search warrant, which made his job easier. Sander's office was on the ball.

"Let's go," Matt said when he disconnected the call. Matt and Kip walked up to the door and knocked.

A young man opened the door and Kip showed him his badge. "My name is Officer Peterson, and this is Chief Parker. We are from the Blue Cove Police

Department, and we have permission to speak with you and any other occupant in the house."

"Is there a problem, Officer?" the man asked his eyes glancing at the others standing outside in his yard.

"There could be. We had the bloodhound there"— he pointed at Radar—"checking out a murder site not far from here off the reservation and he led us to your door. We have some questions we'd like to ask you, Mr.—" Matt waited and hoped he'd tell them his name. "Would you have any idea why he might pick out your house?"

"I have no idea." The man shook his head. "I hope it's not my wife. She's been missing." The man motioned them in and sat on the edge of the chair.

"Did you file a missing person report?" Kip asked him.

"I didn't but maybe her parents did." He rubbed his hands together.

"Weren't you concerned about her?" Matt took note of the man's sweaty palms and shifting glances.

"Not really. She runs off whenever she has a mind to." His foot tapped the ground beneath his chair.

"Why is that? You never did tell us your name," Matt told him.

"Didn't I? Ben Tso, sir," he said.

"Mr. Tso, you mentioned your wife tends to run off. I'm wondering why. Aren't you, Kip?

"I was thinking the same thing. Ben, you don't mind if I call you Ben, do you?"

"No." Tso looked down at his feet.

"Ben, did you knock her around when she made you mad?" Matt's hands fisted at his side. "You know we'll ask her parents the same question. They'll know if you ever hit her."

"How do I know if she's even my wife?" He smirked leaning back in his chair.

"I have a photo of her right here. Of course, it's not a beauty shot but I think you'll get the idea." Kip pulled out the coroner's photo from the morgue. "I'll ask you again—did you ever hit her?"

Tso blanched when he saw the picture. "That's her." He gulped. "I might have hit her once or twice when I got drunk, but that's it. The last time I saw her she was alive."

"Did you hit her the last time you saw her? Maybe more than once?" Matt asked him.

"I might have. I don't remember that night. I was pretty wasted. I lost my job, and she started harping on me. I hit her and she said she was going to her mom's. I wouldn't let her have the keys. She said she would walk and left."

"And that didn't worry you to have your pretty young wife walk the several miles at night alone to her mom's house? It sure would worry me. Wouldn't it concern you, Chief?" Kip frowned at the man.

"It sure would. Let me tell you what I think happened, Ben. You hit her more than once. The fact is you beat her pretty bad. She suffered several blows and what looks like a few well-placed kicks to her torso."

"I don't remember that." He turned his eyes away from Matt's intense look.

"I think you do. She has DNA under her fingernails. We'll know soon enough if you're guilty." Matt walked closer to where Ben sat. "Tell me, how did it feel to watch your bleeding wife stumble out of the house and run away?" Matt studied the man's body language.

"I passed out. I'd remember that if it happened. She was alive." He wiped at the tears in his eyes. "I swear she was alive."

"Alive, barely. I hope you don't mind if we search your premises?" Matt said when Dylan came through the door and nodded at him.

"I would rather you didn't without a search warrant. Don't I need a lawyer present? I have rights."

"Yes, you do. You can call your lawyer if you have one. But he doesn't need to be present at the moment for a warrant to be served. Officer Mitchell signaled me that the judge has issued a search warrant for this location," Matt told the man. Ben jumped up and began to pace especially when Frank came inside with his dog. "Kenny, why don't you keep Mr. Tso here company while we check out his house."

****

The store was quiet most of the morning which gave her way too much time to worry. She wanted to go on the track today with Matt and Frank, but Jessie had to work. Audrey couldn't come in until the afternoon. At least she could run with Peyton before dark.

Instead of going, she settled for waiting. Patience wasn't one of her strengths. She paced, sat, and paced every time the phone rang even though Matt had told her she wouldn't hear anything from him until later in the day.

When Peyton arrived and he hadn't called yet, she knew something was going down. She had her phone, and he could reach her even if she were running.

"Are you ready to go?" Jessie asked Peyton the minute she came through the door.

163

"No, and from the looks of it neither are you. We both need to change into our running clothes. You couldn't have chosen a more beautiful day for an outdoor run. It's our first real taste of spring weather with no chill. Although, knowing how fickle the weather can be, it won't last long." Peyton walked into the back room and changed into her running clothes.

"My turn." Jessie went to change her clothes. "Audrey, if Matt stops by, tell him we went out for a run, and I have my phone," she told her employee on her way out the door.

"Will do. Enjoy the weather." She waved.

"We will," Jessie called over her shoulder. "Let's take your car, Peyton, since it's right here. You can bring me back to get mine later."

"Sounds good to me. I like driving mine. Jaxon picked out the perfect car."

"He sure did. I think the guy might like you a little bit." Jessie laughed.

"Hopefully, but he likes hot cars too. He says he loves me, and I know I love him." Peyton sighed wistfully.

"We're hopeless romantics." Jessie smiled at her cousin and gave her the directions to the path she had discovered. "Isn't this beautiful?" Jessie said when they pulled into the parking spot.

"Gorgeous. You described the spot perfectly." Peyton jumped out of the car, locked it, and stuck the keys in her pocket. She followed Jessie to the trail and let her cousin set the pace.

"See what I mean about the view of the ocean and woods." Jessie took a deep breath. "I love moments like this. Everything seems right with the world, at least for now." Jessie picked up her speed.

The girls got into the rhythm of their pace. They had gone a couple of miles when they found themselves on the part of the path that went straight through a grove of trees. The silence around them seemed almost magical. Jessie thought about the description in Cara's diary about the door in the woods. She turned to tell Peyton about what she was thinking. That's when Jessie saw the door. The door opened, a bright light blinded her eyes for a moment, and she lifted off the ground and was pulled through to the other side.

Chapter Twenty-One

"What do you mean, she's gone?" Matt rushed into the station and grabbed Peyton's arm. "I knew something was up. How could I not have seen this coming?" Matt frowned at Peyton, his voice getting louder with each statement.

"Don't yell at her." Jaxon stood between Peyton and Matt. "She'll tell you if you give her time."

"She couldn't tell you." Peyton's chin edged up. "She promised not to tell anyone."

"What do you mean she couldn't tell me?" Matt roared.

"She was told she could only tell me. She didn't even tell Reba. And she was also told I could tell you the whole story when the time was right. I'm beginning to understand why." Peyton muttered the last sentence under her breath rubbing her arm where Matt had grabbed her.

"Now had better be the time." Matt sat on the edge of the chair, hanging his head in his hands. "I don't understand why she couldn't tell me."

"Look at your reaction. You wouldn't have let her out of your sight." Jaxon put his hand on Matt's shoulder and Matt knocked it off.

"Anyway, the time has come for you to be told." She stood in front of him. "First, you need to know she's fine." She glanced at Jaxon.

"Go ahead, sweetheart." Jaxon pulled her into his side as he stood beside her.

"A few days ago, Jessie told me what happened." She explained to them how Kimama came into the store and told Jessie she was needed. "Because of my cousin's dreams and her concern for the number of Native American missing and murdered young women, Kimama wanted her to experience it through their eyes." Peyton paused. "Before you ask, neither one of us had any idea how Kimama's visit was possible. She never told Jessie how or when this improbable journey would take place but what happened while we were running tells me it has started, I guess." Peyton shrugged.

"You guess. That's the best you can give me." Matt jumped up pushing past her and started to pace. "I should have made her tell me."

"She wouldn't have told you. You couldn't change what happened any more than Jaxon could have stopped me from being sucked back in time. There was a portal in that grove of trees, and she was pulled through the gate. She'll be back when her time is finished. For now, we wait, and when she returns, she'll have a great story to tell. The families waiting for the missing daughters will find closure, and a nation will be made aware of a great tragedy happening in the shadows."

"Damn, does she have to go through a portal to get the story? Can't she just do research like every other writer?' Matt asked.

"Such is our life. She'll be back." Peyton touched Matt's hand as he walked past for the second time. "I know she will."

"You sound sure." Matt scrunched his face and stopped in front of her. "Thank you. I'll have a few things to say myself when she returns."

"I am sure, but be nice. You have before you a person who traveled through time and came back, and she will too. She's on a special mission," Peyton told him. "I can't wait to hear what transpired."

"Okay then. It's back to work for me because I won't stop worrying until she's back in my arms. I'll have to keep busy." Matt turned to look at Peyton. "What about the store? Will we need to close the doors?"

"Jessie and I talked about that and planned. I'm working to make sure the store is covered for a few days. Reba, Audrey, and I will keep it humming along. I'll also let you know if any of us hear or see anything. Does that work for you?" she asked.

"Other than her being with me, it'll have to do." Matt raked his hand through his hair.

"It's what she wanted because she's invested. You know Jessie. She never gives up, and she'll give this story all she's got."

"That's my girl, and I had better be doing the same." Matt walked toward the door. "I'll catch up with you at the house later, Jaxon. Frank will be doing another track tomorrow. Hopefully, we can find Sofia. The one today took all day. I'd like to have some good news for Jess when she returns." He started down the hall to his office. Matt stopped and turned around. "Thanks, Peyton. I'm sorry that I yelled at you. I appreciate your restraint, Jaxon. If that had been you yelling at Jessie, I might have hit you and asked questions later."

"You could try." Jaxon laughed.

"Don't egg him on." Peyton covered Jaxon's mouth with her hand. "No worries, Matt. I know it took you by surprise." She smiled and pulled her hand away.

"My little diplomat." Jaxon kissed her cheek.

****

"Wow, that was a trip." Jessie found herself standing in a strange setting. She had no idea where she was but what an awesome way to get there. Hopefully, Peyton figured out where she went. They had been running through a grove of trees when the strong light pulled her into its energy force. The next thing she knew she was lifted off the ground and pushed through some kind of energy field to where she now stood. She wondered how many times a person could do that before it physically messed them up.

A bit scary and a whole lot of cool was how she would describe the ride. The more she looked around her the more the area seemed familiar, which made little sense. "Get it together, Jessie," she told herself.

With no instructions to guide her, she started to walk, and that's when the woods came alive with chants and swaying dancers. The more she walked the louder they became, not unlike her dreams. When the music reached its peak that's when she saw the body lying motionless on the ground. The woods became silent and suddenly Jessie found herself standing in a small living room observing a young woman on the phone. When the woman hung up, a look of fear crossed her face as she rushed around stuffing a few items in a bag. That's when Jessie noticed a young man stumble through the door. He was drunk and angry. When he saw the bag in her hand, he ripped it from her throwing the bundle against the wall.

"Make my supper. You're not going anywhere. Do you hear me?" She ducked when he raised his hand. "I'm your husband, and you'll do what I say." His hand clenched and he punched her square in the jaw.

She dropped like a stone to the floor. Jessie thought for a moment that she was dead. The woman rolled into a fetal position to block what was coming next, the several forceful kicks to her head and body area.

"Please, no more," she begged.

Her pleas seemed to enrage him more, and in his rush to kick her one more time he lost his balance. He staggered back tripping over the coffee table and falling to the ground. He was too drunk to get back on his feet and she had enough time to stumble out the door. Jessie followed her to where she fell to the ground broken and exhausted. All Jessie could do was watch her die. Murdered by her husband, the young woman died alone. Jessie sat near the prone figure and cried.

He couldn't get away with his crime. No way, not if she had anything to do with exposing him. Jessie remained by the young woman's side. She had no idea how long she sat there but she didn't want to leave her alone. Would anyone find her? Matt would, and that thought brought her peace.

The woods were filled with the sound of drums beating in a hypnotic pattern. Dancers in their traditional garb moved toward where she sat, moving in cadence with the chants and the drum beats filling the night's air. The moonlight filtered through the tree branches casting eerie shadows on the ground. One dancer reached out and grabbed her hand and she was caught in their ever-growing circle. Whirling and floating through the air she observed their ritual until one by one the dancers left her, and she stood alone in a vast open space with vistas of rock formations in all directions her eyes could see in the distance. She noticed a pickup truck parked near one of the formations. She continued to watch until the truck moved, rattling over one of the dirt roads between a small cluster of houses. For some odd reason, the truck seemed familiar to her. Where had she seen it before? Whoever was driving seemed to be in a big hurry as the truck picked up speed. She followed its progress until the truck was merely a small dot on the horizon.

Keeping the rock formation in her sight, Jessie moved with urgency toward where she had first seen the truck. She increased her tempo breaking into a run when she sensed there was something not quite right. The closer she got to the area the more she knew what she was about to find. Searching between the rocks and a few short bushes she stopped when she saw the foot. Only a few seconds had passed when she saw the face and body attached to that foot. The girl was dead and had been dumped. Jessie wiped the tears already forming in her eyes when the vision rolled through her mind like a movie.

The young woman walked on the shoulder of the highway with her long black hair blowing softly in the breeze. Dressed in jeans and a tee, she was on her way to town about ninety miles away from her home on the reservation. Like she had done hundreds of times before, she lifted her thumb hoping to hitch a ride from one of the many pickups headed into town. Her first paycheck from the trading post seemed to burn a hole in her pocket, itching to be spent. She had never had her own money to spend, and it was a heady feeling. After lunch at the local café, she would maybe buy a new pair of shoes or something at the local store. A movie might be nice too. She could always find a ride back home later if she decided to spend the whole day in town.

The first truck that came along had several people crowded into the front seat and the driver pointed to the back where two other passengers were. Happy for the ride, she continued to plan out her day. The first thing she had to do was to get her check cashed. Once in town, the girl jumped out of the back, thanked the driver, and headed toward the store everyone knew cashed checks. Her smile grew as the woman behind the counter handed her the wad of money. She was excited to begin her adventure for the day.

As the vision moved on Jessie became aware of someone in the pickup she had seen viewing the girl's movements. And after lunch and her shopping spree, which included candy for her siblings, she began her trek toward the highway headed back the way she came earlier. The first truck to approach her was the one Jessie had seen. She wanted to warn her, but it would do no good. She was seeing what had already taken place and it couldn't be changed.

The truck slowed turning on his flashers and a man called out. "Hello, little lady. Hop in and I'll be happy to take you as far as I'm going." The man's heavy southern drawl caught Jessie's attention. She only wished she could see his face.

"I should wait. I have family coming this way soon." The girl hesitated.

"It will be dark before long and the road can be dangerous at night. I won't bite. I promise," he told her.

The girl's hesitancy was gone. She hopped into the front seat of the pickup and began the journey to her death. All Jessie could do was watch the tragedy unfold before her and know the fear the girl experienced in the last moments of her life.

Jessie slumped to the ground with the memory of the young girl's face etched into her mind. Leaning her head into her folded arms Jessie cried herself to sleep. Altering between sleep and the sense of being overwhelmed, at some point she stretched out on the hard earth. Giving no thought to what might crawl on the ground or if she was even really there at all she went into a deep, exhausted, dreamless sleep.

The sound of drums awakened her. Taken by surprise by the strange surroundings where she awakened, she rubbed the sleep from her eyes. Standing slowly, she ran her hand through her hair expecting it to be tangled but it wasn't. Her jogging pants didn't have a smidge of dirt on them even though she slept on the ground. How could that be?

The memory of the day before slowly returned along with the faces of the two young women. She had to be in some kind of travel bubble. Jessie had no idea how any of this worked. As she stood there reasoning, a group of dancers began to gather from the north and encircle her. They looked different than the last ones had. They had bells on their moccasins, feathers on their headdresses, and beaded belts around their waists. The warpaint on their faces made them look fierce and yet somehow beautiful.

She knew that the man in that truck was a serial killer who looked for his prey as he roamed in his pickup. Darn, she wished she could remember where she saw the truck before or what the man inside looked like. *Find him and you will find more victims.* Which were her last thoughts along with Matt's handsome face to race through her mind before the next phase of her journey began. She was soon whisked off to another location.

Chapter Twenty-Two

Matt stretched out on his bed. Today's track and search led to the arrest of Ben Tso for the murder of his wife. He told Jaxon about how good it felt to put the abuser behind bars and at the same time sad. In some ways, Ben was himself a victim. Ms. Tso's parents were heartbroken but not surprised. They had begged her to leave her husband many times. Alcohol put her life in jeopardy more than once.

Matt knew alcoholism was a big problem where Tso grew up. *But how do you break the cycle of alcohol and substance abuse? It calls to people everywhere from a young age as they navigate the hard years of growing up.* It was a story he had heard more than once in his career and not given to one particular ethnic group either. Poverty didn't help the situation. No wonder Jessie fought hard for women's rights. Peyton and her sister both had suffered abuse from their father because of his alcohol and substance abuse. Greater minds than his were working hard to come up with ways to solve the abuse crisis in families before they led to crimes.

Though today's track was a success on one level, it also exposed the continuing crisis that they faced in law enforcement. At least tomorrow's track might end more positively if they could find Sofia. He wanted to have some answers for Jessie when she returned. Once again, he found himself trying hard to be positive in the face of the unknown. He tried to imagine where and what Jessie was doing but his brain didn't work on that level. For him, logic, facts, and the law made sense not ghosts, dreams, and trips to unknown places.

Jaxon knew what he was feeling. They talked for a few hours before calling it a night. Matt had to find a way to deal with the nagging fear in the back of his mind. That apprehension seemed reasonable enough in light of this recent event. How many times could he hear the words "she's gone" and not be undone by the thought that this time could be forever? Jaxon could relate, and that helped. At least, he knew that he wasn't alone in his thoughts or hesitations. One positive, at least to this point—Jessie always found answers in the process. Hopefully, that's what this was all about now. Answers to some of the questions they had in the case and the big one which was the reason for her dreams.

"Goodnight, sweetheart, wherever you are. Sleep well, my love." Matt rolled onto his side.

He wondered if she went to sleep or if it was some strange alternate state. His mind drifted naturally to when Jessie went through the mirror and was in the hospital at the same time. She lived in the sixties while she remained almost comatose in the hospital during the present. The only difference this time was that she was gone and not here at all. Only her return would tell him what she experienced.

He couldn't imagine what she might be seeing this time. Peyton had told him Kimama wanted her to see the murders through the eyes of the victims. Kimama wanted to help her people who once again were suffering.

"Hopefully, Jess, you know I'm thinking about you." He could see her smiling face in his mind.

Jaxon had told him earlier that Reba had instructed him to talk to Peyton and she would let him know in some way that she was okay. He could do that too. Matt started to tell Jessie about his day. He went into all the details that he knew she would like to hear. It was a good rehearsal of his day's activities for him even if she couldn't hear it. Somehow, he thought at the very least she would know she was on his mind.

****

Jessie remembered this scenery from her dream. The open spaces and tall grass blowing in the breeze. Unless she missed her guess she was not far from the site of Custer's Last Stand. She walked to the place where the body was hidden in the tall grass. Searching the area, she noticed the tire marks that had flattened the grass. Though the grass was starting to stand once again, the path the vehicle had taken could be seen. She followed the path the tracks made out to the main road. From the size of the tires, it had to be a pickup or SUV, and not a car.

She found a mound of dirt back from the highway where she sat. Trucks and cars passed by where she lingered. She knew there was something for her to see because the dancers hadn't arrived and there were no drums. The sun was hot in the sky, and she knew the body wouldn't last for long in the heat. Had the body been discovered yet, or was she still waiting for her remains to be to be found?

The familiar pickup approached the area slowing down to turn. The truck went past where she sat. The girl in the front seat flopped around and he shoved her lifeless body back against the seat trying to hold her in place. He stopped and pulled her body from the front seat and dumped her where Jessie had seen it. The scene of her murder flashed through Jessie's mind. Another girl was given a ride to her death. Jessie grieved for yet another girl.

She closed her eyes. The images of the three young women were fixed in her mind. How could she get away from what she had seen? The trust, the betrayal, and the fear they felt when they faced the fact of their imminent deaths. Their lives had been expendable to their killers. Jessie wished she could erase the images and the emotions that came with them, but she knew on some level she had been given a gift. She could write their story to highlight the hundreds of others that were still unknown. "Remember me," their voices cried out to her. No matter where they rested, their lives could not be forgotten.

Jessie heard the rustle of the grass. When she opened her eyes, Kimama was there.

"You still have much to see before you return to tell the story." Kimama reached for Jessie's hand. "We must hurry, for we both are given only a window in time. Every life has value whether they are my people or yours. We are all a part of the human family, and sometimes we are allowed to step into each other's shoes for a moment in time."

Jessie found herself once again moving through the air, only this time Kimama was her guide. She tried hard to take mental notes. She didn't want to forget the power of the emotions racking her. She wondered how many people are touched to see beyond their own lives to the plight of others each day. Before she could finish the thought, she found herself standing alone in the desert of the southwest. The sun was high in the sky, the earth parched from the heat. Yucca trees, saguaro cactus, and Joshua trees dotted the landscape as far as she could see. The area seemed too desolate for anything to live there. She watched a small lizard scoot across the ground. She sat on the only rock she had seen. Why had Kimama abandoned her?

Left with only her thoughts until she knew her purpose for being at this location, she recalled each of the victims she had seen to this point. Each of the bodies she had seen, except for the woman beaten by her husband, had bruises on their hands and knuckles. They might have been defensive wounds. But she had also noticed pieces of what looked to be skin and hair under their nails indicating a struggle and possible offensive wounds. Hopefully, the DNA could prove helpful in finding their attacker.

"Matt, I wish you were with me." He would have to notify authorities in the areas about the possibility of victims there. How he would tell them he came by the knowledge he would have to figure out. She sat on the rock and waited for the next step she was supposed to take. "I need to talk things over with you. You would know what to do."

****

"Have you heard from Jessie?" Dylan knocked on Matt's door. "I didn't say anything to Katie. She wouldn't understand."

"I appreciate that, I know Jessie doesn't tell Katie about this part of her life anymore. I think she needs to have a bit of normalcy and Katie offers her that." He motioned him to come in and sit. "She isn't back, if that's what you mean. I can't believe I'm saying that calmly. I don't get this part of her life either."

"It's a package deal. You love her, and this comes with her. Believe me, I'm not sure what normal is anymore. It's constantly changing, isn't it?" Dylan asked. "I mean, passing out traffic tickets might be routine, but road rage takes traffic issues up a notch."

"I know what you're doing, Dylan. Let's cut to the chase here. My girl takes strange trips, sees ghosts, and gets visited by the spirit of the past like in a Dickens novel. It's okay in a book of fiction but a bit overwhelming in real life if you know what I mean."

"Well, when you put it that way, it sounds crazy to me too. But the evidence she discovers and the cold cases that are solved because of these little side trips would be buried in the past and left unsolved. Who is to say that she's the strange one and we're not because we can't see beyond the visible?" Dylan chuckled. "I mean there are times I wished I could see what is motivating someone to do what they do."

"I know you're right. I'm sure she'll have a feasible answer when she gets back but until then I'm merely speculating." Matt stood as Frank stood in the doorway. "Hey, Frank. Are we ready to give this next track a try?"

"We're ready. We might find a general route she traveled without finding her or maybe we'll be lucky and find the girl alive and well." Frank leaned against the door frame. "Radar is in the car, and he's ready to get to work.

"I'm holding out for the second one," Matt told him. "I know Jessie would like to see Sofia alive and well when she returns."

"Speaking of Jessie, have you heard from her?" Frank asked.

"Not yet. You know how this goes. When she's done, we'll hear from her."

"Yep, and we'll all be blown away once again. Lead the way. Let's see if we can bring this girl home, and maybe Jessie will come home too." Frank followed Matt and Dylan down the hall.

Jess, wherever you are we're looking for Sofia. Don't forget I'm waiting for you to come home to me, sweetheart.

Chapter Twenty-Three

The team arrived at the gym and dance studio and got ready to get to work. Frank took Radar from his crate. He attached the dog's leash and put several dog treats into his pocket. Frank gave him water in a bowl while they waited for their orders.

"I'm going inside for a minute to hand them the warrant. I want you to be able to work him inside unimpeded. Give us a few minutes and then the rest of you come in." Matt and Dylan walked inside the building and handed the owner a copy of the search warrant. If body language was an indicator of guilt, there was plenty of it to go around in the small group standing near the office.

As soon as the team came in, Matt gave them their assignments to question the owners about Sofia and some of the other girls they had interviewed. He wanted them separated during the interviews. He didn't want them aiding each other with answers. Matt had asked the judge to consider a separate warrant for the team doctor's files and business files at a later date. The judge agreed but wanted to see how the track and interviews went today. He wanted solid evidence of probable cause before he issued the next warrant. Matt agreed with him. The case was building slowly, and Sofia was important to the process.

"You're free to do your job, Frank. Dylan and I

will have your back." Matt patted Radar's head.

Frank stooped down beside his dog and let him smell the scent item. "Find the girl, fella. Let's bring her home." Radar walked through the gym, stopped at a locker that had Sofia's name on it, and moved on until he came back to the entrance of the building. When Frank opened the door, Radar went out to the parking lot stopping at a parking space and then proceeded onto the road. He followed the road for several blocks and then turned right onto a side street.

"What do you think?" Matt asked.

"She must have come this way at some point, whether by car or on foot. I think he's on to something. I'm not sure if he'll find her or a dead end. Either way, at some point she came this way."

"That's good enough for me," Dylan told him. "This dog always amazes me. To even know the direction she took is mind-boggling to me." After a few more turns they came to a large brick house halfway down the block. Radar showed interest in the area moving down the driveway toward a small building toward the back of the building.

"Frank, hold him back a minute." Matt walked up to the front door and knocked. When the door opened, he showed his badge. "I have a warrant for this dog to track. We're looking for a missing child. The dog has shown interest in the building at the back of your property. Could you tell me what the building is?"

"It's a carriage house that we use for family and friends when they visit. I have a key. You're free to look around. I'd be happy to open the door for you."

"That would be great. Thank you." Matt followed the homeowner out to the building. As soon as the door was open Radar raced in and made his way to a room at the back of the small cottage. On the floor huddled in the corner was Sofia.

"Young lady, what are you doing in here? Who let you in?" The homeowner shook his head. "I had no idea she was in here."

"Sofia, would you like to answer the man's question?" Matt encouraged her with a smile.

"Jenna, your granddaughter, told me I could stay here," she said softly.

"That sounds like something my granddaughter would do and not tell me. How long have you been here?"

"Several days, I guess. She brought me food and told me to lie low for a while."

"We talked to Jenna a few times trying to find you, and she maintained with a straight face that she had no idea where you were." Matt helped Sofia to her feet.

"That also sounds like my granddaughter." The man shook his head again. "Is this girl in trouble?" he asked. "My granddaughter may be after this stunt."

"Oh, please no, don't be mad at her. She was only trying to help me. She even made a call to tell Jessie I was all right and to tell my mom."

"That's true. That's how we made our first contact with her. She never did give away Sofia's hiding place. Why is that, Sofia?" Matt asked.

"She was afraid for me and my family. They threatened to kill my family if I said anything to anybody. I couldn't tell my parents, and I never wanted to go to that place again. I was afraid I guess." She sniffed and then started to cry.

"It's okay. I don't know who the people are that

you're talking about but I'm glad that you are safe from them," the elderly gentleman told her as he awkwardly patted her back.

Radar nudged Sofia's hand. "Who is this?"

"This is Radar. He's the dog that tracked you from the gym to here. Your parents are worried sick about you."

"What about my parents?" Sofia petted Radar.

"We'll keep them safe. Right now, we want to get you home to your parents," Matt told her. "Thank you, Mr.—"

"Simpson. Hank. My son is Jenna's dad. I'm glad she helped her friend, but I wished she would have let us all know. We could have saved her parents some heartache."

"Thanks again, Hank." Matt shook his hand. "I wouldn't be too hard on your granddaughter. She did keep her friend safe after all."

"There's that at least. I wish kids would tell you when something is wrong." Simpson shook his head.

"Not all adults listen and not all are trustworthy either. I guess they hatched a plan they thought would be the best for everyone involved," Matt told him.

"I guess you're right."

As soon as they were outside, Matt called for Kip to pick them up in the SUV. He gave them the address with help from Hank. While they waited, Matt called Mrs. Barton to tell them they had found Sofia and she and her husband could pick her up in an hour at the station.

"Frank, your dog did it again." Dylan helped him lift Radar up into the crate. "Is Carlene going to be another great tracker?"

"She has all the earmarks of one. She's a hard worker and picks things up quickly." Frank handed Radar a treat. "But this guy is my best friend. He won't ever be replaced in my heart."

"Dogs have a way of doing that." Matt helped Sofia get into the car. He couldn't wait to hear what had happened at the gym with the interviews and what Sofia had to say for herself. One thing he knew for sure was that Jessie would be happy to know Sofia was fine.

****

Jessie was still waiting when she noticed a cloud of dust following a vehicle in the distance. The truck was coming in her direction and seemed to be moving at a fast clip. He pulled off the road and drove across the dirt near where she sat. He opened the door and shoved the body out letting it fall face down in the dirt. He backed up, turned around, and sped off, the dust choking her as he left.

When Jessie got closer to where the girl lay, she found herself distraught once again. It was the same MO she had seen before. The pickup was the same. She had more questions now than ever. How did this girl feel in the moments before her life was taken? The grief she experienced was overwhelming.

Suddenly, she rode in the truck with another girl. Fear rose in her chest when he turned off the main road onto a rutted dirt road in a remote place. The girl searched for anything she could find to hit him with. The continuous bouncing gave her the perfect opportunity. Her sweater fell from her lap when her body bounced up. She bent down to get it and grabbed the first weighty item she found under the seat, hiding the item in her sweater. She waited for the right moment when she had gathered her nerve and then she hit him as hard as she could in the head. He slammed on the brakes, and she flew forward hitting her head on the dash. Dazed, she yanked the door open and took off running. Stumbling over the rough terrain, her shoes filled with sand and tiny rocks. "Keep running," she whispered as she looked back over her shoulder. She knew he would follow but she had to try to get away. Breathing hard, with a stitch in her side, she ran, staying off the dirt road. She kept on the soft sandy area where she knew the tires on his truck would sink and get stuck. She had stunned him. His head wound had bled. The truck still hadn't moved because she could see the lights were farther away and weren't moving closer. She had to put some distance between them because he would come. Of that, she had no doubt. She had seen that look on someone before. He enjoyed the hunt and the kill.

She heard the truck as it once again rattled closer to her. She struggled to pick up her pace. Fear raced through her forcing her to trudge forward through the sandy dirt when her body screamed for a break. She had no idea where she was running to. She could no longer see the landscape because darkness had settled in with no moonlight to brighten the night sky. She could hardly see her hand in front of her face. She fell, got up, and fell again scrambling over rocks and grabbing at tumbleweeds and sagebrush within the reach of her hands. Feeling her skin wet with blood from the scratches, she pressed forward until she fell over a ledge, reaching out to grab onto anything to stop her fall until she landed with a thud on her back in a gully. She didn't move; she couldn't. Struggling to catch her breath, she strained to listen. The man cursed and yelled for her, but he sounded far away. She forced herself to remain still until she heard the truck move on. She had survived, but she had no idea if he would return or where she even was.

Jessie shook herself and sat up, glancing at the girl who lay beside her. She had fallen about fifteen feet. Thankfully, it was into a sandy wash. The water must run through the area when it rained. The young woman had been brave, and it saved her life. The girl was one of the few lucky enough to get away. Jessie knew she had experienced a real event in the life of this young woman. Jessie cried and once again found herself alone. All these were shadows from the past. She couldn't change the results of what she had seen; she could only hope to change the future for the girls still living. She closed her eyes.

When she opened them again, Jessie found herself in the safety of her cottage with Kimama by her side. She had seen and known fear through the eyes of the victims. Once again, she cried. She wasn't sure if it was from relief or grief.

"How did this happen?" Jessie asked when she stopped crying.

"You are a traveler, and you are needed to bring attention to what is going on among my people across the country. I can only come through the door for limited reasons, and you can only cross through to help others. That is how it works. Tell the story you saw and lived. Help them discover those girls. They need to go home to their families. Cara was my friend in this life, and now we have you too. Sleep well, my friend. You will need your strength tomorrow." Kimama hugged

Jessie and disappeared.

Jessie spent the next hour making mental notes and writing down details of everything she had seen and the emotions she experienced. Especially, those of the girl who got away. If the girls were going to take rides, then they needed to know how to protect themselves from predators. Peyton knew all about self-defense. She taught women how to defend themselves for the PD in New York. She would get Peyton involved.

Jessie needed to remember the details of where the bodies could be found. At least the general area. Tomorrow would be soon enough to call Matt. If she called him now, he would rush over, and she was way too tired to talk. Coming and going through the portal had to do something to your insides. She laid her head back on the pillows and fell into a deep sleep with her running clothes still on.

Chapter Twenty-Four

Matt sat on the edge of the bed going over last night. He had questioned Sofia until her parents took her home. She refused to tell them much. She kept saying she would talk when Jessie was there. Hell, he wanted to have Jessie in the room too, but life didn't always give you what you want. The one thing he had learned during their conversation was that someone had threatened the girl to keep her mouth shut or they would make her family pay the price.

Sofia wouldn't tell them any names, but she gave small hints. When Matt mentioned one of the owners or the coach her reactions were informative. The team doctor's name was the clincher. He had enough circumstantial evidence to request a search warrant, but he wanted more. This case had been messed up years ago, and this time every step needed to be done by the book. He didn't only want to know who, but he wanted to understand why no one was held accountable.

His scheduled teleconference with the girls' legal team yesterday went well. The firm agreed to wait for a few weeks before filing the paperwork for their civil lawsuit case with the court. A criminal investigation would only strengthen their civil case. The delay bought Matt a couple of extra weeks before the defendants in the case were notified.

He had asked Jeremy and Gary to research the

center's business practices. He wanted a list of all the complaints against the company or any of its employees. The FBI was closing in on Zach Johnson's part, if any, from prison. The one thing working on their side was that Zach was a braggart and quiet wasn't one of his strongest suits.

Matt reached for his ringing phone. "This is Matt."

"Oh, yeah, that's good to know," Jessie's voice sounded over the line.

"Where are you?" He jumped up. "I'll be right over."

"At my place. And no, you won't come right over. I need to shower and get dressed. I'll meet you at the station in a while and we can talk." She hung up.

He took one look in the mirror and was glad she had stopped him from racing to her house. Besides a shower, he needed coffee and plenty of it. Even though he trusted he would see her again, that hadn't kept his mind from doubt. In his book, he had reacted better this time but still not without stress. He continued to do his job and remained somewhat patient. Yep, he was growing. He turned on the water and stepped into the hot spray. Damn, the warmth felt good. She was back and all was right with his world once again.

****

Jessie dried her hair and dressed with care. It was important to look her best today when she saw him. One of the most important discoveries she had made in the past few days was that Matt was a great guy and she wasn't going to take him for granted anymore. There were some awful men out there, but he was one of the good ones.

Jessie called Peyton while she made a cup of tea.

"Hi, cousin, I'm back." Jessie placed the teabag in the cup and poured the hot steamy water in.

"Audrey is opening the store this morning while I work. I thought you might want to know. I'm sure Matt has a lot of questions to ask," Peyton told her.

"I want to talk to you later. I'll be at the store. You'll never believe all that happened to me. Gosh, I can hardly believe what I saw, and I experienced the whole thing." Jessie took a sip of her tea. "You know, since moving here I've learned there are lots of good folks and bad folks in this world. I've managed to see both. How you and I were so lucky to meet two great guys is beyond me, but it's the truth."

"I agree. Do you mind if I ask you, what brought this on?" Peyton asked.

"I'll tell you later. I wanted you to know I'm back. We live a charmed life, and we should never forget that. See you later." Jessie disconnected the call.

Jessie checked her hair one more time before she slipped on her jacket. Shoving her phone in her purse, she grabbed her keys and headed out clicking the lock behind her. She sorted through her mental notes trying to figure out what to tell Matt and in what order. Hopefully, Sofia was home safe and what she had to share with Matt this morning would be mostly confirmation.

Seeing what happened to those women had made her more conscious of the man who was angry with her and left her notes. She would be more careful. She owed that much to Matt. She honked as she passed the inn on her way out to the road into town.

Her first stop was the bookstore. "Good morning, Audrey. If you are okay to work for a while, I need to stop by the station and fill in some details. As soon as a get a scone and a coffee that is."

"I'm glad you're back. Peyton told me you were called away suddenly regarding a case you were working on. It's been busy but fine here the last couple of days. I can work until noon when Sadie is scheduled to be here. Take your time."

"I'll be back before then. I've missed my store, and I can't wait to get back to work. I'll hurry," she said as she walked into the coffee shop.

"Hey, Molly. I hope you're feeling less nauseous this morning." She leaned close so only she could hear.

"About the same." Molly shrugged her shoulders. "It is what it is. Was your trip a success?"

"Yes, I think it was." Jessie looked at the menu. "I don't know why I'm looking. I want a decaf coffee and a scone. You know, my favorite."

"For here or to go?" Molly asked. "One of these days I'm going to convince you to try one of my new breakfast sandwiches."

"But not today. This is to go. I have to get to the station and talk with Matt."

"Sounds good. Here's your cup." Molly handed her the empty cup.

Jessie filled it with hot coffee and added cream. She paid for her order, grabbed the bag that Molly placed on the counter, and put a tip in the jar. "I'll see you later." She waved as she rushed out the door to her car.

He had to have been watching for her. Matt came out the door as soon as she pulled into the parking lot. He was ready to open the door as soon as she stopped the car. "Thank you." She stepped out of the car. "I've missed you too." She smiled at him.

"That's one way to put it." He pulled her into his arms and kissed her.

"Matt, can't you hear the guys in the background?" Jessie chuckled.

"Sure, I hear them, but I don't care. I haven't missed them." He kissed her again and the bantering got louder. He pulled her into his side and draped his arm around her. "Damn, I missed you."

"Wow, you sweet talker, you have such a way with words." She glanced at him, and he pulled her tighter.

"Wait. I forgot something." She pulled out of his arms and went back to get her coffee and bag. "Okay, I'm ready."

"Let me guess." He took her free hand. "Decaf coffee and a scone perhaps?"

"You know me well."

He pulled her into his office and shut the door. "One more, and then we'll get down to business." He took the bag and coffee from her hand and placed them on his desk. Hands free, he pulled her into his arms and kissed her again. "I don't like it when you suddenly go missing." He nibbled on her ear. "And I don't like that you couldn't tell me. There had better be a good reason for Peyton, and not you, telling me." He leaned his chin on the top of her head.

"Sorry about that. I was trying to follow the directions that were given to me. I don't think you would have handled it well. I mean you don't exactly like things you can't control. We are a lot alike in that department." She pulled out of his arms and sat. Reaching around him she grabbed her coffee.

"Haven't I for the most part been understanding

when it comes to this strange part of your life? I try not to complain or worry too much. This time I even trusted that you would be back and continued to work the whole time. You would have been proud of me." He sat on the corner of his desk. "We found Sofia and she is home with her parents. She said she wouldn't talk until you were present."

"You found the murder victim, didn't you?" she asked. She held up her hand to stop him from telling her what happened. "Her husband murdered her." She proceeded to explain everything she had seen.

"You got that right. He's sitting in jail right now. It felt great to put him behind bars." He brought her hand up to his lips and kissed it. "Tell me what you were thinking when you watched the scene play out. And for the record, do you see how I've grown. I didn't question your ability to see or even ask you how."

"I am impressed." She took a sip of her coffee and reached for the bag with her scone in it. "Sorry, but I'm hungry. I didn't eat while I was gone, and I have no idea why."

"What else did you see?" he asked.

"The next part is important because you will need to notify the police in the areas where the bodies might be found." She bit into her scone.

"Take it slow and easy, and let's get down to work." He sat behind his desk and reached for his pen and notebook. He took notes as she began to describe the first murder site she visited. She went on to tell him about the man who picked up the girl. She described the truck and the fact that she saw the same truck at two other sites. "I'm sure he's a serial killer. What's equally strange is I may have seen the truck or possibly heard the man's voice somewhere before. Although, I'm sure I would've remembered his southern drawl if I had. Something about what I saw or heard seemed familiar to me, but I have no idea what or why. It could just be me mixing my dream up with reality."

"Look over my list." He pushed the notebook toward her. "See if I have the details the way you saw them. Especially the mile marker numbers, the states, and monuments you mentioned that were nearby. Those details will be important to the authorities."

Jessie looked over the page. "Is this a one or a seven?"

"It's a one. That's the way I was taught to make my ones." He grinned.

"As long as it's a one you've got it right." She smiled at him. "This time was strange for me. It was hard not to talk to you. And what was even worse was knowing something was going to happen but not knowing when or how. The stress level seemed intensified."

"Why?" he asked.

"Good question. I tried to figure out how I would go on the journey Kimama talked about. But running with Peyton was never on my radar. To be with her and suddenly pressed through a portal was strange."

"I don't know how you do it. At least once I got used to the idea, I handled the situation better than I normally would." He leaned back in his chair. "Of course, I might have scared Peyton when she told me, at first."

"I don't believe it. Not you." Jessie stood. "You're an old softy at heart." She traced his cheek to his chin with her hand. "What happened to those women was awful. I won't ever forget what I saw. Now more than ever I have to fight for women's rights."

"You'll get no argument from me. That's one of the many traits I love about you."

"Good, because I'm a package deal." She leaned against him.

"Did I mention to you that I like the package?" He kissed her. "I guess I'd better behave myself. Before I forget, I would like you to sit in when I question Ben Tso and Sofia. I'll text you the times as soon as I know them."

"I need to work at the store since I've been gone a few days. Peyton may be able to help out at some point." She drank the last sip of her coffee.

"I'll make it work. Enjoy your day." He opened his office door for her. "I'll let you know how these contacts go. I'll mention that I'd like to be notified if they find a body."

"Thanks, that would be helpful. It would be nice to know I'm not a total nut job." She waved at Dylan walking down the hall. "I'll see you later."

"Hey, Jessie, it's good to have you back," Dylan called over his shoulder. "I didn't tell Katie anything." He stopped so she could catch up to him. "I thought it would be better for her not to know. She seems quite upset by this side of your life."

"You're right about that. We've managed to remain friends through it all."

She smiled while driving back to the store. Opening her latest order of books, Jessie got busy. After she entered them into the computer and priced them, she placed them on the shelves. A few made their way to her display table at the front of the store. This simple repetitive action seemed almost comforting to her. There was a lot to be said about routine.

When Peyton arrived, Jessie told her the details of her short jaunt in time and space. Peyton could be counted on to stand with her. She understood abuse and having to fight for everything she had. Jessie was grateful to have her cousin living in Blue Cove. Between the two of them, they were a formidable force for women's rights, especially when it came to abuse.

Reba and Sadie stopped by to be filled in on all the details. By the time Jessie had gone over the story the second time, her workday was almost done. The store would close in less than an hour and she hadn't heard from Matt yet. She scrolled through her text messages and there wasn't one from him.

She started her closing practice which included straightening the bookmarks. They always got so messy by the end of the day. Once Reba and Sadie left, the store seemed empty. Those two brought such joy with them, and Matt was the icing on the cake.

Chapter Twenty-Five

Matt spent the day on the phone with tribal police departments in several states. The only thing he could give them was that the information had come to him as an anonymous tip but had been specific. He figured that Kimama was about as unknown as he could get. How did you tell someone your girlfriend got a tip from a ghost? Matt knew the words that he could use to ring the alarm and still have what he said seem credible. A police chief told him today that abuse and missing girls were a big problem on their reservation. They had several missing persons with too few officers to send out looking for each one. A body was a different story. He would get two of his officers on it right away. The directions were good enough to steer them in the right direction. He was the first police chief to call back and tell him that they had found the victim.

He scheduled the interviews with Sofia and Ben for tomorrow. They had questioned Ben Tso already but Matt wanted to go through the items gathered during the search one more time before the next interview. He needed to let Jessie know and dialed her number.

"I thought maybe you forgot me," she said when she answered the phone.

"Not a chance. The interviews are scheduled for tomorrow afternoon. I hope you can work out the time." He waved at Dylan when he passed by his door. "I want to take you to dinner. I'll meet you at your place around five-thirty."

"Works for me. See you in a little while."

Jessie's car was there when he pulled up. Matt walked the familiar path to the door. Sooner rather than later he hoped she lived with him. Maybe he should simply tell her they could be married or not—either way she would be living with him. He knocked on her door.

"Are you ready?" He held the door open locking it as soon as she stepped out. "I thought we should go to that new restaurant everyone is talking about. It's in the resort area. I often forget about the restaurants there because during the height of the tourist season they're too busy. Dylan told me it's a great bistro with a nice atmosphere for dining."

"Sounds perfect. Especially, if it's quiet. The last few days have been taxing. The whole trip impacted me more than I realized." She slipped in the passenger's seat.

"I'm sure. Seeing a person murdered can't be easy, but seeing the scene through the victim's eyes must be horrific." He glanced at her. Hearing her appealing voice was music to his ears.

"I ran beside a woman who fought her attacker and got away. I tripped when she did and fell in the gully when she went over the edge." She shivered and he put his arm around her shoulder. "It seemed as real to me as you are."

He glanced at her before he started the car. "Are you sure you're okay?"

"I'm fine, but emotional. I will never be the same. Somebody has to care about all the girls out there who are being abused by their fathers, husbands, or boyfriends. Or, just as sad, by a person in a position of trust, a family member, or a stranger with issues against women. We're not that scary. Most women are out to take over the world but if they are strong at all, a lot of men feel threatened by them. Why? Don't get me started on the fact that women have been taking it from men since the beginning." She touched his arm. "Sorry, I get frustrated about the inequities I see in the world sometimes."

"I get it, sweetheart. That's why I do my job. The system isn't perfect but it's better than most. We fight to get these criminals off the streets one crime at a time. Do I wish we could stop it before it escalates to murder? Hell, yes. All we can do is our best."

"Yeah, I get it. Change comes slowly. Well, for the families of girls waiting for them to come home it doesn't seem good enough." Jessie dabbed at the tears in her eyes with a tissue.

"I know. At times, the wheels of justice seem to hardly turn at all. But one piece of good news that I heard today was that one of the girls had been found. The police chief called to let me know right before I left." Matt told her about his talk with the chief earlier. "Your directions led them right to her. At least she'll be going home once they can ID the body."

"Where does the case here stand now? You found one body and got her killer. What about the studio and the girls there?" she asked.

"We are slowly building our case while doing an internal investigation. I want to know who's tampering with the files. Whoever it is, I'm sure they are working with Zach Johnson and he's telling them what to do.

Tom Maxwell's guy is on the inside working the Johnson angle." He backed out of the parking space and drove past the inn. "I have a question for you." He stopped before turning onto the road into town.

"I'm listening," she said.

"Have you thought any more about the man stalking you? Any guesses about his identity?" he asked as he began driving again.

"Not a one. But after the past few days I'm more clear-headed regarding the whole situation. I won't be cavalier about his threats. I am going to take them seriously."

"Good to hear. The guy troubles me. He's the unknown factor that can change the equation of a case with one action."

"That's true. I'm also thinking about the possibility of a serial killer roaming the country. I'm sure there are probably more than one, but I only know about the one I watched."

"I can't imagine how many are roaming around out there. They have the thrill of the kill. That's scary to think about." Matt pulled into a parking space. He opened her car door. "No more work talk. You need a break." He took her hand and closed the door.

"Agreed. What do you want to talk about?" she asked while they waited to be seated.

"Us." He smiled at her. They followed the host to their table. After giving the waiter their order, Matt took her hand in his. "I've made a monumental decision today."

"Oh yeah, what's that?" she asked.

"You know I love you." He grinned and toyed with the ring on her finger.

"Yes, I do." She smiled at him.

"You also know I've been patient about the whole marriage thing." He stroked the palm of her hand with his thumb.

"So you say." She chuckled and pulled her hand away.

He grabbed it back. "Yes, I do say, and you know I'm right, sweetheart. I'll give you more time to see things my way and then I'll enact my plan."

"That's thoughtful of you. I have my own plan." She fluttered her lashes at him playfully. "Mine will win the day."

"Challenge is accepted. You know how I love a good challenge. The game is on. If I have my way, we'll both come out winners."

"Funny, I was thinking the same thing." Jessie thanked the waiter when he placed her meal in front of her. "This looks good. I'm hungry."

"Enjoy." He loved observing her eat something she liked. She didn't hold back and the expressions on her face said it all. Yes, he was going to love this challenge even better than the first one to get her to go out with him. This one involved their future happiness.

"I will." She took a bite of the Tuscan chicken while closing her eyes. "Perfection." She licked her lips.

Matt smiled. He couldn't help it.

****

When Jessie opened her eyes, he was smiling at her. "What?"

"You hold nothing back." He took a sip of his wine.

"I'm glad you're entertained." She blushed and her

face heated under his continued regard. "I aim to please."

"I don't think I tell you often enough how beautiful you are to me. It's more than your physical assets, which I find quite appealing, but it's you. I find you utterly fascinating and refreshing."

"And now thoroughly embarrassed." Her face was a deeper shade of red. "Thank you."

"Wow, I didn't know a face could blush that red." He grinned. "I'm sorry if I made you uncomfortable. I only realized the fact that I love everything about you."

"I'm sure to disappoint you eventually." She sipped her water.

"Anything is possible but, at the moment, I can't imagine it. I rather think of you the way I see you right now."

"Doesn't it concern you that life will change us, and our feelings toward each other?" She wanted for him to answer and yet she didn't.

"What if life's challenges push us closer to each other rather than apart? My parents' love endured three crazy boys, plenty of sad times, and an empty nest. Married for over forty years and they still love each other. There's something to be said about that kind of relationship. I know it doesn't always work out, but I couldn't imagine not trying."

"I guess you're right. You can't give up because of what might happen that may never materialize." She smiled when he reached for her hand. "You've given me something to think about.

"Nothing is perfect, but what we have is close to it as far as I'm concerned." He took another sip of his wine. "I missed you, sweetheart, everything about you."

"And how will you feel when it continues to happen after we're married? Because it will." She placed her napkin on the table and waited for him to answer. He seemed to be taking longer than normal.

"That's true, but I've come to understand that it's a part of who you are." He stroked his chin. "I find your gift a fascinating piece of you. I can't imagine our lives ever being boring. Can you? With you, the mystery will always be present."

"True." She thanked the waiter when he took her plate. She watched as Matt pointed out something to the waiter.

"I ordered a special dessert in honor of another successful outing for you. Already one girl is being ID'd, and soon her family will be able to find closure and lay her to rest. It might have been years before somebody stumbled onto her body."

"Yeah, that's good news." She smiled. "Now, about the dessert, I hope it's chocolate."

"Would I order anything else for you?" he asked.

The waiter placed a huge piece of chocolate deliciousness between them and handed each of them a fork. "Enjoy. What are you celebrating?" he asked.

"A successful trip," Matt told him.

Jessie sighed when she closed the door after Matt left. The night had been perfect from beginning to end. Matt reassured her more than he would ever know. He loved her, she was convinced.

His kisses could make her forget what troubled her. He made sure she had plenty of them tonight. She leaned against the door and sighed again. Jessie had no clue what movie they had been watching because Matt had pleasantly distracted her. Love was both wonderful and scary. You gained and lost at the same time. But as Matt said, she couldn't imagine not trying.

Chapter Twenty-Six

Opening her store the next morning, Jessie was struck again with a sense of contentment. At home among all the books, she enjoyed talking with the people who came and went each day. The friends she had met since moving to Blue Cove were numerous. Molly was one of them. Jessie waved at her when she opened the doors to the coffee shop.

The people at the church where she first went to work were among some of her best customers, and of course, Reba. She made living with her gift a bit easier to swallow with all of her encouragement. Jessie mused as she walked to the front of the store. The church across the street looked as grand today as the first day she drove into town. A lot had happened in her life in the past year. Who would have thought that a girl from the Midwest would grow up to be an investigative reporter who could see ghosts? It wasn't something she would have said when asked what you want to be when you grow up. But truth be told she couldn't imagine doing any other job or living anywhere else. She couldn't see the church without thinking about Melissa—or Red, her pet name for the custodian—her one-woman welcoming committee who told her about the church ghost on her first day of work.

She turned the sign to open and unlocked the door, waving at Reba crossing the street from the church.

Jessie held the door open for her friend and squeezed her hand as Reba rushed past into the store.

"I've come to hear details, my dear. I heard you were back. There's a storm brewing over the town and it has nothing to do with the weather." Reba placed her purse on the table.

"What do you mean?" Jessie asked giving her a befuddled look. She lifted a piece of hair twisting it around her finger.

"Dear, I haven't seen you twist your hair in a while. Is something troubling you?" Reba slipped off her jacket and sat patting the chair next to her.

"When you say there's a storm brewing, I take that seriously." Jessie sat beside her with a grave expression.

The bell above the door rang and a tall man wearing a cowboy hat came in. His boots were scuffed Jessie noticed. "May I help you?"

"I'm just looking." He smiled. "Well, howdy, Ms. Lawrence. It's always nice to see you." His tipped his hat. "Don't get up, young lady." He gestured at Jessie. "You gals enjoy your visit. I wouldn't want to intrude on your little tete-la-tete."

He walked around the store, looked at a few books, and picked up a travel magazine. "You have a nice store here." He handed her a hundred-dollar bill. "Keep the change, sweetheart. I'll be back. You can count on it." He took his bag and walked by Reba, tipping his hat again. "Enjoy your day."

When he left Reba glanced at Jessie. "I don't like the man."

"Who is he?" Jessie asked looking at the bill in her hand.

"Sonny 'Tex' Webster, or at least that's the name he goes by. I don't believe he's married, or I've never heard him mention a wife. He owns the hardware store in the strip mall right off the highway. His brother owned it before him, and Sonny took over when his brother died of a heart attack, or so the story goes. He's always annoyed me."

"Why?" Jessie asked. "He seems smitten with you."

"That's ludicrous. He hardly knows me." Reba shook her head. "I won't go into his store unless Lawrence is with me. There's something off about the man and I'd rather not be near him. Plus, I've heard my share of gossip about him." She leaned close and told her some of what she'd heard. "Has he ever been in your store before?"

"I don't remember seeing him before. I would remember that cowboy hat. Not that many men wear them around town, much less in my store." Jessie chuckled. "It was a bit over the top for me."

"Everything about him is over the top. A braggart would be my description. And that's why we must put our heads together and figure him out." Reba frowned. "It's like the man isn't who he pretends to be."

"That's not a great recommendation coming from you. You know people. Not only by their appearances but by who they are. Their heart, if you want to call it that, or what makes them tick." Jessie glanced at her friend.

"I'll have to think about why he bothers me for a while. I don't feel put off by many folks," Reba said.

"That's true. You are gracious and caring." Jessie patted Reba's hand.

"We'll talk about it more another day. Be sure to let me know if you come up with anything." Reba stood pushing in her chair. "I'm going to get a box of Molly's goodies for dessert. Lawrence always appreciates when he gets something special."

"I'll let you know. Don't forget to get at least one lemon bar for yourself." Jessie smiled.

"If I only could forget." She patted her stomach as she reached for her purse. "I'll be back to get my jacket."

Jessie had a few hours before Peyton would get here to watch the store. Matt wanted her to be there for his interview with Sofia and to watch the one with Ben. He wanted to see if Ben's story jived with what Jessie saw.

As she waited, she entered more new inventory into the computer. Reaching for the list she added the numbers next to the title of the books. While she was at it, she needed to place an order for several books that consistently sold out every time she got them in. Conservative was her word of choice for how she stocked inventory. The demise of many small bookstores was an overstock of merchandise that failed to move. But in the case of these books, she might need to add a few more copies of each of the titles to have enough for her customers. They were her most frequently requested titles. Word of mouth seemed to be a good selling point for an author.

"Hey, cousin, have you been busy today?" Peyton asked when she walked in.

"Not with customers, which gave me time to get caught up on paperwork. I have a few more entries and I'm done." She smiled at Peyton.

"A good feeling, I'm sure." Peyton leaned her hip against the counter.

"Yes, but I have this nagging thought at the back of my mind that I'm forgetting something. I can't for the life of me think what it might be. I think Reba's concern earlier might be impacting me more than I want to admit." Jessie scrunched her face.

"I'm early. Fill me in. Reba doesn't throw words around lightly." Peyton sat in one of the chairs.

"That's what has me worrying. First, she said there was a storm brewing over the cove that had nothing to do with the weather. We didn't spend much time on that before a man walked into my store." Jessie told her about Sonny Webster and what Reba said.

"Do you think the storm and the man are somehow connected?" Peyton asked.

"There's an angle to consider. I didn't think of a connection and Reba never made one. Anything is possible, I guess. Reba didn't seem to like him much."

"Did she say why?" Peyton pushed her hair behind her ears.

"She thought he might be hiding something. He's one of the business leaders in town and most people seem to think highly of him. But you know me. I tend to trust Reba on all things strange in the Blue Cove."

"You and me both. She has a great track record. Even when she doesn't make sense at the time."

"You can lock up at five." Jessie handed her cousin the keys. "I'll stop by your place and get them from you when I get home. I know I won't be back to close on time."

"Sounds good." Peyton waved as Jessie rushed out the door.

"Remind me that I need to make you a set of keys." Jessie called over her shoulder.

****

Matt stood at the station door waiting for Jessie to get there. First on the agenda was to listen to their interview with Ben Tso. He trusted what she had seen because they could prove most of it with evidence except for Tso's condition at the time. His story kept changing and he now maintained that he wasn't drunk, and she had hit him first. Witnesses had seen him drinking and had called his wife to warn her. Ben was known to be less than a stellar husband by even his closet friends.

He walked out the door when she pulled into the parking lot. "Hi, sweetheart," he said when he opened her car door.

"You're the second one who called me that today. It means more coming from you, though."

"Who else called you sweetheart?" He frowned.

"No one important." She explained about Tex Webster and Reba's feeling toward the man. "He seems harmless enough even if he looks out of place in our town with his cowboy boots and hat. You have to admit we don't see that every day. My guess is he thinks of himself as a ladies' man."

"I've been in his store. I might need to check him out." He took her hand. "Are you ready for this?"

"Yes. I can't wait to see Sofia. Tso not so much. I get mad every time I think about what he did to his wife. I'm sorry if a man is angry or doesn't like his spouse but he should walk away. He doesn't have to stay and most of all he doesn't need to kill her."

"Agreed. Let's get this over with." He held the

station door open for her.

"Sounds good to me." She followed him to the room where she could watch the interview.

"I'll be back at some point to hear what you have to say," he told her.

Tso was brought into the room and sat in a chair across from Matt and Dylan. He leaned back in his chair, folded his arms across his chest, and a smug look crossed his face.

"Are you charging me with something?" He glared at Matt. "I have rights."

"Yes, you do, and you were read those rights and signed a release to be interviewed." Matt showed him a copy of his signed waiver. "We want to hear your side of the story before there are any formal charges. If we make charges, you can have a court-appointed attorney since you said you don't have one."

"Okay, it's like this." Ben explained his side of the story leaving out several details that Matt already knew to be facts by evidence alone.

"You say she left to go to her parents after you accidentally knocked her down. You fell backward after she shoved you. Is that right?"

"Yes, that's right." He nodded.

"I have a problem with your story. We have several witnesses that say you were fired from another job and had been drinking most of the day. You could hardly walk when you left the bar much less drive. Several people we talked with said they called your wife and told her to get out of there before you got home because you weren't in your right mind."

"They were lying." Tso leaned backed in his chair.

The interview went on for a while and Matt

listened to Tso's ever-changing story. At one point he denied even being home. Matt told Dylan to continue to question him some more while he went to check on something. He left the room and went to see Jessie.

"What do you think?" he asked when he walked in.

"He's lying, of course. I wonder what would happen if I jogged his memory."

"I have an idea." Matt discussed the plan with her for a few minutes. "Give me ten more minutes with him and then come in and do your thing."

****

Jessie waited ten minutes and put the time to good use. She recalled the details of her journey.

When Jessie entered the room, she inserted details she had seen into a casual conversation as possible scenarios and not as facts. Matt would back the statement with evidence found at the scene.

"She didn't deserve to die alone," she said quietly. "Her blood spilled on the ground where they found her. No woman deserves that." Jessie wiped the tears from her eyes.

Ben became quiet and then he broke down and cried. The confession rolled out of him. In some odd way, he loved his wife and lived with the guilt of what happened that night.

To say Jessie was frustrated was an understatement. When did it become okay for a man to use his wife as a punching bag because he had a tough day? She walked out of the interview room before she said something that would mess up Matt's investigation. She understood he had to do it by the book or Ben Tso could get off. She was thankful that she could go home and turn her frustration into words on paper and tell the story.

Maybe if she wrote about abuse against women often enough one woman somewhere could be saved.

"Are you okay?" Matt asked.

"I will be, but I get tired of the same old story. Now he cries because he got caught, but did he search for his missing wife for all those days? No, he did not."

"I understand how you must feel." He hugged her.

"Do you? I don't think any man fully understands what women go through. There's always been a double standard when it comes to us. A boy grows up and makes a mistake and we hear people say, boys will be boys. We hear a good girl would never do that or my favorite—it is your job is to keep the man in line. As if he's not responsible for his actions. I know you're different, but it doesn't make it any easier for me to accept this junk." She pulled out of his arms.

"I hear you and if I do other men will too when they read your articles. We don't understand how our words impact people." He took her hand in his and pulled her close again. "Remember, change comes slowly but it does come."

"It seems to be often one step forward and two steps back." She stepped forward and then back to emphasize her point. "I know women don't always understand men either. But we don't have the same brute strength to punish you with. We can get snarky with our words and quite petty at times. I know it's a two-way street. But right now, all these young women are on my mind. I give you permission to ignore my ranting." She rested her head on his chest.

"Jess, sweetheart, I love how you care about others. I understand your frustration. I wish I could do more.

My dad tried his best to educate us to do the right thing and to feel a sense of shame when we went against that code of conduct. A lot of the norms have broken down in society. But believe it or not, progress continues to be made," he told her.

"I know, but sometimes it seems to move too slowly like the wheels of justice you're always talking about." She pulled out of his embrace. You would think we'd all wake up to the fact the most common thread running through everything in life is our humanity and our need for one another."

"Now that's something I can relate to. I need you." He smiled at her. "Get something to drink. Sofia should be here in a few minutes to talk to you. This time I'll watch for a while."

A few minutes later, Jessie pulled Sofie into her arms and hugged her. "Tell me what happened."

"A man I had never seen at the gym before threatened me. He had heard me tell my trainer I wouldn't go see the doctor about my injury and why." She gave Jessie the details her tears. "The man squeezed my arm really hard and promised he'd hurt my family. I waited until he wasn't watching me and slipped out of the gym. Thankfully, Jenna promised to help, or I don't know what I would have done." She sniffed.

"Were there others threatened or afraid of the doctor too?" Jessie handed her the tissue box.

"I heard rumors of what he did to some of the older girls when he treated their injuries. He never did anything like that to me until a few months ago." Tears filled her eyes. She went on to describe how he made her uncomfortable and how he often touched her inappropriately. "The guy gives me the creeps."

"Was there anyone else involved?" Jessie asked her.

"There's something squirrely with all of them but there's no way I will ever trust my trainer again. I know he was told by the other girls many times, but he kept sending them to the doctor."

Sofia's parents were angry and in shock. They were ready to join the lawsuit with the other parents they had talked to. Jessie could only imagine how they felt. She was angry for each of the girls who had to face this. By the time the Barton family had left, Jessie's frustration level had reached a whole new level.

"I know you heard her say the same thing I did. Tell me, what are you going to do about this?" She frowned.

"What I always do, sweetheart. Follow the leads, find more evidence, and develop my case. It takes time and believe it or not this one is picking up steam. I learned a lot listening to Sofia that jives with what other interviews have revealed. We have some more evidence that we're waiting on. Arrests will come soon. But you know how it goes, Jess. It's got to be done right. Facts rule in a court of law and not emotions."

"I know," she said softly. "I also know you'll get these guys. You're good at what you do. But justice was delayed for these girls once before by the system there to protect them."

"Not this time." He reached for her hand. "Let's eat."

"I have my car," she reminded him.

"I'll follow you home and we can take mine from there." They walked out of the station hand in hand.

Chapter Twenty-Seven

Jessie could see Matt behind her as she turned out of the station. She had no doubt he would do his job. But nothing happened quickly enough for her. What she needed was to get a life. Not that she didn't have one, but she couldn't spend the next many years being concerned about justice. She would go nuts. It was the lack of concern that seemed to be the problem but on the other hand what could one person do?

"Don't go there," she told herself. "There were plenty of examples in history of one person doing amazing things. One woman saved over twenty-five hundred Jewish children during the Holocaust." Jessie remembered reading her story. Because of her job with the Social Welfare Department, the woman was authorized to enter the Warsaw Ghetto. Under the guise of performing inspections, she would sneak in food, medicine, and clothing into the ghetto but never left empty-handed. She loaded babies and small children into packages and suitcases to be smuggled out. One person could do a lot if they're determined to sacrifice their comfort to help.

Owning a bookstore meant she had plenty of material to read. There were lots of stories to inspire her or make her feel better when she wanted to give up. Just like that, she could snap her fingers and recall a story to remind her one person can make a huge difference.

Jessie stopped at the light. Matt was right behind her. He loved and cherished her all the while making her feel secure. He seemed to take her soapbox stands in stride and never was condescending about it. She couldn't ask for anything more in a man. The question she needed to answer was why she was on the fence. She drove toward the inn when the light changed.

She pulled into her parking space and got out of her car. Peyton and Jaxon were walking her way. "Hi, you two."

"I have your keys which you'll need in the morning." Peyton dug them out of her purse and dropped them in Jessie's hand.

"Thank you. That means one less thing for me to do later." Jessie stuck them in her pocket.

"I found this letter when I sorted through the mail at the store. It looked personal and I thought you might want it." Peyton handed her the envelope.

"Thanks." Jessie had a bad feeling the minute her hand touched the envelope. "What do we have here?" she muttered under her breath. "Where are you guys off to?"

"To dinner," Jaxon said. "For some reason, we both thought the diner sounded good. It's the rolls that are calling to me." He chuckled.

"They're good but it's the pie that does most of the talking." Jessie smiled. "I thought Matt was right behind me." She glanced toward the inn. "We're going to dinner too."

"We'll wait. I wanted to talk to Matt anyway," Jaxon said.

"I have a bad feeling about this." Jessie held the envelope in the air. She waved to Matt when he pulled up.

"Do you want me to open this for you?" Jaxon asked reaching for the envelope.

"Yes, please," Jessie told him.

Jaxon opened the letter carefully and began to read the contents. "Matt will want to see this."

"Good, or bad?" she asked.

"Not good, not good at all." Jaxon handed the letter to Matt when he walked up. "I think you might want to see this."

"Damn, Jess, he's back and at the worst time possible." He handed her the note to read.

I'm back. Did you miss me? I can't wait to teach you a lesson that you'll never forget. I promise you won't hear me coming until it's too late.

"Great." She handed the note back to him. "I guess you need to keep this. I sure don't want it."

"Sorry, cous, I should have left it at the store," Peyton said.

"It doesn't matter. I would have seen the letter eventually. At least Matt is here to see its contents with me." Jessie leaned against him. "They are headed to the diner. Do you want to tag along?"

"As long as you're there I'm in." He draped his arm around her shoulders. "Let's go. I'm starving."

****

"Thank you for driving." Jessie leaned close to him.

"My pleasure." He opened the car door for her. "Tom Maxwell told me today they are considering having Jaxon work with me on this case for the next few weeks. He'll let me know tomorrow. The FBI has an invested interest in it because of Zach Johnson's suspected involvement."

"How do you feel about that?" she asked.

"Truthfully, I'd be happy to have his help. I have several fronts on this case open and I could use more hands. My guys are busy with follow-up interviews, and I'd like Jaxon to snoop around the station. He can see what those of us working there regularly might not be able to see. Someone working there is feeding Zach information and covering for him. All the files regarding the gym and dance studio and many of the other files that Chief Anderson signed off on have been altered a few times since his death. I'm hoping Jaxon can ferret out the mole if we have one."

"Let's enjoy dinner with our friends and let tomorrow take care of itself." Jessie turned to look out the window.

****

Franny had the night off according to her stand-in, Libby, a platinum blonde with dark green eyeshadow and a southern twang. A unique sound to their ears not heard often in the northeast.

"What would you young fellas like?" she asked Matt and Jaxon. After they told her their order their unique dining experience was off and running.

"Young fellas. I'll have to remember that one. I've never thought of you as a young fella, Matt. It sounds to me like she called you little man, which I know isn't true." Jessie fluttered her lashes at him playfully.

"Thank you, sweetheart. Franny calls me son and Libby just called me young fella. I haven't seen myself that way in years. Almost makes me think I should be in short pants and suspenders." He chuckled.

"Let's leave it as a unique way to be addressed."

Jaxon changed the subject quickly. "These rolls are the best around. They taste like the ones my mom makes around the holidays." Jaxon slathered on the butter and took a big bite. "They'd be great with a spoonful of homemade blueberry preserves on them. I can taste it now." He smacked his lips.

"They're the best. And you can't beat the blue plate special." Matt pointed at his plate. "They've had some of the best specials every time we've been here. This is a good pork chop."

"Comfort food like mom's." Jaxon took a bite of his mashed potatoes.

"You guys are fun to watch." Peyton laughed. "You talk about food like some boys talk about girls."

"Never. The two aren't even in the same category. But hey, this is man food." Matt grunted and Jessie laughed.

"If you're eating man food then what is this?" Jessie pointed at her salad.

"Rabbit food." Matt rolled his eyes. "Not fit for humans to survive on as far as I'm concerned."

"I would call that the first course and look forward to the rest of the meal." Jaxon took another bite of his roll.

"Well, I call salad smart eating and saving room for what matters most." Peyton smiled. "Dessert." She took a bite of her banana cream pie.

"We think alike, cousin." Jessie turned to thank Libby when she placed her slice of chocolate cream pie in front of her. She took a bite of the pie and closed her eyes. "Yum, wow is this good. The servers make this restaurant fun, but the pie makes it worth the drive every time. Which is also the reason I can't come here often."

"Like Sally's milkshakes are for me. They're great but mean I'll be running a lot more." Peyton laughed.

"Did you see that look on Jessie's face, Jaxon? I'll know I've finally arrived when my kiss will make her look that way." Matt waited. "Ouch." Her foot kicked his shin.

"That's personal, and you know how I feel about your kisses. Chocolate pie can't hold a candle to them." She nudged him with her foot again for good measure.

Jessie asked Peyton about what happened at work after she left. It was always nice to hear she had several customers who bought books.

She glanced at Matt who seemed to be in deep conversation with Jaxon. Wow, she loved that man. To think she thought his rugged good looks weren't her type. Was she ever wrong! Everything about the man appealed to her. Matt asked her on the drive here if she was worried about the note she got. The truth was she wasn't; she knew Matt would do everything he could to keep her safe.

"Are you still mad at me?" Matt asked on the ride home.

"I was never mad." Jessie glanced at him. "I don't like talking about personal things in front of others. Besides, I have a lot on my mind."

"A more accurate way to have said it would have been that's the look on your face after I've kissed you. Satisfied." He reached for her hand.

"Now you're being cocky. Truthful but cocky." She squeezed his hand.

"Babe, I was trying to put you at ease. I know this has been a rough day. No one has ever accused me of being smooth. I'm a bit rough around the edges but you make me want to be a better man."

"I love you, Matt. You're almost perfect the way you are." She smiled at what she knew was coming.

"Almost?" His brows rose with his question.

"No one is perfect, but you're as close as they come." She patted his arm.

"I can live with that. Near perfect works for me." Matt glanced at Jessie.

"What were you and Jaxon talking about tonight? You both forgot you brought dates to dinner."

"Shoptalk, and you know how I get when I'm working a case. One of your many wonderful qualities is understanding my preoccupation with an investigation I'm working on," he told her.

"I get it. I can get lost in my world and so can Peyton. That's what we were talking about when I thought I heard you mention Zach Johnson. Would you care to elaborate?" she asked.

"I'll fill you in when we get back to your place."

"Fair enough." Jessie turned to look at her store as they drove by.

She loved how it looked with the low light showing on her small window display. Her store was her pride and joy.

Chapter Twenty-Eight

"Hey, sweetheart, I didn't mean you had to stop talking altogether. Is everything all right?" Matt stopped at the light.

"I was simply admiring my store as we drove by, and one thought led to another." Jessie turned to look at him. "I can wait until we're home. I don't mind a little silence."

"That's another quality I like about you." He turned onto the road leading back to the inn. "We're a great fit." He parked beside her car and walked her to her cottage. "We need to talk over a few subjects. Zach is one of them and that note you got earlier is another. I didn't forget." He unlocked the door.

"I didn't think you had. I've been waiting to hear your verdict." She took off her jacket and sat on the couch.

He sat close beside her and reached for her hand. "I don't like the idea of the stalker sending you another note. My guy watching him was supposed to give me a heads up when he was on the move. Either he slipped our tail, or he's playing games from a distance. If you'll give me a minute, I aim to find out." He texted the guy he had in charge of the suspect.

"Be my guest. Do want some hot tea while you wait?" she asked.

"I prefer mine iced if you have some," Matt

answered his phone when she went into the kitchen. He learned all that he wanted to know during their conversation.

She placed the iced tea on the table near him and went back for her hot tea. "What did you find out?" she asked when she sat beside him again.

"He moved to a different location but not near the cove yet. We sent Jeremy a photo of the man. Jeremy sent me several photos back that he found. He has changed his looks and aliases several times over the years." Matt opened his emails on his phone. "Do any of these look familiar to you?"

She studied the various facial shots of the man. "This is how he looked when he came into my store that day." She showed him the photo. "Other than that, I don't recognize him right off."

"That makes it more concerning to me. He holds a grudge against you, and you don't even know who he is. Does the name Dexter Hoffman ring a bell?"

"I can't say that it does." She shook her head.

"Jeremy is looking into if he showed up in any of your stories. So far he's not on anyone's radar. Neil Dempsey said Dexter complained once to him that you always scooped him on stories and that you were the reason he never got published. Neil told me that Hoffman was never published because he worked in the mailroom and wasn't hired as a writer."

"Wow, that's news to me." Jessie sipped her hot tea. "I guess you never know who you might offend without knowing it."

"Believe me, I don't like that idea. What it means is that he has built a case against you not based on reality. How do you deal with a truth based on a manufactured offense or lie in his mind?" Matt frowned and looked at the photo again. "Nothing about him stirs a memory?" he asked. "Look again through the photos and concentrate."

Jessie studied each photo. She kept returning to the same picture. "Do you notice where this one was taken?" She glanced at Matt.

"It looks like a police station." Matt looked more closely at the photo.

"I used to go there often when I worked as a reporter in the city. You talked to Lieutenant O'Malley once if I remember. This is his precinct and Hoffman is sitting there. Why?" she asked. "The guys there looked out for me and helped me with any of the stories I worked on. I gave them information that I found that was news to them too."

"I remember the lieutenant. He's the one who told me to let you into the case, that you could get people to open up and talk. O'Malley said you were highly respected among his men, which says something since most cops don't like journalists." Matt reached for her hand and held it tight not wanting her to hit him. "He's also the one who told me about the way you put things together but that you were tenacious and got to the truth." He chuckled. "Little did he know how strange you would get. From the beginning, sweetheart, you've messed with my head."

She tried to wriggle her hand out of his grasp. "You're pushing it. I'll show you how I mess with your head."

He laughed. "I don't think we're talking about the same thing. You've given me a good suggestion, though. I'll call O'Malley and send these photos to him.

Maybe it will stir a memory in him. He also warned me to treat you well or I would have to answer to him. Have I?"

"The jury is still out on that one." She grinned at him. "Let me call O'Malley. It might be nice to talk to him."

"Be my guest. I'll email you the photos, but I still need to call him in my official capacity." He leaned his head back against the couch.

"What about Zach?" she asked.

"Johnson is still being a bad boy. He's up to his neck in the coverup we're working on now. Money is being funneled in and out of his hands to a special account under a bogus name. I guess he thinks he'll get out of prison a rich man. He'll get more time if the FBI has any say in it. They're involved in the case too."

"At least, that's someone I don't need to worry about." She leaned her head back against his arm behind her.

"Not so fast. It seems your name was on his lips a lot when he talked to Tom's inside guy. He is half in love with you, which I get, and at the same time blames you for his being in prison. Between the Harvest Club and his involvement in the Collector's Club, he won't see the outside for a while. If this gets added to his time, he'll be on the inside for a long time." Matt traced her cheek.

"He can't hurt me from prison and besides, he would have to get in line." Jessie leaned forward to glance at him.

"That's where you're wrong. People are working for him on the outside. I'm wondering if your note writer might be."

"How could he be?" Jessie asked.

"We know that Zach has done recruiting from prison before. He could have met up with your boy on an innocent-looking chat forum online. You'd be surprised how active criminals are online. The internet is a smorgasbord of activity."

"Well, that's great. Not! What should I do?"

"Be smart. I have people looking into any connections now. Between Gary and Jeremy, that area is covered. You need to watch out for yourself. I'll help you with that part."

"It makes me weary. Will the endless parade of criminals ever end?" She slapped her hand to her forehead dramatically. "It does make me wonder what club he operates now though."

"You and me both." He squeezed her shoulder. "Let's change the subject for a while." He massaged her tense neck.

The rest of the evening was quiet, maybe too quiet. Jessie wasn't happy about Zach having even a remote connection to Dexter. He couldn't reassure her because from what Jaxon had told him the possibility of a link was quite high. Zach was using the prison computer and library under the guise of continuing his education as a part of a prison reform program.

Matt went home when Kip texted him that he was there to watch her house for the night. He would leave that piece of news a secret for now. Although Jessie handled the news better than she used to, she still didn't like it. And one thing Matt wanted was for her to be happy. His girl deserved that much. He would let her call O'Malley but so would he. Call it a gut feeling—he had several questions he wanted to ask one cop to another.

****

To say she wasn't happy was an understatement. This whole Jessie is to blame game was getting on her nerves. *Someone needs to get a life and find a new punching bag.* She tossed the throw pillows off her bed onto the floor. She wasn't going to be an easy target anymore. *What was it with these men anyway?* She yanked the bedspread back and flipped it to the foot of the bed instead of neatly folding it. Did they think every woman was an easy mark? Two could play at this game. If the past year had taught her anything, it was that she was a lot tougher than she thought possible. "Bring it on, Zach boy, I'll be ready," she growled.

She propped up the pillows behind her and opened her laptop. The first email she opened was from Matt. She had the face of Dexter Hoffman staring back at her. "No offense, bud, I've had enough of your face for one night," she muttered while closing the email and moving on.

Next, she opened an email from Jeremy. He had some interesting tidbits to add about Hoffman that had her trying to recall if she had ever had any contact with the man. It wasn't until the last part of Jeremy's email that something started to click in her brain. There was a photo of Dexter when he first came to work at the office as Poindexter Hoffman. She rarely had any interaction with him, but he always seemed to be somewhere nearby with his mailcart.

She had overheard him talking to one of the guys near her workspace about some of his ideas regarding several known conspiracy theories. She dismissed it as office gossip when she heard him talking but maybe he was more dangerous than she thought. At the time, he seemed like a nice enough guy. He was from the Midwest like her, or so he said. His whole life seemed to be based on a lie. A lie seemed to be at the heart of most crimes. "Truth matters," she repeated to herself.

After going through her emails, she shut off the computer. She stretched out on the bed and pulled her covers up to her chin. Sofia was home and that was positive. Zach was a nuisance but still dangerous because his influence stretched outside the prison. Dexter was an unknown commodity. She wasn't sure how dangerous he was but a fact she did know was that a serial killer was murdering Indigenous women across the nation. She wanted answers and a plan would be nice too. She closed her eyes and soon she fell asleep.

Chapter Twenty-Nine

Jessie awakened with a start. The nightmare's residual effect was still fresh in her mind. A tangled mess of disjointed images raced through her memory complete with the sound of beating drums, scary faces, and otherworldly screeches. Taking deep breaths to calm herself, she sat up and turned on the light. There was a nagging voice that pervaded the dream, one she was sure she had heard before, but where? The twangy southern drawl didn't seem natural and she couldn't put a face with the voice. A voice that reminded her of nails scratching on a chalkboard sending chills racing down her back, one she would never forget. Somehow his voice was tied to all those terrible images that she wanted to put out of her mind.

She turned off the lamp but lay awake unable to go back to sleep. Sitting up again, she opened her computer and began to write more in her article for Neil Dempsey, who had once told her to write facts but let them come through her heart. "Make your readers want to care about what you care about. Don't let your mind build a wall from your heart." Matt, on the other hand, told her she couldn't let herself care too much. Somewhere between those two statements was where she needed to write from.

She had always considered herself a caring person but looking back now she was more of an activist. Not that she still wasn't empathetic, but the past year had taught her to care about people and their personal stories. People were what made life worth living. It had all started with Gina Martin's ghost asking for her help on her first day in Blue Cove. Jessie had no idea what that help would cost her, not merely physically, but emotionally as she learned Gina's story and met her children and her parents. The more she learned what the young pastor had suffered the more she found herself invested in her story. No one knew the tears she had cried over her story or her quest to find Abigail, the little girl who reached out in her thoughts for help. It was a race against time to find the little girl.

Jessie's life had been scarier this past year but much more satisfying as she found herself caring about others and not only herself. Their stories had reached into her heart and altered her life in ways she was still learning about.

It helped that her cousin was on the same journey. They not only bounced things off one another all the time but they found a way to help each other balance everyday life while doing so. She needed to spend some time with Peyton and Matt tomorrow. Peyton would understand the strange aspects of what was happening, and Matt would ask her the questions that needed answers. He had a way of making logical observations out of even the strangest situations. More important, he had believed her almost from the beginning. He didn't understand any of her strangeness, but he still trusted her judgment.

Jessie thought about each of the events of this past year that she had shared with Matt. With each investigation and near-death experience, Matt became more entrenched in her heart. Sometimes it was her in the crosshairs; sometimes it was Matt. The year had sped by but the one constant through it all was Matt, her charming hunky cop who encouraged her to be exactly who she was. He had learned to trust her ability, lecture her less, and ask her and not tell her what to do. How she loved that man. He had more faith in her than she had in herself.

Thinking of Matt, what would he ask her about the dream? She needed to think about it. The answer was how she would come up with her answer for him. Unlike in the past, she wouldn't keep this from him. He would ask her about the voice. What made it familiar? He would want details. She would give them to him. One by one she made a mental note of said details. Smiling, she could almost hear his reaction.

With her plan made for the next day, Jessie turned onto her side and closed her eyes. With any luck, her dreams will be filled with Matt, a far better subject to dream about. Crossing her fingers she whispered, "No more nightmares, please."

****

Matt got to work early the next day with Jaxon by his side. They had a teleconference scheduled with Tom Maxwell. Jaxon was told to be at the station for the call and that he would get his next assignment.

During their call, Maxwell told Jaxon that he was assigned to Matt's case with the blessings from the higher-ups. Tom wanted Jaxon involved because of the agents who had screwed up the case with the girls. Jaxon could clean up the mess that was left behind, which was a black eye on the agency's record.

"We don't want to leave a bad taste in the mouths

of the locals when an agent blows it," Tom informed Matt. "Jaxon seems like the perfect candidate to help since he's living in your house and he's a congenial guy. He puts a good face on the agency." Tom laughed as he hung up.

"Looks like you're working with me again. You may as well be one of my guys." Matt glanced at him.

"Maxwell is my boss and if he says I'm working here then it's my job." Jaxon sat down in front of the desk. "I know what my assignment from the agency is but what do you have for me?" Jaxon leaned back in the chair.

"We're looking for our inside person working with Zach. I'm hoping you can see what is hard for us to imagine. We're too close to the situation. Who is feeding information to Johnson? How is he paying them and how is he disseminating his orders to the outside?"

"Our guy is listening in on Johnson's phone calls, tracking his online presence and visitors. We should know more soon. Johnson is seasoned and nobody's dummy. He can cover his trail."

"Luckily, we both know someone who can follow the money better than anyone and knows how to get around the strongest firewalls. I'll call Jeremy and get him involved." Matt wrote himself a reminder. "Tell me what you're thinking."

Matt and Jaxon talked for the next hour. They went over all the evidence they had to this point. They talked to Jeremy who promised to speed up his research. Matt remembered how Johnson had set up the promotion site for the Harvest Club and recycled it for the sale of illegal weapons with the Collector's Club. Johnson was capable but by no means the best out there when it came to covering his tracks. Jeremy thought he could get the information they needed within a few days. He already knew some of the accounts Zach used before and maybe he was using them again. It was worth a shot.

With that settled, Matt went on to talk to Jaxon about one of the areas troubling him the most. He wanted to know who was changing the files and funneling information from the station. "The one thing I consider most important in our field is being able to trust the men and women you work with. You've got to know they have your back—your life might depend on it. Someone is handing out info that has the potential to harm someone. I want to find out who it is and want them behind bars."

"Here's the file you requested, sir." Bev, one of the two new people they hired to enter data, knocked on his door.

"Thank you." Matt reached for the file in her hand. "How are you doing with all the data entry?"

"It's moving along quite well. The program is easy to work with but a bit tedious at times," she replied. Her smile was pleasant. "All the recent cases are in the database as well as the past two years."

"That's great, Bev. Jaxon here is the guy who turned us onto the program. In the long run, it will make keeping files much easier."

"Oh, yes, sir. You'll be able to find your case files a lot easier in the future. Do you need anything else?"

"No, that will be all." Matt scrunched his face in thought. "After we brought the program when you told us about it, I had Gary go for training. We hired three new people to start inputting the files. Janet Olson, Bev, who you just met, and Carry Masters are all new in the past year. One works on recent cases keeping us up to date. Two are working on the backfiles. You don't suppose Zach could hack into the system?" Matt asked.

"Anything is possible, especially if he has one of his people giving him passcodes. It's something to have Gary and Jeremy check out for sure. I will check out these ladies quietly."

Matt sent a text to Jeremy and to Gary to get them on it pronto. He had no idea how Zach was getting the information but at least he had a developing theory in his mind. Matt and Jaxon tossed a few more ideas around and then they went down to the records department together. Matt introduced Jaxon to the person on duty.

"This department is open from seven to five. We have four people who rotate on two shifts and have access to the records. Anyone wanting to see an old file case or check one out must sign in and out along with logging any case files we take." Matt looked around. "This room is supposed to be locked when it's unattended. You can see how someone could mess with the files."

"Most PD systems for old case files work about the same," Jaxon stated. "We had a similar system in Phoenix. Even when files are on computers you still require boxed evidence. This room archives your cases and it's an important part of your history. Trusting the people who work here is important. I'll keep my eyes open. Do you mind if I take a copy of this log?" Jaxon lifted the clipboard.

"Be my guest. There's a copier right there." Matt pointed at the machine.

"Chief, I hope you found what you were looking for. I had to use the facilities. I'm sorry I wasn't here when you arrived."

"You need to shut and lock the door when you have to step away, Mark. It's the rules," Matt reminded him.

"I get lax sometimes. Very few people come down to this area. I'll not do it again, sir." He stepped behind the counter. "Can I help you find something?"

"No. I was bringing Agent Kincaid up to speed on our system. He'll be going over our protocol and checking out our operations."

"I hope everything is okay." Mark frowned.

"I'm sure there's nothing to worry about." Jaxon handed the man back his clipboard.

Matt and Jaxon walked out of the evidence storage room together. "That was enlightening."

"Maybe the log-in sheet will add more light," Jaxon said.

"I'll leave you to work. I have a few calls to return." Matt left Jaxon in the interview room and walked down the hall to his office. There was a mounting stack of messages.

Chapter Thirty

After Jessie opened her store, she found herself looking over her shoulder every time someone came in the door. Glancing at the clock, she was happy that Peyton would be here soon. It would be nice not to be alone. Between the voice she kept hearing in her mind, the note she had received last night, and that strange little man who ran through her store she had no idea what might happen next.

With time on her hands, she checked through her emails, and before long she found herself surfing the web. She read through the ads about the gym and studio. She read through the bios of the coach, trainer, and team doctor along with the dance instructor. With references like these who wouldn't want their talented child to belong to such a prestigious organization?

Was the business legit, a front for something else, or had it simply got into trouble over time by hiring the wrong people? Maybe there were money issues like bribery or embezzlement. "Hmmm, I wonder what you're hiding," she muttered pursing her lips as she scrolled down the page.

She tried to remember some of the tricks that Jeremy had taught her to get around the security system. Getting nowhere fast she sent a quick text to her friend to ask him how to do it.

—I'll call you when I get a free minute and walk

with you through the steps. I'm intrigued by what you're trying to find.— His quick reply came back.

Jessie minimized her open window on her computer when Sonny walked into the store. Something about the man was annoying. It wasn't his cowboy hat either. She only hoped that Peyton would arrive soon.

"I'm only looking, sweetheart. Go about your work." He tipped his head but never removed his hat.

"That's fine." She frowned as she answered. *I'm not your sweetheart. No southern accent which was too bad. At least then, she'd have a good reason to suspect him.* The bell rang above the door and another customer walked in causing her to breathe a sigh of relief. The woman had a list of books that a friend suggested, and Jessie got busy showing her where the books were located.

"Have a nice day." Webster winked at her as he walked toward the front of the store. "I'll be back."

Thank goodness he was gone. She learned the hard way to trust her instinct when it came to people but Sonny gave mixed signals. On one hand, he seemed like a charming older man who simply liked people, but on the other hand, there was something that set off warning bells in her mind. Why? Maybe she was simply paranoid. Either way, she was grateful the woman came in when she did. Not only did she buy several books, but she also kept her from being alone in the store with Sonny Webster. The fact that he sported a large gauze bandage that showed under his hat and was wearing an eye patch on his right eye didn't help either. Another man with a patch. What's up with that?

"Hey, cous, how was your morning?" Peyton asked when she walked into the store.

"Better now that you're here. You always brighten up the day." Jessie smiled at her. "I have a lot I want to talk to you about. Grab a chair. I could use your input." Jessie sat next to her. She told Peyton about the voice that seemed distinct yet familiar, and her questions about why Webster made her skin crawl, and of course, her concern over Dexter Hoffman, her stalker. "Tell me what you're thinking. I could use a different viewpoint."

"If the voice rings a bell, then you must have heard him somewhere before. You'll know when you hear again. Let's just hope you're with others when you do." Peyton reached for Jessie's hand. "Sadie always used to tell me if you sense something off go with your intuition. It's almost always right."

"I remember Grams saying that too," Jessie said twisting one of her curls around her finger.

"For now, if anyone comes in that makes you uncomfortable while you're alone go near the open doors and alert Molly." Peyton glanced into Joe's where Molly stood. "You can count on her, as you already know."

Jessie nodded. "I vaguely remember Dexter. The man who fits the voice is still an unknown commodity, and as for Webster, so far he's been nice. Maybe he's simply a flirt. Some men can't help themselves, and you know how I feel about men like that." Jessie shrugged her shoulders. "You're right about Molly though."

"Everyone knows!" Peyton laughed. "Have you thought that all of these people may be connected?" Peyton asked shifting forward in the chair.

"I believe they are," Jessie told her.

"I guess we'll know soon enough." Peyton jumped up. "I have a strange feeling the connections are stronger than we can imagine, which is a bit scary."

"What makes you say that?" Jessie gave her cousin a bewildered look. "Why, scary?"

"To me, it means someone is orchestrating the whole crime. How powerful that person must be." Peyton shuddered. "Of course, I could be wrong. I've been off the mark before." Peyton compressed her lips together.

"I doubt it, cousin. You're rarely wrong when it comes to this new life of ours, and neither am I, for that matter. Talk about coordination. I feel like I'm an actor on a stage." Jessie walked to the counter with a dramatic flair. "Someone else is managing my movements, or how else can you explain Kimama or traveling back in time for that matter?" Jessie clasped her hands behind her back. "I wish I understood the whys."

"The whole reveal seems to be on a need-to-know basis. So, we wait." Peyton straightened a book on the shelf facing the wrong way.

"Can I help you find something?" Jessie asked a young woman who walked in.

"I'm only looking right now but I'll let you know if I have any questions." She flung her shiny dark hair over her shoulder as she kept glancing out the front window.

"Let me know if I can be of help," Jessie said. But as she watched the woman move around the store Jessie had the strangest sensation. "You're not here for a book, are you?"

"How did you know?" She glanced around the

store. "I had this strange guy following me and I ran in here hoping he would leave." She stood behind a shelf and peeked out at the street. "He drove down the street and started to make a U-turn."

"Would you like me to call the police?" Jessie asked the girl.

"I don't know what to do. But it bothers me. There was something creepy about the man." The girl flopped down in the nearest chair.

"I think we should call." Peyton grabbed her phone out of her purse. She told Kenny when he answered about the girl in the store. "He's sending a couple of officers."

"If nothing else they can be on the lookout for his vehicle. Can you remember what he was driving?" Jessie squeezed the girl's shoulder.

"It was a pickup truck. I don't know the model. I'm not good at that." She shrugged her shoulders gesturing with her hands. "We have a lot of trucks on the reservation where I live but I've never seen this one around there before. The truck was an older model, but it looked shiny and new. The guy driving wasn't from the res, that much I do know."

"Are you sure?" Jessie asked.

"One hundred percent. It's a small area and we all know each other. Besides this guy was a white dude."

"My name is Jessie, and this is Peyton." She pointed at her cousin. "I'm sorry. I didn't even ask you your name." Jessie sat in the chair across from the girl.

"Winnie, my name is Winnie." The girl's head snapped toward the door when the bell rang. Her shoulders relaxed when a woman walked in.

"Nice to meet you. You've come to a good place.

My cousin will fight heaven and earth to help you if she can. Believe me, I know." Peyton placed her hand on the back of the girl's chair.

"Thank you. I don't come to town often. I brought some of my mom's crafts to the local gift shop. She likes to sell them when the tourists start to come."

"I've seen some of the local artisans' crafts in there. What does your mom make?" Jessie asked.

"Jewelry and dolls." Winnie turned in her chair to look at Jessie. "The money she makes helps." She showed them pictures of her mom's creations on her phone.

"Tourists love to buy souvenirs and gifts to take home from the trip. I know I do." Jessie smiled at her. "When did you first notice the man?"

"When I came out of the store. He whistled and made some crude remark, but I put my head down and kept walking."

"What happened next?" Jessie's hand fisted at her side.

"He drove slow beside me telling me to get in and he would take me home. As another car came up behind him, he had to speed up. That's when I came into your store. I didn't flirt with him. I tried not to look at him at all." Winnie looked away from Jessie a blush tinging her face.

"I'm sure you didn't," Jessie told her as the patrol car pulled up in front of the store. "I know these officers who have just arrived, and they will do everything they can to help you."

When Kip and Gary walked in Jessie introduced them to Winnie. They sat in the chairs beside her and talked for a while. Jessie heard Kip call in the description of the vehicle the man was seen driving. After they finished their conversation Kip motioned for Winnie to follow him.

"You did the right thing calling us, Peyton. We've had someone else report the same truck. We'll drive Winnie home and be on the lookout for the suspect. She gave us a good description to work with." Kip lifted his chin as he walked past them and winked.

"Do you see what I mean, cous? It's all tied together. Winnie is from the reservation. I wonder if the man you saw is the same one who moves around the country attacking these young women. It's possible don't you think?" Peyton's hands reached out to straighten the bookmark basket. "Nothing happens by chance."

"I was thinking the same thing. I wonder how she described the man or his truck. I've seen Webster in a truck but his is a brand-new model." She wrote a reminder to herself. "I'll have to ask Matt later." Jessie waved as Reba walked in the door. "What brings you our way today?"

"I wanted to get dessert for dinner tonight and I always have to check in with my favorite girls and catch up on all the news. And before you say there is nothing new, didn't I just see a patrol car leave from in front of your store?" Reba pointed out the window.

"Yes, you did as a matter of fact." Jessie smiled at her. "And knowing you the way I do you have something to offer besides a simple visit."

"You could be right about that, dear. Get comfy. I'll give Molly my order and be right back to join you. Of course, I'll bring tea too." Reba placed her jacket neatly across the back of the chair.

"It's safe to say we're about to learn some new truth that we're going to try to make sense of long after she leaves." Jessie laughed. "And drinking tea to boot."

"She has a way of messing with my mind." Peyton sat across from where Reba placed her jacket. "I might as well get comfortable. I can always use a good cup of tea."

"I hear you." She thanked Molly who help carry the cups for Reba.

"Enjoy, ladies." Molly thanked Reba who handed her a ten-dollar tip.

"Of course, dear. You're always so helpful." Reba sat in her chair. "Isn't this lovely, girls?"

"Your visits always are a welcomed event." Jessie reached for her hand.

"That's sweet, dear. I know my visits can be somewhat trying at times, and you girls are nice to put up with the ramblings of an old lady which often make little sense but are usually quite accurate." She took a sip of her tea. "Oh, my, I do love a nice soothing cup of tea, don't you?"

"The tea is good, but I know you have something you're simply itching to tell us. You may as well lay it on us." Jessie looked over her cup at Reba.

"I see what you're doing, dear. But as you know these things can't be rushed. They must come at the right moment. There's always the right time and the right way." Reba smiled and took a deep breath. "I guess now is as good of a time as any."

"We're as ready as we'll ever be." Peyton leaned back in her chair and waited.

"It's like this, girls, everything you're facing is all connected. The ghost, Kimama, and what happened in your store earlier. The Barton girl, the murders of the young Indigenous women, and the girls at the gym. They're all connected in some bizarre way. I know you've been thinking about the possibility, haven't you?" Reba patted her hair. "I tell you there's a common thread that runs through them all."

"I believe it, but I don't see how as of yet." Jessie pursed her lips.

"I found it hard to put it together in my mind too until I think about the man who is angry at you, Jessie. His story will show you how when you learn it." Reba leaned closer to them and whispered, "Bottom line, my girls, you are living for such a time. You're needed. Consider yourself drafted. There is a man who is connected in some way to every aspect of the case. One you know, and others you don't. One you'll be shocked by his identity."

"Do you have any ideas who?" Jessie threw out the question grasping for an answer.

Reba shook her head. "I can only see what I can. Know this though, the fact that the door was opened and you were given sight through a window in time is amazing enough. When you connect the dots to the investigation how remarkable it will be." Reba slipped into her jacket. "Kimama could not have traveled here if this wasn't the time." She hugged Jessie and then Peyton.

"Wait up, Reba. I'll walk you out to your car." Peyton rushed ahead and held the door open for her.

"We're drafted," Jessie told Peyton. "Now there is a word picture I can live without."

Chapter Thirty-One

At lunchtime, Matt stopped by the interview room to check on Jaxon. "Have you found anything of interest yet?" he asked leaning against the door frame.

"I see some interesting names that have turned up in your log sheet. See what I mean." Jaxon pointed the names out to him. "What are they doing going over your files?"

"Good question. This guy here is a lawyer for the city." Matt put his finger on the name. "But he should've gone through proper channels to view the files. He would have had to fill out a sheet requesting the information and the file would have been brought to the interview room where an officer would have sat with him as he viewed the files. A rule was put in place to keep people from viewing or changing files without authorization. Who told him he could search through the evidence room and files?" Matt frowned pushing away from the door.

"That's what I'm going to try to find out. Peyton texted me about the girl that came into the store. Did Kip fill you in on the details?"

"He hasn't got back yet." Matt wanted a copy of the log that Jaxon had made notations on. He made a quick copy and gave it back to him. "Let's visit Jessie. I want to hear her take on the girl who came into the store earlier."

"Sounds good. I can always use food and with any luck maybe Peyton will be there too." Jaxon reached for his jacket and followed Matt out of the station. "I find it strange that I'm always told to work on a case with you."

"Maxwell used to have to come here, and now he sends the newbie. I'm glad to be working with you. You may as well be on my team." Matt unlocked his car.

"Yeah, so you say, but then Tom would have to send another guy." Jaxon laughed as he got in the passenger seat.

"True, but he wouldn't get Peyton without you. Those gals make us look good." Matt started the car and pulled out of the station parking lot. "I know Maxwell would hire Jessie or Peyton away in a minute if he could."

"That's a scary thought. It's bad enough what they've had to deal with since moving here but what we deal with on the national level would be brutal. I wouldn't want Peyton near the place." Jaxon latched his seat belt.

They continued to talk about the case's stranger elements and speculated about who might be connected. Matt had the sense that Johnson would turn out to be one of the key players and it wouldn't be long before they knew exactly how he fit into the picture.

At least he could tell Jessie about the conversations he had earlier. Two more Indigenous girls were found and once identified would be on their way back to their families. Hopes would be destroyed in the process, but at least there would be closure. A word that often brought sadness to the families and a little resolution for a season. For many, it was only the beginning of the nightmare that they would find themselves going through. Matt pulled into the first open space he saw. He and Jaxon walked first to the bookstore.

"After you." Matt held the door open for Jaxon and followed him.

"Looks like I'm in luck," Jaxon told Matt as he saw Peyton.

"Hey, sweetheart, Kip told me you had a bit of trouble here." Matt kissed her cheek. "He hasn't got back to the station yet. Fill me in with what you know," Matt told her.

Jessie told him about Winnie coming into the store. "She was scared, and I don't blame her. The guy sounded a bit creepy." She touched his arm. "Did you notice she lives on the reservation, which makes me wonder if our serial killer might be in the area?"

"That's a bit of a leap, don't you think?" Matt shook his head. "Look who I'm asking. I'll think about it."

"While you're trying to digest that, let me give you something else to think about." Jessie told him about Reba's visit and what she had shared with them. "What does your cop instinct tell you? Could there be one person who is the lynchpin in all of this? I mean, I think one person can orchestrate or at least have their hands in each part of this case somewhere."

"I don't know about that, babe. Anything is possible, though. I do know that two more victims were found that are being ID'd as we speak."

"That's good but sad news. I want you to give serious thought to my theory. I also believe the girl who got away was a recent event since I dreamed of her alone." Jessie held his face between her hands. She went on to explain why she thought her idea was valid.

He listened because he had to. "Okay," he said. "I admit your idea makes some sense but it's still a long leap from here to there." He took her hands from his face. "I know you well enough to listen and eventually I'm sure you'll probably be right. Let me get there in my way. Okay?"

"All right." She pushed him toward Joe's. "Go eat. We can talk about this later. But I'm right, and you know it." She smiled at his frown.

Matt walked into Joe's with Jaxon. "Damn, she's right you know. I don't know how I'll ever prove it logically but I'm about to find out."

"You've got that right. Sit back and enjoy the ride." Jaxon chuckled,

"Could you?" Matt asked.

"Hell, no." Jaxon stepped up to the counter and gave his order.

****

"Well, cousin, you gave Matt something to think about." Peyton laughed. "They both still look quite perplexed."

"That's because they know I'm right." Jessie carried a stack of books to place on the shelf. "I've sold several of this book in the past few days. I might have to read it." She flipped the book over to read the blurb. "Word of mouth seems to be one of the best free marketing tools of all. Sounds like a good read."

"Bring me a copy too. I need a new book to read." Peyton reached for the book Jessie handed her. She pulled money out of her wallet and paid for the book. "Have you heard any more from the guy threatening you?"

"Matt's got someone keeping an eye on him. He says Hoffman is still not in town. Which is great unless he slipped out of their watchful eyes without being seen."

"Do you know any more details about him?" Peyton asked.

"I'm still waiting for a call back from Officer O'Malley. The only picture I have is of him sitting in O'Malley's precinct." Jessie pulled the picture of Hoffman up on her computer. "You need to memorize his face in case you see him around."

Peyton looked at the picture. "Hmmm, I wonder how he ties into all of this. If I've learned anything in the last few investigations, everything is connected in some way. No matter how far out or improbable it seems. The weird seems to follow the two of us around."

"You've got that right." Jessie smiled at Matt when he walked in from Joe's. "Did you guys solve the world's problems?"

"Hardly." He chuckled. "We might have added a few more. Before I forget to mention it, I put a call into O'Malley and I'm waiting to hear from him. I'll let you know what he says."

"I did too," Jessie told him.

"I'll talk to you later. I'm bringing dinner to your place tonight." He kissed her and rushed out the door after Jaxon.

"He's not much for sweet talk, but boy does he look good coming and going." Jessie followed his exit fanning her face playfully.

"I need to leave too. I'll see you later, cous. I have

a manuscript waiting for a response on my computer at home." Peyton grabbed her purse and headed toward the door.

"Don't forget your book." Jessie handed the book to her. "Why did you buy it anyway?"

"You gave a good recommendation, and I liked the cover." Peyton stuck the book in her purse and took her keys out. "Call me later or better yet, I'll call you."

The rest of the afternoon was quiet except for the few customers who straggled in. Jessie had plenty of time to do some research. Using the coordinating sign markers, she was able to determine the nearest reservation to each of the victims. Of course, as soon as she had the names, she would contact the families to get more information. She wanted to paint an accurate picture of each of the victims according to their loved ones.

Jessie discovered some more gems after Jeremy called and showed her how to get around the firewall of the training center's website. Jeremy promised to call Matt with his findings. Could the gym's owners honestly believe they wouldn't get caught? Of course, not everyone had a Jeremy helping them to find what she was able to see in the fine print in their application process and that was only one of the trouble spots Jeremy had pointed out to her. She doubted many parents who signed their kids up were aware of all that they were agreeing to. Jeremy often cautioned her about leaving a cyber footprint in searches online that can be followed by someone who knows what they're doing. Parents were giving away some valuable information to crooks.

She had no idea. Could she be more dense, or were

criminals getting more sophisticated? How many times had she traipsed around a website leaving her electronic footprint without a care in the world? Jessie shook her head. Thank heavens for Jeremy. His talent was needed more now than ever.

As Jessie began her closing routine, she tried to connect all the pieces she had learned. Sofia, along with the other girls from the gym, gave them valuable information. Marcia's ghost reminded her of the cost of an interrupted life. "Remember me," echoed through her mind. There wasn't a doubt these events were connected if only by nature of the crime.

Chapter Thirty-Two

While Jessie waited for Matt to get there with dinner, she picked up the book she bought earlier. She wanted it because her customers said it was a great book but also because of the title. She flipped the book over in her hands. What is the likelihood of this being a coincidence? "Remember Me" was written in bold letters on the cover. *What little gem do you have hidden for me to find between your covers?*

She was hooked from the first words on the page and even more when she learned it was based on a true story. She reached for her phone.

"Peyton," she said when her cousin answered. "Have you started reading the book yet?"

"I have. I was about to call and ask you the same question," she said.

"Matt is on his way here. Keep reading and tell me what you think. I'll call you after he leaves."

"I'm waiting for Jaxon. We are having dinner and a movie night. I'll keep reading until he gets here. What are the odds?"

"When it comes to us, that's a loaded question." Jessie laughed. "We'll talk later."

****

Matt headed to Jessie's with dinner and some bad news. He found out before he left the station that Hoffman was on the move. He was holed up in a motel out on the highway ten miles out of town. To this point, there was nothing Matt could do about him. He was sending threatening notes to Jessie but hadn't acted on them, which left Matt in a bind as to what to do. They would keep an eye on him, and hopefully he would lose interest. Matt shook his head. Like that would ever happen. His sweet girl attracted trouble like flies to honey.

Matt grabbed their dinner from the car. Jessie had told him to get whatever sounded good to him, and Sally's was the first place that came to mind. She would lecture him, and he would nod as he drank his chocolate shake. He walked the path to her cottage carrying a few mouth-watering treats. He was hungry and the day had been a long one. How many times over the past year had he walked this path? Figuring that out would keep his mind busy for a while. He would walk the same path over and over again as long as she was waiting for him when he got to the door.

He must be tired. Matt never considered himself a poet or a philosopher, but damn, Jessie made him feel like he could always aspire to be a better man. This had been one crazy year. Before he could ask her to marry him, she asked him. And then he surprised her and asked her to marry him in front of all of their friends. Patience wasn't one of his virtues, but he would wait. She was worth it. He lifted his hand to knock on the door. What surprise awaited him tonight? With Jessie, life would always be exciting no doubt. He still was trying to figure out how he won her heart, and how he would keep it.

"Hey, sweetheart." He kissed her cheek as he walked through the door that she held open on his way to the kitchen. He placed the bag containing their dinner on the table. "You said anything that sounded good." Matt had noticed her frown when she looked in the bag.

"Yes, I did. But honestly, Matt, if I eat like this often, I'll never be able to stop running."

"You won't stop anyway because you love it. And I won't stop because well, I love a good cheeseburger and your lectures. I have to give you a chance once in a while to instruct me. It's only fair. I like that you care enough to say something." He gave her a lopsided grin.

"You're incorrigible." She tapped the top of his head.

"I'm all that but you still love me." He tickled her chin. "You know you do." He took a huge swig of his chocolate shake. "Besides, I did get you a side salad instead of fries, and a grilled chicken sandwich. I didn't want to corrupt you. But if you're really nice to me, sugar, I'll give a sip of my shake." He laughed when she grabbed it out of his hand and took a big gulp out of his cup. "Well look here, I bought another one." He took a second cup out of the bag and placed it on the table.

Jessie kissed the top of his head, and he pulled her into his lap. "Just so you know, this is how I want to be kissed." He proceeded to show her.

He shared some of his fries and she gave him half of her salad and chicken sandwich. They shared the first shake, then the second one, and settled down to watch TV. Matt didn't want to bring up Dexter Hoffman. He wanted to enjoy being with her. Mostly he wanted to hold and kiss her whenever the mood struck him. Which happened through every commercial and during some of the movie they weren't really watching too.

When the movie ended, Jessie told him about the book she bought today and about what she had found with Jeremy's help. When their conversation turned serious, he knew he had to tell her about Hoffman.

"How did you hear about the book?" he asked, stalling for time.

"Several of my customers told me about it. Peyton is reading the story too." She laid her head on his shoulder. "There is something to be learned from the story, I'm sure. I heard the voices calling out the words remember me, and that's the title of the book."

"Weird. Your life is one long strange adventure, isn't it? Speaking of coincidence…" He paused.

"I don't think we were talking about happenstance," she said as he placed his fingers over her mouth.

"Maybe not in so many words, but at least let me pretend there are." His hand brushed her hair away from her face. "Now for the not-so-good news. You need to know Hoffman is on the move and getting closer to the cove. I have my guys keeping an eye on him. Let me know if you get any other menacing notes, calls, or if he shows up."

"I will. But maybe he'll just give up and go away." She pursed her lips.

"Do you believe he will?" Matt held her gaze.

"No, but one can hope."

"I talked to O'Malley earlier and he is checking into a few things for me. He seemed to remember Hoffman. He also told me to tell you not to worry your pretty little head over it. He will be calling you back. He was pressed for time today."

"Naturally, he would call you first. You are being

the chief of police and all, and I'm little old insignificant me." Her lips twitched. "I won't worry my pretty little head over it," she muttered. "That's such a male thing to say."

"That's one of the reasons I love you. You're sensible and know your place." Matt grinned and knew what was coming next. He ducked in the nick of time.

"It's a good thing you're fast. I almost had you." She laughed and then slapped him upside the head. "You deserved that and another just because."

"That's mean, and you cheated." He grabbed both of her hands and held them tight in his. "Two can play at this game." He kissed and tickled her.

"Uncle," she sputtered and couldn't stop laughing. "Stop!" She pinched him.

"Are you going to behave?" he asked wiggling his fingers in front of his face. "Do you want more?"

"No more, please, "she begged. "What else do I need to know about Hoffman?"

"I don't have a lot more information on him. He's been under the radar but seems to have an issue with women. Who knows what that's about?" Matt shrugged his shoulders. "But he's hit a couple of women and has a couple of arrests for assault on his record. You need to be aware of that." Matt took her hand in his. "Which means if he comes into your shop again don't egg him on. He may not play fair, and I don't want you to get hurt."

"I'll try not to hurt him but I'm not making any promises." She doubled her fists and held them in a boxing position. "I'm teasing, of course. I'll be careful not to push him, but I will hurt him if I have to."

"I'll take that." Matt nodded and grinned.

"Is there anything else I should know?" she asked. "The reason I'm asking is I believe that this investigation is about to take off. You know how these things work." She glanced at him.

"I do. The authorities are still trying to find the girl who escaped her abductor. She would be able to identify or at least give them a great description of the guy. Your description of the scene narrowed down the area if the girl lives near where she was abducted. That's the big question. She will be like finding a needle in a haystack." His brows furrowed.

"Due to the fact that the other victims were found, I'm holding out hope they'll be able to find her too. She could help a lot."

"Kip filled me in on Winnie. Her situation sounds familiar to what you saw with the girl who escaped. I don't know how they could be related because of the distance where the attempted crimes took place, but nothing is impossible. Kip notified the reservation police about the possibility. We likely have a serial killer in our area which isn't a pleasant thought."

"No, it's not." She tapped her fingers against her forehead. "I know I'm missing a key ingredient. The fact is stored somewhere in my head, but I haven't been able to zero in on it yet which perplexes me. It makes me wonder what else I am missing."

On his way home Matt went over everything Jessie had told him tonight and found he had some questions of his own. Her instincts were impeccable up to this point. If the voice sounded familiar to her then it was, and if she thought it was all connected then the proof would come out soon enough. He made a note to talk with Janet Olson about how the data entry was moving along and how the new girls were working out. He needed to ask her to keep an eye out for files that seemed to be tampered with.

The voice had to be attached to the serial killer. Johnson had to be the key. How? Jeremy's breach of the firewall on the studio webpage sounded like Johnson's fingerprints to him. It had the same MO as the Harvest Club. How did Hoffman fit into the scenario? He could be a loose cannon, but his gut told him Dexter Hoffman wasn't operating on his own.

Chapter Thirty-Three

Jessie noticed as the evening wore on that Matt had gotten quieter. She knew him well enough to know the investigation was taking over his thought process. She set the alarm after he left, filled her water bottle, and got ready for bed. She wanted to read more of the book and talk to Peyton before she went to sleep.

Plumping the pillows against the headboard she leaned her back against their softness and began to read.

"They found my friend's body in the most unlikely place. A man leading his sheep to water taking a different way than normal saw her foot peeking out from behind the brush covering her. I had hoped to see her again, but in my heart I knew she was gone. My breath has left me in my grief. I will remember my friend always and tell her story to anyone who will listen to my voice."

Jessie read through the first couple of chapters. She discovered in the pages a friendship like she and Katie knew growing up, a bond that had developed between the two Native American girls growing up on the reservation. As children, they played together and rode the bus to school each day. The girl telling the story was shy, but her friend was outgoing. Her friend loved to learn and perform the traditional tribal dances while the narrator would watch from the sidelines. Different as night from day, they still forged a unique friendship that had lasted for years.

The farther into the book Jessie read the more she understood that behind every statistic was a story to be told, the people whose lives had been impacted and diminished by the murders of those they loved. Rubbing her tired eyes, she set the book aside and called Peyton. They talked about what they had read so far.

"I've come to understand that there are no coincidences for us when it comes to an investigation. Whether it's as simple as a book to read or a ghost that shows up, there's always a reason for each event," Peyton told her.

"I know. Reading this book is like seeing the story of any victim through the eyes of their family or friends. Matt once told me there was no such thing as a simple murder, and now I understand what he was telling me. He sees their story through the evidence he puts together. We tend to see it from a different perspective is all." Jessie leaned her head against the pillows. "You know, cousin, our world is sometimes a sad place. Don't get me wrong—there is a lot to be happy about too, but sometimes I wonder is all. I'm thankful for the stability of Matt."

"I hear you. Jaxon keeps me grounded. I tend to think I should solve every problem. For most of my life, I was oblivious to what was going on beyond my little world. I was trying to survive, and Jaxon tells me that is okay. I was stressed enough trying to keep Madi safe." Peyton paused. "We can only do what we can and find contentment in that."

"Is Jaxon getting used to being wealthy?" Jessie asked.

"He's being super cautious, but he did tell me he's going to buy himself a hot car like Matt's brother Evan before he ends up like Dylan driving a minivan." Peyton laughed. Sleep well. I'll see you tomorrow."

"Goodnight," Jessie told her. Shutting off the light she rolled over and closed her eyes. The next time she opened them it was morning, or at least the light in her room made it seem that way.

There was no apparent reason for the brightness in her room. The lamp was off, the clock said three a.m. when she glanced at it, and there wasn't a fairy or ghost to be seen. *What's up?*

The light swirled around her faster until she found herself being lifted into its strange energy field, or at least that was her first thought. Weightless and euphoric she twirled faster through the air carried by the illumination until she passed through some small opening and found herself standing alone in a field surrounded by sudden darkness and a sense of overwhelming loneliness. She waited. For what, she had no idea. With no way to go back, there had to be a reason she was here. If she were here at all and not sleeping in her warm bed at home. This could be a dream; it had to be.

Forgotten, broken, and wounded—the words swirled in and out of her mind. The sky above her seemed to convulse and the earth beneath her feet vibrated and shifted. The whimpering began softly at first as if the person crying was many miles away. The sound of a woman weeping for her lost child. One by one faces filled in the dark space as the atmosphere contracted and shuddered as the cries became louder. With years and dates marching through the darkness before her Jessie watched the endless parade of nameless faces. Scattered among those faces were heads with no faces at all.

And then she recognized a few among the unknown and she knew what she was seeing. An impossible number to count of those who had been missing, or murdered over time in one country after another, with little regard for their value or life.

"Who made these lives dispensable?" a voice thundered from the darkness. "Who will remember them?"

"I will," Jessie whispered into the noise around her thinking no one could hear her. But one by one the faces faded, the weeping stopped, and the sky brightened with light that began to swirl around her once again.

When she opened her eyes, she found herself standing in her room. She reached for her notebook and began to write their stories. Some had names and others remained nameless, but each had been someone's daughter, wife, or friend. Some were young women cut down in their prime. Each was somebody's world with potential and filled with dreams lost to those who loved them, and some were never to be found.

She couldn't change what had happened to them, but she could help Sofia and the other girls now. She wanted to keep them from becoming statistics. She would help Matt solve this case and then she would decide what was next.

****

Matt had spent a good portion of the night in thought. The way forward seemed clearer this morning. He talked with Jaxon at breakfast, and they planned where to move the investigation next. Jeremy was tracking the money, and how Zach might be getting his messages to those on the outside working under him. The guy was savvy in covering his tracks, but he was also arrogant, which was his major downfall. Matt knew overconfidence could make Johnson slip up.

Jaxon had received a text message from Tom Maxwell with some news from inside the prison. They planned to bait Johnson into a trap. All they could do was wait and see if he took the lure.

Jessie had given him a few ideas without realizing it last night. Between Gary and Jeremy, Matt hoped to have some answers soon.

"Are you ready to leave? I thought I would stop for coffee and one of Molly's breakfast burritos." Matt reached for his keys. "We may as well ride together."

"I'm ready when you are." Jaxon grabbed his laptop case and followed him into the garage. "Strong coffee and a burrito sound good."

Matt drove to Joe's and was surprised to see Jessie's car was already at the store. It was early for her to be there. He could see her through the French doors at the counter busy doing something. He tapped on the closed doors and waved when she turned around to look.

"Good morning," she said when she opened the door.

"Aren't you at work early?" he asked.

"Remind me later to tell you about my night. Anyway, to make a long story short, I wanted to get some work done while I'm full of energy." She stroked his hand as she answered him.

"Did you eat? Let me buy you a coffee and scone."

"Sounds good. Hey, Jaxon." She waved at him.

"You know me. You piqued my interest, and I want to hear about your night. I'll be in to talk. Watch for me and open the door."

"I will." Jessie closed the door and went back to her computer. A few minutes later she opened the door again so they could come in.

"You're at it early this morning, Jessie." Jaxon placed his coffee and bag on the table.

"I wanted to get a few things done before I open this morning." She thanked Matt for the coffee and took a bite of her scone. "Yum, blueberry with a lemon icing drizzle. My favorite since my first day in town." She closed her eyes and enjoyed the flavors.

Matt smiled as he watched her. "I believe you have something to tell me about an unusual night."

"Right." She adjusted herself in the chair and went on to explain about all she saw the night before. "The experience left me thinking of a few possibilities regarding the investigation. I'm researching a few of them now. I'll let you know if I come to any conclusions." She took another bite of her scone and a sip of her coffee. "Is Frank still in town?"

"No, he left a few days ago but said he could come back at a moment's notice." Matt devoured his breakfast burrito in a few bites. "Why?"

"Did you even taste any of that burrito?" She gave him an odd look when he nodded. "I don't know how. Anyway, I was wondering if Hoffman tries anything stupid, which I'm sure he will, we might need Radar to either find me or him."

Matt jumped up overturning the chair. "Don't go there. It's not going to happen."

"I'm not saying it will, only that we should be ready for every eventuality." She reached for his hand to calm him.

"She's right, Matt. The dog might be able to track our suspect if he's on the move," Jaxon told him.

"You're right but I don't have to like it." He frowned. "I'll call Frank and get him back here."

Jessie changed the subject. When he was ready to leave, she walked Matt to the door and kissed him. He promised to call her if anything new came up and she told him that she would do the same. After she closed the door, she locked it until time to open again. Her heart told her that she would make the call sooner rather than later.

****

Matt pulled out of the parking space in front of the bookstore. "Have you ever noticed the closer we get to ending an investigation the more those girls seem to perceive?"

"What do you mean?" Jaxon asked.

"Think about what we're talking over this morning. Her ideas came from another level, but she had some of the same ideas we have. Consider her discussion about one person coordinating the whole crime; it sounds the same as our conversation earlier. Jessie sees the personal price of what crimes do in people's lives. We concentrate on the evidence to put the perpetrator behind bars. It's amazing to me how close we parallel sometimes." Matt turned on the street back to the station.

"You're right. The same is true with Peyton. Although, you have more cases you've experienced together. I've been stunned on more than one occasion with Peyton."

"Not to change the subject but have you spent any of your money yet?" Matt glanced at him.

"I've invested some, put some into savings, and ordered myself one item I've been wanting for a while."

"Let me guess—you bought a car." Matt chuckled. "I remember you drooling over Evan's."

"Between your brother's car and Dylan talking about a minivan I figured I wouldn't have forever to drive a sporty car. I ordered one with all the extras." Jaxon whistled. "She's a beauty and you know I haven't made a dent in my money."

"True. We aren't getting any younger. I wouldn't mind being a family man, but I draw the line at a minivan. I would want a manly SUV." Matt flexed the muscle in his free arm.

"I'm with you on that. The interest only that my money makes is more than I've had in my bank account at times." Jaxon laughed. "I'm going to remain cautious. I like seeing the money in my accounts. It adds a bit of security."

"I'm with you there. Tuck it away for a rainy day." Matt pulled into the station. "Time to get to work. We have a serious crime to solve and a serial killer roaming around our area."

They walked into the station talking over their plan of action. Jaxon went to the interview room to get on his laptop and Matt went to Janet Olson's cubby to set an appointment to talk to her later in the day. He had a teleconference with the lawyers for the girls on his agenda, a reminder to call Frank, and a talk with Dave Lewis to get the final autopsy report for Ms. Tso. Instinct told him the results would debunk Ben's many sides of the story. By the time he reached his office his first call was waiting for him.

Chapter Thirty-Four

Jessie went through her morning routine and opened her store. She could see Reba talking to someone in the church parking lot. Something was up. The shivers started at her neck and ran down her back and arms. She had no idea why. Sure, there was a ghost or two in the cemetery but that was nothing new. Her reaction to whatever was out there was new though. Hadn't she told Peyton nothing is a coincidence, or maybe Peyton had told her. Jessie kept her eyes on the action at the church while trying to do her work. She didn't hear anyone until she felt their presence behind her.

"I'm sorry, young lady, did I startle you?" Sonny Webster stood in the open door into Joe's.

"Sorry, I didn't hear you." She gave him a tight smile. He oozed a snake-like charm as he tipped his head in her direction. "Woolgathering I guess."

"Well, now that's all right, sweetheart. I got myself a coffee and came in through your open doors. I thought I would read my magazine. It's quieter in here than in the coffee shop." He sat in one of the leather chairs and placed his coffee on the table beside him.

"Be my guest." Jessie gagged at the thought of being alone with the man for five minutes much less as he read leisurely. *Please come see me, Reba.*

Jessie walked behind the counter to get closer to

her phone. She tried to analyze why Webster bothered her so much. Truth is, he made her skin crawl. Why? She had no immediate answer. All she knew was that he did. She rubbed her arms. Throw in a few ghosts at the cemetery and her day was off to a rip roaring start.

She sighed with relief when the bell above the door rang and two women walked in. Jessie got busy helping them. The taller of the two women asked her where a book was located. Jessie glanced at the paper the woman had written the title on. Jessie smiled to herself and showed her the book on the display table.

"My friend told me it's an awesome book." The woman with reached for a copy of the book and read the back cover.

"I agree with your friend. I'm reading it now and so is my cousin." Jessie handed the other woman a copy. "The book is well written. The story captures you and breaks your heart at the same time. It resonates with most people."

Reba waved and smiled at Jessie when she walked in. Jessie also noticed her instant frown when she caught sight of Webster sitting in the chair. The man in question stood and nodded at her. Jessie noticed once again that he didn't remove his hat and had a black patch covering his right eye.

"You're almost as busy as your neighbor. I think I'll be moving along." Webster smiled as he walked by Reba. "Have a nice day, Mrs. Thomas." He tipped his head at her.

Reba's lips pursed. "You, too." Reba sat in the nearest chair with a frown on her face.

After Jessie checked out the two women she walked over to Reba. "You must have heard my plea for you to come in today. I was alone when Webster came into the store. I felt his presence before I saw him. I was busy watching the action across the street. Being alone in the store with him here gave me the creeps."

"Ah, I wondered if you had noticed the odd gathering across the street. I guess you answered my question." Reba shook her head. "Sonny Webster is trouble and I have no idea why. He's always polite, kind, and almost charming in every way, but, and there is always a but, when I see him… There's a shadow around his aura making all the rest of him seem like a façade." She exhaled. "I know I sound silly but that's how I feel, and I like most everyone."

"I agree and have a theory about why. He is a real ladies' man. No proof, only a theory." Jessie went on to explain more about her idea. She hadn't told anyone but Peyton what she was thinking. Reba would tell her if she was too far off base.

"You might be right. I've never seen him with a woman but that doesn't mean anything. He bears watching." Reba stood. "I need tea. Would you like a cup too? All this troublesome talk has left me parched."

"Yes, I would. Make mine iced tea, please." Jessie went to help someone who wandered in from the coffee shop.

Jessie's afternoon was an improvement over the way her morning had started. She always enjoyed Reba even when she came with one of her crazy thoughts and today was no exception. Peyton showed up and added hers. And just when she felt the day was perfect as she talked with her friends, everything changed in an instant. When Jessie tried to tell Matt later after he came running into the chaos, she found it hard to explain how it all began.

"The three of us were talking and had just finished our tea when a few visitors, not of the earthly variety, came into the store. Soon afterward they were followed by Sonny Webster, who returned for some absurd reason, followed by Dexter Hoffman several minutes later." She grabbed Matt's hands before he could hit something.

"And you didn't call me?" he asked shaking his head.

"There wasn't time. The ghosts were instantly agitated by Webster's presence or Hoffman's. I'm still not sure which one. Sonny backed into Hoffman knocking him off balance into the bookshelf." Jessie motioned at the books that had fallen off the shelf when Dexter hit it. She wiped the tears rolling down her cheeks.

"What happened next?" Matt asked, his fist clenched at his side.

"Of course, I had to make sure he was okay. I'm always thinking about lawsuits," she muttered shaking her head.

"Jess, honey, focus please." Matt turned her face toward him.

"As I approached him, Dexter lurched at me pulling a gun out of his jacket. Reba saw what he had and grabbed his arm to stop him. He swiveled around hitting her head hard with the butt of the gun. Oh, Matt, it sounded awful." She buried her face in her hands and cried.

Matt handed her a tissue. "I'm sorry, Jess, but I need for you to tell me what happened next." Matt squeezed her hand.

She dabbed at her eyes. "The minute he struck Reba—" She stifled another sob. "Peyton jumped up, kicking his gun across the room, and body-slammed him. Seeing Dexter being lifted over her shoulder and knocked to the ground was a beautiful sight. My cousin was amazing." Jessie started to stand. "Just so you know, Peyton has promised to give me lessons."

"I need you to concentrate a little longer, sweetheart." Matt pulled her back. "Where's Hoffman?" Matt asked.

"He hightailed it out of here mumbling under his breath. Webster stood there dumbfounded with three ghosts spinning around him like blades on a fan. The air turned cold, and the atmosphere was creepy. I know how strange this sounds but that's how it went down."

"Hell, he got away." Matt turned to Jaxon and told him.

"I heard. Hoffman's damn brazened to walk in here and try to abduct her with customers around. He's either not thinking right or his arrogance knows no boundaries." Jaxon walked over to the paramedic. "Is she going to be okay?"

"She's got a nasty lump and cut. That's why there's so much blood but her vitals are good."

"Does she need stitches?" Jessie watched the medic at work. She wiped the tears forming in her eyes all over again.

"Because of her age, we're going to transport her for observation. She's doing fine considering the blow she took."

Matt squeezed Reba's hand. "Thanks for standing up for my girl. I'm sorry he hurt you, but I promise we'll get him."

"I know you will. Now, don't you fret, Matthew Parker. These two girls are like my daughters. He surprised us and he hit me before I knew what happened. But bless this girl's heart. She was my avenging angel." Reba smiled at Peyton. "Remind me never to get on your bad side, dear."

"Never going to happen." Peyton handed Reba her purse when she was secure in the ambulance. Stifling the sob in her throat she wiped the tears from her eyes.

Jessie wrapped her arm around Peyton, and they watched until they could no longer see the vehicle. "I think I'll close early. I want to go to the hospital. Do want to come with me?"

"Of course." Peyton followed Jessie inside.

Matt asked them to tell him what happened again. By the time he was through with all of his questions, Jessie was ready to scream. She knew he was doing his job, but she was done. Before she locked the doors into the coffee shop, she went in to tell Molly thank you for calling the police.

"It all happened too fast and there was no time for my training to kick in. Besides, everything went out the window when I saw him hit Reba. Thank heavens for Peyton's quick reaction or this day might have ended differently."

"I'm glad to help. Your store has had more than its share of characters. I've learned to carry my phone on me just in case." Molly pulled her phone from her pocket to show her. "I couldn't believe the nerve of that guy."

"Us either," Peyton chimed in.

"Is Reba going to be okay?" Molly asked.

"They said she was doing okay, but I know it was a

shock for her. I'm closing early because we want to go check on her. Thanks again." Jessie closed the doors and locked them.

****

Dexter had been sure he could pull off the abduction without any problems. He'd planned for the past several months, but every last step of his strategy went out the damn window the minute he walked into her store. What the hell went wrong? He mumbled scurrying to get out of town hiding among the trees as he went. The authorities would be looking for him. They already had his car. Before he got back to where he had hidden it the cops had it surrounded. Someone had to have tipped them off. But who?

Not a good choice to hit the old lady. He shook his head. That seemed to push the women to fight back. Taken down by a damn woman. Hell, he hadn't seen that coming. That redhead was one strong broad. Damn, what a mess he had made of this job. It all went south in a matter of minutes.

The cops would know his identity. He left his detailed plan, suitcase, and ransom note in the car. "Looks like you'll be spending time underground for a while," he muttered.

Loser, his mother's voice screamed repeatedly in his head. He grew up hearing her call him that. Damn loser was her pet name for him, and it never seemed to go away even though she had left him years ago. His father took up where she left off. *You're a loser, like your dad. He wasn't any good either.* He had learned to live with the insults and proved them both wrong. But some days like today they came at him loud and clear.

He wasn't a loser, but he had messed up again, which was the ultimate insult of his disastrous day.

Chapter Thirty-Five

Reba was shaken but thankfully okay. Jessie and Peyton spent an hour with her until she went to sleep and Lawrence came in to sit with her. The doctor was keeping her overnight for observation. Every time she thought about what happened Jessie got angry all over again.

She remembered Dexter Hoffman as soon as she saw him on the ground and Peyton standing over him. That weasel was the guy who followed her and tried to scoop a story away from her every chance he got. He was snide, sneaky, and a stalker, but forgettable. She hadn't thought of him since she left New York.

His problem was that he was hired in the mailroom but wanted to be a reporter. Neil told him he could submit work and he would read it. The challenge was that he never did a thorough job investigating a story and Neil wouldn't use his work until he submitted something worth printing. Dexter got mad at her for his rejections and also blamed her when he didn't get a promotion but remained in the mailroom. At the time she didn't think much about it. People got upset all the time when things didn't go their way. Hoffman accused her of using her looks to get ahead which at the time made her mad, but she didn't think it deserved a response. He couldn't accept the fact that she did a better job than he did.

She worked hard and he didn't. End of the story. She was a better investigative reporter, and Hoffman couldn't live with the idea of being bested by a woman. In her heart, she knew this wasn't over, but next time he would hear the truth.

"Tell your wife we love her when she wakes up," Jessie told Lawrence as she kissed Reba's cheek.

"The doctor gave her something to help her rest. She should be out for a while. I'll tell her but she already knows and loves you girls too." He stood when they went to leave. "Thank you, Peyton, for taking on that guy for me."

"I wish I wouldn't have let him get away. He's still out there." Peyton frowned. "I turned my back to check on Reba and he took off through the coffee shop. It all happened too fast."

"Fast maybe, cousin, but you were a thing of beauty. You got rid of his gun and disabled him long enough. I for one am grateful." Jessie looped her arm through Peyton's.

"I am too." Lawrence walked with them out into the hall. "Chief Parker will take care of the rest. Go home, girls, and please be careful."

When the elevator doors opened Jessie was happy to see Matt standing there. "Hi, there." She smiled at him.

"Hi there yourself. I was waiting for you. I didn't want either one of you driving home alone. Jaxon should be here any minute." Matt glanced down the hall. "He went into the gift shop to have flowers sent up to Reba."

"That's nice of him," Jessie said.

"They're from all of us at the station. We signed a

card and everything. I figured Jaxon would be good at picking out the right flowers." Matt reached for Jessie's hand.

"I'll be right back." Peyton went into the gift shop.

"You know, you don't give yourself enough credit, Matt. I don't know anyone more romantic than you are." She kissed his cheek. "Are you blushing?"

"Not me. Tell me about Dexter Hoffman. Do you know why he is angry at you?"

"He is not half as angry at me as I am at him. If I see him again, he will get a piece of my mind." Jessie led Matt over to one of the chairs in the hospital lobby. She explained what she could remember about the man. "Truthfully, I thought he was a nuisance, but I never worried about him hurting me. In general, I think that's a brand-new concept to me. I thought people liked me, and that shows you how aware I was." Jessie exhaled and frowned.

"I like you, sweetheart. You can't account for some men's taste though." He stroked her cheek. "I digress. Tell me what you know about Hoffman again."

Matt was in his case mode, and she knew he would keep asking her questions and she had better not give him an attitude. Right now, her attitude wasn't good. The last person she wanted to talk about was Dexter. "I'll start at the beginning but for the record, I don't want to talk about the guy at all."

"Okay, my little hothead, I'll give you a break for a few minutes. But I'll be asking questions all evening. Be prepared to answer, my sweet girl." He chucked her chin. "How about I take you to dinner?"

"I could eat." She smiled at him. "Especially, if you're with me."

They said their goodbyes to Jaxon and Peyton in the parking lot and Matt drove Jessie's car. As soon as he turned the key in the ignition, he grinned at her. "You know I love to drive your car. But your reprieve is over." He began to grill her again.

She glanced at him and rolled her eyes. "I'll tell you one more time and then I'm done with the subject." She paused when she saw his expression. "Unless, of course, I can think of something else that might be important. Dexter Hoffman was a bit of a pain as my memory serves me."

"Nice save. Do you know if he knew his way around a computer?" Matt signaled and turned out of the hospital parking lot.

"I'm sure he did. Why?" she asked him.

"I'm working some details that I've learned about him out in my mind." Matt turned toward the Seaside Village. "If it's okay with you, I thought we'd go to Sally's. I wanted to show you the sweet storefront that will soon house my brother's photo gallery. I couldn't be prouder of Evan and all the strides he's made in his life."

"Oh, I'm glad he got the place. He mentioned he was looking. Sally's would be great because I want to see Evan's future business site. I've always liked the village, but I know I got the right spot for my bookstore."

"Yeah, your place is in a perfect spot. Great foot traffic and high visibility mean added customers. Add the coffee shop next door, and it's a win, win." He pulled into a parking space, walked around to the passenger side, and opened the car door for her. "And no, our conversation about Dexter isn't over yet."

"I didn't think so, but I was hoping." She swatted his hand away.

"Oh, no you don't." He took her hand in his and held it tight. "You know how this works."

"Naturally, but I have to insert myself from time to time to keep you on your toes. I don't want you to fall back into the pattern of lecturing me." She turned her face away to hide her smile.

"Well now, I'm offended." He put his hand over his heart. "I've worked hard to ask and not tell you. I might be letting you off too easily. Do I need to pull rank?"

"I was teasing." She laughed brushing his cheek with her hand.

He pulled her to his side and changed the subject. "There's the storefront. With the high volume of foot traffic, it seems like a good spot. But I don't have a mind for business. That's Evan's and your department. Tell me what you think."

"It seems like a perfect location." Jessie stopped to look in the window. "It's a nice space and the businesses around this location are places that tourists love to shop. I can see it. Evan does amazing work. I can see him doing quite well here."

Matt asked her questions all through the meal. Jessie found it strange that he wanted to know about her days working for Neil Dempsey in New York, and about the police officers who helped her with any of her reports from O'Malley's precinct. Something was bothering him, and she wasn't sure what. She continued to think about their conversation long after she dropped him off at the station to pick up his car. There was something she was missing. One by one she worked back through all the details of their investigation. She started with Sofia Barton, worked her way through Kimama, and on to the missing Native American Women. She finished with Sonny Webster who still left big questions in her mind along with one big warning flag. And of course, Dexter. Why now? He could have acted on his anger long ago. Round and around she went. The best analogy she could use to describe the sensation was a dog chasing his tail. When she thought she had caught the answer the chase began in her mind all over again. She picked up the book on her nightstand and started to read. Maybe she would see the connection if she stopped trying so hard to see it.

****

Matt slapped his hand to his head. He had what seemed to be four or five separate investigations and Jessie believed they were somehow all connected. *Hell.* He rubbed his temple. She was always right, but even she didn't know how each of the investigations were connected. Jeremy always said when in doubt follow the money. There had to be a money trail, and more than a few people on the payroll.

When Jaxon came in, Matt handed him a file and they pored over the facts. Jaxon added some further details that Tom had sent him in a text earlier concerning Zach Johnson. Matt told him about his conversation with O'Malley regarding Hoffman and showed a new email from Jeremy with more spreadsheets.

"I can't see any connection yet. But if Johnson is involved, and I think he is, we will crack the code before long. The evidence must be somewhere on his cyber footprint." Matt reached for the remote.

"He's there all right. Not up-front but on the dark places of the web. He put out the call, and he has folks working for him," Jaxon told him.

"I'm ready to give my mind a break. How about you?" Matt waved the remote in the air.

"Sounds good. I'm going to grab something to drink. Do you want iced tea, soda, or a beer?"

"A beer sounds good to me," Matt replied.

"Two beers coming up." Jaxon walked into the kitchen and came back with two bottles of cold ones.

Matt turned on the TV and flipped to his favorite station. He was content to watch sports highlights. "This is a nice way to end the day." He took a swig of his beer and put his feet up. At least for this moment, he could relax and let his mind chill.

Chapter Thirty-Six

Famous last words. As soon as his head hit the pillow, Matt's mind kicked into gear. The craziest conversation of the many he had with Jessie came back into his thoughts. At one point a man came into her store wearing a patch and walking with a limp. He might need to remind her of their conversation. When it came to Jessie, nothing happened by chance. She instantly researched the legend of Blackbeard's ghost. The man fit into their investigation somewhere.

One by one he went over the details Jessie had talked about over the past several days. The ghosts, the messages Reba had given her, and the strangers who had popped into her store. She was right—her place was a gathering place of sorts. He glanced at the clock. She would be asleep, but he sent a text to her anyway.

—*Call me in the morning when you read this.*—

He was surprised when his phone rang. "I thought you would be asleep," he said when he answered.

"My mind won't let me. The thoughts just keep going and going." She laughed. "I continue to go over details again and again. I feel like I'm spinning my wheels."

"Do you remember the day the man with the patch came into your store?" he asked.

"How could I forget? His visit prompted me to study everything I could find on Blackbeard and his ghost." He heard the laughter in her voice.

"I don't believe his visit was a fluke. I think he fits into our investigation more than we realize."

"Strange that you would say that. I was thinking the same thing tonight. I'm still wondering how, but I'm sure I'll put it together soon."

"Let me know if you do. We should attempt to sleep, sweetheart. But I want you to be on the lookout for Dexter. I don't think he'll give up easily."

"I agree. I don't know how I can stop him if he does," she told him.

"Frank is coming back to town in a couple of days, and we will try to track his location before he does. We're going over his car and the contents and hopefully will have more information on the man soon." Matt stretched out on his bed leaning up against the headboard.

"Remember, we exchange any info we get. It goes both ways," Jessie reminded him.

"I remember, and you know I'll give you what I can. Goodnight, Jess. I love you."

"I love you too. Be careful. I wouldn't put it past Dexter to go after someone that I love."

Matt thought her last warning was closer to the truth than she probably realized. After reading some of Hoffman's writings, Matt knew he had been watching her store for a while. Hoffman knew that Jessie was close to Reba, Sadie, and Peyton. Dexter was also aware that Jessie had a cop boyfriend. That's what he wrote it in one of his online rants.

Gary was going over Hoffman's computer. Dexter had been bragging in several online chat rooms. He also had been visiting several sites on the dark web. Jaxon explained the details to Matt tonight. Zach Johnson spent a lot of time there also. Now all they had to do was connect the two of them.

Matt closed his eyes. "This is one time I wouldn't mind a bit of unconventional help with a case," he muttered before he drifted off.

****

Was it a dream, her mind playing tricks on her, or a nightmare that wouldn't go away? Jessie could hear the whispers in the darkness from every corner of the room. "Remember me. Don't forget who I am." The voices started as a whisper and increased in intensity as the room seemed to move around her, pulsating and alive with an energy that seemed hard to describe. The atmosphere was animated with some unnamed presence reaching out to her grasping for her to hear and understand.

She found herself a passenger as the story unfolded in front of her. One fact connected to another until the picture of the destruction of lives became clear. One crime built upon another until the lines blurred and she could no longer tell where one ended and the next one began. In the darkness, the schemes were forged and committed in the shadows until forced into the light. All it took was someone who cared enough to listen, ask questions, and search for the truth.

Jessie turned on her light and began to jot down notes, listing several names that she needed to research their backgrounds. The connection was clearer than ever, and she hoped Matt was coming to the same conclusion.

Not sleepy, she grabbed her laptop and began her search jotting down notes as she went. It was amazing that a bit of digging beneath the surface could turn up little-known facts about someone's life. *I wonder what I would find on myself if I searched.* She might have to try a search on herself one day soon, or then again, maybe she would rather not know. She sent a quick text off to Jaxon asking about the dark web. He had mentioned the cyber world being the next big frontier of crime. She believed their investigation had online activity. Most of it was being conducted in chat rooms and web recruiting sites along with the payouts. Figuring out the conspirator behind the scheme was easy enough. How he was managing to pull it off might be harder to discover. She might need Jeremy's and Jaxon's help to find her way around the internet sites without leaving a trail for someone to follow her.

Jaxon's reply to her text was to give her several articles to read on the subject. "Geeze, doesn't anyone sleep at night?" she muttered. "Look who's talking." She sent an email to Jeremy, and she didn't expect an answer until tomorrow. She turned off her computer and light. She wanted to try her hand at sleeping again or at least pretend to.

****

Matt awakened to the smell of coffee and bacon. He could live with both. After a quick shower and shave, he got dressed, strapped on his holster, and stuck his badge in his pocket before heading for the kitchen and the great aroma that awakened him.

"You're up early," Matt said pouring himself a cup of coffee.

"Jessie texted me wanting to know about the dark web." Jaxon filled Matt a plate with bacon and scrambled eggs. "She's figuring things out, I'm sure of it. I should know by now that the Reynolds girls are one step ahead of us, but I still find myself surprised by them."

"You and me both. What is she on the trail of this time?" Matt sipped his coffee and took a bite of his eggs.

"She knows Zach is involved, but she figures he is operating on some remote online site on the darker side. She's right, of course. We simply have to find out how and where."

"My girl is a marvel. If I know her, she's way ahead of us in figuring out peoples' connections and motives. If she doesn't have the answers yet, she soon will." Matt poured himself another cup of coffee. "I'll call her today and try to catch up with the details. If she was texting you late it means she had a dream or an idea that wouldn't let her sleep."

"Sounds like a good idea to me. I have a few theories on what is going on, but I still can't imagine how each segment of the case is linked. I have a feeling we're about to find out."

"You've got to admit this is the point in an investigation where it gets exciting. It's also the point where anything can happen. I for one am still concerned about Hoffman. He may not be done with Jessie yet."

"I guess we'd better keep our eyes open," Jaxon said on the way to his car.

Matt backed out of the garage. Damn, but he wished it were as simple as that. Every case seemed to have some surprise hidden somewhere. Reba, for example. Matt hadn't expected Hoffman to attack her. Thankfully, she was okay, but he wouldn't want to risk anyone else or her again. Hoffman knew who was important to Jessie. If he couldn't get at her again, he would be willing to use someone else to draw her out. He wasn't afraid of getting caught either. The bottom line was, that Dexter Hoffman had gone after Jessie in her store, in the middle of the day, with people in the coffee shop able to see his actions.

With his car and his computer in police custody, Dexter must be feeling backed into a corner. Not a good position to be in and the thought made Matt's concern grow. A criminal could get desperate, and desperation added extra danger to the equation. Anticipating his next move was not going to be easy.

Matt pulled into the spot in front of Jessie's store. The store wasn't open yet, but he could see her behind the counter. His need to see her hadn't diminished with time, but only increased. He rapped on the glass with his knuckles. Matt loved watching her face light up when she saw him. She came toward the door waving and smiling at him, a scene he hoped to see repeated often over the next many years and one he would never tire of.

"I wasn't expecting you this early, but I figured you would drop by at some point," she said as she opened the door.

He pulled her into his arms and kissed her. "Now that's the way to start a morning." He kissed her again.

"Hmm," she sighed leaning her head against his chest. "Why are you here?" She glanced up smiling sweetly at him. "Not that I mind your kisses, but you have something on your mind, Chief Parker, so spit it out."

He grinned. "Are you always this sassy in the morning? I like it, and you're right. I want coffee first and then we'll talk." He walked over to the doors, and she unlocked one to let him go into Joe's. He returned with two cups of the steaming brew. "Now we can talk." He placed the cups on the table. "Jaxon told me he got a text from you late last night." He pulled out a chair and sat.

"Yes, I want to understand the dark web. I know people communicate and recruit on certain sites. I also sent a text to Jeremy. I want to know how to search for them without having an audience. Until I know that I won't even try." Jessie paced. "People often maneuver into one of the sites to find others who believe like them or agree with their latest rant."

"Why even go there?" Matt patted the chair beside him. "Sit. You're making me dizzy watching you."

"Sorry, I think better when I'm moving. I want to go there because that's what links all of these cases together in some bizarre way. I know it." Jessie told him about her experience the night before. "I can see their connections but not all the people involved." She sat beside him.

"If you think they're linked then they are most likely. Damn, I wish I knew who was sending information to Zach from my station. I can't see any of my guys being guilty, but I was wrong before."

"Yeah, but you also cleaned house. Could it be a woman? You know, a secretary or someone more vulnerable financially. Johnson is a charmer, and he might be able to manipulate information out of a woman." She sipped her coffee.

"You think Zach's charming? Really?" Matt's forehead furrowed.

"I don't, but some women might find him that

way." Jessie patted his hand.

"I never thought of it from that angle, but you could be right. I need to take another look at some of our support staff."

"Good idea. I think Dexter is connected through the web somehow. I'm sure Gary and Jeremy will find info on his computer."

"You've given me plenty to chew on. I love that about talking with you. You know what else I love about you?"

"No, what?" She glanced at him.

"I like how you twist your hair around your finger when you're thinking or worried." His fingers lightly stroked her cheek to her chin. "I especially like your dimples when you smile at me and this…" He leaned over and kissed her. "Yeah, I love that most of all. I'll see you later, and call me if you see or sense Hoffman within miles of your store." He stood and pulled her up beside him. "I'm going to mull over what we talked about. If you think of anything else let me know. I'll do the same."

****

Jessie stood at the door and watched until his car was out of sight. "Matt Parker, you're a gem," she muttered locking the door until it was time to open. She went over their conversation in her mind as she read through Jeremy's email. He wanted her to send him what she was looking for. He told her that she would need more training before she wandered onto any of those sites. Jessie had thought that was probably true, but she wanted to know. *You can't blame a girl for trying. Even one in over her head.* She sent him the names and what she was searching for.

—This may take some time, but I'll get back to you if I find anything.— Jeremy texted her.

In the meantime, there were searches she could do online that she didn't need to be concerned about. She glanced at the clock. At least for the next thirty minutes, she could see what she could find.

She found plenty of information that kept her following from one trail to another. Nothing that would put someone behind bars but made her think about the person differently. You could learn a lot about a person by simply reading their social media posts. Sonny Webster seemed to be a colorful character along with a few others that she checked out. Her posts were dull in comparison. She did have an exciting life that she would rather keep quiet. She wanted the people in Blue Cove to like her not run away every time they saw her walk down the street. She could see it now. Instead of the cat woman she would be known as the ghost lady.

Jessie laughed to herself. "Some things are better kept secret." She opened the doors into the coffee shop waving at Molly as she did. Walking to the front door she turned the open sign around but paused before unlocking the door. The truck driving down the street at that moment reminded her of one she had seen before. She was more positive than ever that a serial killer was in the Blue Cove area.

Chapter Thirty-Seven

Matt spent the morning in teleconference calls. Pieces of evidence were coming together and widening the circle of their investigation. This was his favorite time in a case. All of the moving parts started forming a clear picture of the crimes and the suspects. The thought of taking a few criminals off the street and putting a few more out of business made perfect sense to him.

As Jessie had told him loud and clear on more than one occasion, women and children got the raw end of the deal. The case he was in the middle of and the evidence to date more than proved her point. It was a damn shame. Men, more often than not, were the ones causing the pain. The scenario made him want to knock a few heads together. He was tired of making excuses for actions that could no longer be justified.

"Hey, Frank. I appreciate you coming on such short notice." Matt stood when Frank came into his office.

"I hope we can at least find the direction the guy went in when he ran from the store." Frank shook Matt's hand.

"He left a virtual gold mine—his laptop, plans, and plenty of other gems." Matt told him about other items they found. "If you want, we can get started right away."

"Sounds good to me. There is plenty of material for the dog to scent off." Frank followed Matt out of the office.

"Let's see what Radar can find." Matt got in the passenger side of Frank's car.

"Give me directions and we'll get this track started." Frank started his car.

Matt was always amazed by how Radar tracked. With two small scent items from Hoffman left behind in his car Radar tracked his movements around town. He had skirted the main street after his escape by going through the cemetery and the wooded area behind the town. At some point, he must have hitched a ride and left the area. Matt felt confident that at the moment he was nowhere in town.

He could be on his way back but at least he wasn't here now. Jeremy sent Matt some background material on Hoffman, and the guy had some issues. It made the task of getting him off the streets more important than ever. Matt needed to have a serious conversation with Jessie about him.

Frank was on his way to another track but promised he would come back if needed. Jessie was convinced that a serial killer was roaming around the area looking for his next victim. After hearing Winnie's story, Matt was sure that Jessie was on to something. The guy or a copycat was in the area. There was no doubt in Matt's mind.

Sofia Barton's last few interviews had gone better. The victim's advocate had got her to open up about what happened to her. It was repeated in the stories of several of the other girls from the training center. Some of the girls had suffered more than others. With their stories more pieces were added to the investigation, and charges were being written up.

He still had questions about who could be leaking information or working with Zach Johnson. Matt knew his officers and trusted them thoroughly. But he had also once trusted Chief Anderson. Matt jotted down a note to himself to give everyone at the station a second look in case he was missing something.

Jaxon knocked on his open door. "Are you busy?"

"Not really. I'm going over what I've learned the last few days." Matt motioned him in.

"Gary called and told me to come down to his office. He thinks they've found Zach's handiwork online. I thought you might want to come along." Jaxon leaned against his open door.

"You bet I do. Let's go." Matt stood and followed Jaxon out the door.

After an hour spent in Gary's office Matt's head was spinning. He didn't understand a lot of what Gary had explained but he knew enough to know Zach was operating and recruiting from behind bars. Gary and Jeremy were working together via the phone to find out who was working with Zach.

****

Jessie waved at Peyton when she walked into the store followed close behind by Reba.

Jessie jumped up. "Are you sure you should be up and out already?" A look of concern passed between her and Peyton.

"I'm fine, dears. We need to talk. I'm glad you're both here." Reba took a deep breath and sat down gingerly.

"What is so important that you needed to come

today? You just got out of the hospital." Peyton patted her hand.

"The whole time I lay in that bed I couldn't let go of thoughts that kept coming to me. It involves you two girls. You need to embrace the gift that's been given to you. Learn all the ropes and don't be afraid of where it will take you. You won't be led astray, and you'll be helping people along the way. You asked me how I know things. Well, girls, you're about to find out."

"What do you mean?" Jessie asked.

"After this adventure ends, another one will begin taking you to faraway places. You'll learn more about your past and your future, and new truths await you."

"I'm curious about the faraway places." Peyton tapped Jessie's shoulder.

"I hear you, cous. That phrase caught my attention too. Maybe Ireland—that would be great after our last case—or maybe some place exotic." Jessie placed her hand over eyes peeking through her spread fingers. "Tell us, Reba, what you haven't said yet." Jessie glanced at her friend pointedly.

"In my mind I saw you on a journey of discovery. Not forever, of course. Where and how I can't tell you, but you will learn the reason for and the strength that comes with the gift you've been blessed with. You won't be questioning why anymore after you find out what you need to know."

"Sounds intriguing. We'll see." Jessie smiled at her. "Hopefully, you weren't hallucinating after being hit on the head.'

"I was doing fine and was lucid when the idea came to me. You girls have been wondering about many things and you need answers to your questions. I want you to be able to embrace your new life and live it fully. I had such an experience when I was younger too. It helped me to understand who I was and my purpose. I called it my journey of self-discovery. I'm excited for you." Reba smiled. "I can live with me no matter how oddly people perceive me. I know you both have wondered about me."

Jessie shook her head. "No…"

"Don't deny it. I already know you do and rightfully so." Reba reached for Jessie's hand. "I've simply tried to make your transitions simpler. But I know I left you more questions than answers at time."

"I guess if we go, we go. I'll cross that bridge when I get to it but right now, we have a crime to solve." Jessie stood and started to pace. "I'm ready to figure out the puzzle of this investigation." She smiled when the idea came to her and wanted to tell Matt soon. "Perfect."

****

Dexter Hoffman drove the backroads outside of the Blue Cove area hoping to escape being noticed. If the last few days were any indication, he should quit while he was ahead. Besides blowing his first attempt and being bested by a woman, he left his car with his computer and plans in it for the cops to find. And now word on the street was the cop had a bloodhound coming to try and track him, which meant they were on to him. He didn't want to get caught by the cops. The only thing worse was the guy who hired him. The man had promised him a big payout if he could deliver Jessie scared but unharmed. Dexter had no problem with messing with her, but his contact also promised retribution if he messed up, which Hoffman hoped he hadn't already heard about. The man seemed to have eyes and ears everywhere.

The whole proposal the man made had worked into his plan perfectly. Dexter was sure it would be easy but now he had lost all confidence. As he made his way closer to the cove, he needed to rethink his plan. The boss man said she was tricky, and not to take her ability for granted. But he also told him, he'd kill him if he let her mess up their gig.

"No worries," he said confidently. What an idiot he was to get involved with the guy. He personally had never met the man but he had met his minions. He should have kept to his original plan. He worked better alone. Living sounded better than the other option. He'd better come up with a foolproof alternative. Damn, but he hated the uncertainty. The last person who contacted him had issued more warnings which had unsettled him. Working alone had always been his trademark. Why had he tried to change things up at such a crucial time? He had no idea. "Stupid." He hit his hand on the steering wheel.

Chapter Thirty-Eight

Kimama came to Jessie in her dream. Most of what she saw was fanciful, filled with Native American legends, mixed with Irish folklore and fairies. She was shown the door in the woods, and Kimama told her about the world beyond the barrier.

"On your journey you saw and heard many things," Kimama told Jessie. "Don't forget the sound of his voice. The words he spoke will lead you to the killer." Then scene by scene Kimama took Jessie through where Jessie had already been. "Listen, pay attention to what you hear. It will come to you when you need to know the answer." A white wolf appeared as Kimama walked from her view. With the wolf's appearance she had confidence the killer would be found.

Jessie was reminded of Reba's words to embrace her gift and learn to walk in every new aspect of it. Determined to be aware of her surroundings, she got ready for her day. Matt worked late last night but he promised to charm her with quality time tonight and now she had something to share with him. She loved how his eyebrows would rise in disbelief and then he would sigh while resigning himself to the inevitable.

She could also see what he thought about her idea. She liked it a whole lot. She wasn't sure how he would feel about her suggestion. He would warm up to the idea given time. Presenting the information in just the right way would win him over. Matt was nothing if not predictable.

Jessie grabbed her purse, stuffing her phone in as she rushed out the door. She couldn't wait to tell Peyton. Her cousin would scheme with her, and Jaxon would come along for the ride. He was smitten. The first thing she did when she got to work besides ordering a scone and decaf was to get online.

****

When Matt got to the station. he had a call waiting. Thanks to a rental car company's quick action, they once again had eyes on Hoffman. After that piece of good news, he found out a link between Johnson and an online recruiting site had been established. Gary and Jeremy were currently unraveling the encrypted names linked to the webpage. At the moment, they had evidence the gym and studio were regular visitors to the site. Jeremy's research turned up proof they were still paying hush money directly into Zach's account which Matt found ludicrous. Chief Anderson was long gone, and Johnson was in prison. They could have turned on him. Crime rarely made sense. Later he would call the girls' law team to tell them they could proceed with their civil suit as soon as the criminal arrests were made.

The morning was filled with great news for their investigation. It would be a pleasure to put the team doctor in jail for what he did to those girls and those who covered his actions. As for Zach Johnson, putting him out of business and confiscating his money would bring Matt great pleasure after he heard what Gary told him. With any luck that dirty agent would never get out of prison.

The investigation into Ben Tso was moving along too. Because there was no premeditation involved, Matt was charging Tso with second degree murder and assault. In a fit of drunken rage, he had killed his wife and Matt had plenty of evidence to back the charges. Tso's wife's family were ready to testify against him because he had beaten her on several occasions when he was drunk. The man needed help with his drinking problem and prison would help with that to a certain degree. He wouldn't be able to drink unless someone smuggled alcohol into the prison. Tso was one of the many domestic violence statistics on the reservation that Jessie had told him about.

Jessie was convinced that most if not all their investigations were somehow linked together by a common thread. He was almost there and before all was said and done her point of view would prevail.

Speaking of Jessie, Matt reached for his jacket and headed out of the station. Jaxon called with some new information for him on his way out the door and Matt told him to meet him at the bookstore. He wanted to discuss what he had away from the station. Someone there had ears and was feeding information to Johnson. Matt was getting close to finding the guilty party. He was waiting on Gary's information to confirm what he knew in his gut to be true. Matt decided to drive to Hanover and stop by Jessie's later.

****

As soon as Peyton arrived after work Jessie told her cousin about her dream. "Kimama emphasized that I should remember not only the victims but what I saw and heard."

"Did you hear the killer say anything?" Peyton

asked.

"Yes, and it's got me wondering. I think I've heard that voice since. It could have been here in my store, or somewhere around town. But without the heavy accent it's hard to be sure. I could be imagining that I've heard him."

"Did you tell Matt?"

"I'm not sure. I might have mentioned in passing that the voice sounded familiar. Truthfully, it could be anyone." She shrugged her shoulders. "There were many details from that time on my journey. I find it hard to remember them all. Last night was important, if for no other reason than to refresh my memory."

"I bet. I think we might be growing and becoming more accepting of this gift. What does that say about us?" Peyton stretched her hands behind her back.

"I'm not sure, but I want to understand. I can see how you could use all of this for good or evil." Jessie gestured with her hands. "All you have to do is remember our last case that resulted in a school shooting. Now I want to know what the ramifications are if you do or don't use your powers for good."

"I've been stumbling through each new manifestation not putting too much thought into it. But you're right—not only is there a reason for the gift, it isn't ours for power or to make us feel better about ourselves but to help. There consequences could be dire if we don't understand the purpose." Peyton frowned. "It's a lot of pressure."

"Yes. Think about the cry to 'remember me.' They are counting on us to tell their stories, to solve the crimes committed against them and to bring closure to their families. Matt and Jaxon do that using the power of the law. I like to think of this as the power of love. We see what we do and hear what we hear proving no matter how long it takes love wins over hate. Never giving up until the voices which have been silenced, and stories forgotten by time are resurrected and told, giving value to every life."

"Wow. Do you mind if I quote you?" Peyton chuckled. "We are too serious by half. Still, I'm with you. If I'm to embrace this fully, then I must understand what I'm embracing. Here's to a pact of no more stumbling. Let us learn the skill to walk in the steps of our ancestors." Peyton slapped her hand to her head. "OMG. What if they were bumbling through like we are?"

"There's a thought. We can only do our best."

After Peyton left to run some errands, Jessie found herself second guessing herself with every male who came into the store. Because of Winnie she was certain the serial killer had been in the area and probably still was there. Kimama's words to remember what she saw and heard kept rolling through her mind until she began to go back through her notes and memories of each of the sites she had seen.

No news articles had been written, missing persons' notices sent across the wires, or local news coverages done for most of victims. What a travesty. Too many beautiful Native American girls had been virtually forgotten. Jessie couldn't make everyone a suspect or she would go bonkers before long. But she could do as she was told and pay attention to what she saw and heard both then and now. If the serial killer were around, he would wander into her store at some point, if he hadn't already. Hoffman would be back too.

She was sure, and the next time she would be ready.

****

A prickly sensation began at the top of his neck and slithered down his back. He took a quick glance around but saw nothing. Feeling sure that he was being followed, he tried to lead whoever it was off his trail by turning quickly first right and then left. He repeated the maneuver several times but couldn't shake the feeling. Even though he saw no one, he knew they were there, nonetheless.

"Dex, old boy, you're paranoid." The sweat ran down his cheek unhindered. Nervous didn't even begin to describe his senses. Was it the cop? Or worse yet, had the man who hired him sent someone? He'd rather the first than the second. The shivers running down his back told him he wouldn't like the answer.

Chapter Thirty-Nine

Jessie was finishing up her day when Hoffman raced through the door. The look of panic on his face would be forever etched in her mind.

"You did this to me." His voice faded as he slumped to the ground, pulling the display table over on him as he fell. Books scattered in several directions as the table overturned. Hoffman lay in an awkward position with several books on top of him.

"Did what?" Jessie took her gun out of the drawer and raced toward him. Her action wasn't necessary. Hoffman's eyes were closed, the corners of his lips pinched in a sardonic sneer, and a noticeable blood spot grew on his shirt.

Shocked, Jessie jumped into action calling for an ambulance and then Matt. Matt arrived right before the ambulance.

"Just so you know I didn't shoot him." She went on to explain what had happened when Hoffman entered her store. "I'm as surprised as anyone," she told him. "Who would shoot him and why?"

Matt tended to Dexter who was struggling to breathe. "Hold on, man. Help is on the way." Matt stood as soon as the medics arrived and let them take over. "I hope he can tell us what happened. If not, I'm more worried about you than ever. Something tells me he botched his part in all of this. When he hit Reba and failed at abducting you, he messed up big time."

"Who could he be working for? I have a few ideas but no proof." Jessie began to pace and mused aloud.

"I have a theory, and folks are searching for the evidence to back it up. I'll meet you at your place later. I'm going to head to the hospital." Matt called in his team, gave Dylan his instructions, and gave her a quick kiss as he rushed out the door to his cruiser.

Jessie watched him pull away skirting around the blood pool on the floor. Shaking her head, she knew she could never get used to all the violence. She held the door open for Kip who walked in followed by Evan to take pictures.

"How's my favorite soon to be sister-in-law?" Evan grinned at her. "My brother has his hands full with you."

"You're such a sweet talker." She smiled at him.

"My family can't wait until you make it official." Evan snapped a picture.

"Yeah, yeah. I bet your brother put you up to that." She poked his arm. "You'll know not long after he does."

"Why does it seem like every picture I take here has books in it?" He bent to get a look at one of the titles.

"Duh, maybe it's because this is a bookstore. When he fell, he took the display table with him."

"Did you read the title?" Evan pointed at the book.

Jessie looked where he pointed. "Wow, that fits."

"For the record, I think you're the best thing that ever happened to my brother. You make him happy."

"You've got that right." Jessie pulled the doors shut into the coffee shop and locked them. "Keep reminding him, would you?" She laughed.

"I do all the time." He snapped a few more photos.

"I have to know the title." Dylan glanced at where the book had dropped. In bold letters were the words Murder For Hire. "That fits." Dylan took a few samples.

Another man that Jessie had never seen before cleaned and disinfected the area. Within minutes her store looked like nothing untoward had happened there. She locked up after they left. Why was Dexter Hoffman shot? None of this made any sense to her. The case seemed more bizarre as time went on. Hoffman was obviously upset with her, and she wanted to know why. More importantly, who else wanted her hurt? That person or persons were still out there, and she had no idea who they were. Not a pleasant thought. She frowned.

"No more whining, Jess." She smiled at the name she called herself. How many times since Matt came into her life had she corrected him for calling her Jess instead of Jessie. It was a sticking point with every argument they had when they first met. He did it to annoy her and boy did it. "My, how time can change perspective." Matt still called her Jess and she let him. That man could make her forget her own name. Thinking about Matt, she wondered what if anything Matt had found out. Had Dexter made it? She didn't wish him any harm, but she did want answers. She didn't think she was being unreasonable. He blamed her for his situation, and she wanted to know why.

When Jessie got home, she waited until after six to make dinner. She ate leisurely hoping Matt would knock at the door at any minute. With dishes done and the kitchen cleaned, she still hadn't heard from Matt. What could be taking him so long? She knew he would call as soon as he had information, but she wasn't exactly patient. Pacing, lots of nervous energy, and an occasional twist of her hair were her claims to fame. More often than not all her actions could be accompanied by tears. She flopped down on the sofa and reached for the remote. Flipping through the stations she landed on an old movie hoping the story would grab her interest.

****

Matt glanced at the clock when he walked out of the hospital. Jessie would be wondering what happened to him. He had waited around until Hoffman was lucid enough to talk, and talk he did. The poor man had stored up years of anger against his mother which he took out on every woman that he met. Jessie was one of many. His anger with her was more about the fact he couldn't have her than anything she had done to him.

He hated to tell Jessie or to worry her, but it was necessary. She needed to know all the sordid details but not over the phone. He picked up his to go order and reached for his phone and texted her.

—*Hi, Jess. I'm on my way. I'll be there in a few.*—
—*Okay. See you soon.*—

Matt sorted through the information in his mind that Hoffman shared. Each detail connected to another piece of evidence and opened a whole new area of inquiry. When it came to putting links together Jessie was the best. She probably already knew most of this. That's why they made such a good team. She left him scratching his head the way she saw things, but it all seemed to pan out logically with evidence eventually.

He could live with that.

He knocked on Jessie's door. "Hi," he said when she opened the door. "I know it's late."

"I figured you had to wait until he was able to talk. Will he make it?" she asked.

"I love that about you, Jess. You have every reason to hate the guy and yet the first thing you ask is if he will survive." Matt shut the door behind him. "It looks like he'll be okay."

"Was he able to tell you anything?" She followed Matt into the kitchen.

He placed the bag he was carrying on the table. "I figured you already ate but I'm willing to share mine if you're hungry." He took a fork out of the drawer and took the lid off his dinner.

"Go ahead. I ate a while ago. Can I get you some iced tea?" She took two glasses out of the cabinet.

"Please. You asked me if Hoffman talked. They answer is yes. He had a lot to say. I felt almost sorry for the guy."

"You look tired. You should've gone home and called me."

He shook his head. "I need you to sort through what he told me, but first I need to eat. I'm starved." He took a big bite of his barbecue beef sandwich. "I brought you dessert, so I didn't forget you altogether. Chocolate cake from Patterson, your favorite." He grinned at her.

"Hmm, chocolate cake. Sounds like you have some bad news for me."

"When it comes to the mind of criminals, most news isn't good. We'll sort it out together. I think we are getting close to solving this case." Matt watched

Jessie close her eyes after she took the first bite of cake. He loved the expression she made when she liked a certain food. Watching her was his favorite pastime.

Jessie opened her eyes and saw the grin on his face. "What?"

"I hope you know how much I love you." He reached for her hand and laced his fingers through hers. "Hoffman was hired to abduct you."

"Wow. Talk about a change of topic." She frowned. "Who and why?"

"He's not sure who and now he's scared. He bungled his attempt and that's why he was shot. He has no idea who hired him. Everything was done online, including his payout. Gary is working on the answer to your questions with Jeremy and should have an answer for you soon. As far as who shot him, he never saw anyone." He stroked her cheek. "I don't want you to worry."

"Worry! I'm mad. I want to talk to Hoffman." She stood abruptly almost turning over the chair. "I'm going to the hospital tomorrow and have a chat with him."

"Sweetheart, calm down. I don't think that's a good idea." He reached for her, but she pulled away.

"I have a right to know why he's angry enough at me to walk into my store and hurt my friend. He owes me an explanation. You can either come with me or I will go alone but I'm going."

"Damn, Jess, you're putting me in a bad spot." He stood and pulled her into his arms resting his chin on her head. "I know what happened to Reba upset you but…" His voice trailed off when she put her fingers to his mouth to shush him.

"You don't get it do you? I'm tired of these guys

thinking they have a right to take out their anger on women. I'm mad. Ben Tso's wife didn't deserve to die because he had a bad day and lost his job. Reba should have never been hit, and never mind the man killing Native American woman. I may not be able to get answers from every one of these jerks, but I can at least extract an answer from Hoffman for myself." She eased into one of the chairs in the living room taking her cake with her.

He stood behind her rubbing her shoulders. "I'm sorry, you're right. I don't understand it from your side. Of course, I will take you. You need to hear from his mouth what he told me."

Later when Matt got home, he talked over his evening with Jaxon. He told him what he had learned from Hoffman earlier and Jessie's feelings.

"I get it. If anyone has a right to hear the suspect's reasoning it's the intended victim," Jaxon said. "Peyton is always enlightening me about how men often treat women in the workplace. The more I hear the more I'm grateful that Peyton likes me at all."

"You and me both. Jessie is going to talk to him whether I'm with her or not. I'm going to let her." Matt smiled and added, "As if I could stop her." Matt reached for the remote and flipped to the sports station. "Before I turn up the sound, do you think Zach is behind the online site?"

"He may not be in charge, but he's involved in the operation. There is a group in prison with ties to others on the outside. Maxwell thinks we're close to cracking it. There are agents working around the clock on this one. He has a personal score to settle with Johnson. A dirty agent makes the whole department look bad."

"I understand his feelings." Matt turned up the sound and put his feet up.

Chapter Forty

Jessie agreed to meet Matt at the hospital around noon. Audrey was available to watch the store for a couple of hours. Questions were stirring inside her mind, and she needed to calm down or she would lambast the man when she walked into his room. She saw Matt waiting by his cruiser when she pulled into the parking lot.

He walked over and opened her door. "Are you ready for this?" he asked.

"Yes." She stepped out of the car and walked in step with him. "You don't need to worry. I won't attack him. I promise." She glanced at Matt out of the corner of her eye. She saw him try not to smile.

"I'll go in with you into the room. Then I'll tell him to talk, and I'll be standing right outside of the door. Does that work for you?"

"Perfect." She smiled and walked hand in hand into the elevator with him.

She followed Matt into the room. From her vantage point she had a perfect view to see all the expressions racing across Hoffman's face when he saw her.

"What's she doing here?" He growled out his question.

"You are going to tell her what you told me. You owe her that much after you sent her those letters and rushed into her store hurting her friend."

"You can't make me talk." He smirked and then groaned when he moved wrong.

"No, I can't. But I'm warning you that you'll never meet a more stubborn woman in your life. Believe me when I say she can wait you out and make your life miserable, and rightly so. You deserve it and more. You may as well start talking. I'll be outside the door if you need to be reminded of your manners."

"You can leave," Jessie told him. "I'll call you if I need you." She smiled sweetly and waited until Matt walked out and closed the door. "Now"—she pointed at Hoffman—"start talking. I want to know why you are angry at me."

He started with the loss of his mother who left when he was young. His anger against women was palpable. Jessie found his reasoning slightly twisted and taken to a max by spending time on the internet. He discovered a group which spouted similar rhetoric and held to his anti-women sentiments. The group bolstered him, and he became a big talking man in the group. Eventually someone approached him about abducting a woman. Hoffman had been offered a lot of money to do the job. Jessie learned through his ramblings that he was talking about her.

Jessie had heard enough and took a deep breath. "You rushed into my store and hit my friend, and you think I'm supposed to take it and not be angry. Well, I'm mad. I never did anything to you. Now that I can I see you without your hideous eye contacts, I remember talking to you and being kind. The fact you weren't good at your job isn't my fault. I did my job and Neil used my stories. He would have done the same for you. He was a fair man." She fluffed the pillow behind his back. "I shouldn't do anything for you, but I can't help myself. I don't like to see anyone suffer, even a jerk. Look at the people you've fallen in with, all because you're mad at your mother who left you. Grow up and own your mistakes and succeed despite her."

****

When Matt opened the door, he couldn't believe what he saw. Jessie was holding a cup with a straw close enough for Dexter to sip. All the while she was giving him hell. At least that's what he would call it. She put his lectures to shame. This was one lecture Dexter would never forget. Matt snapped a picture with his phone and tried hard not to laugh. She never ceased to amaze him and fill his life with meaning.

"Did you come to rescue me?" Hoffman pleaded with his eyes.

"I warned you, didn't I? What do you have to say to her? You do know this is my girl and I don't like anyone making her feel bad."

"I figured as much." He reached for Jessie's hand holding his cup. "I'm sorry for everything. I guess these people I thought of as friends aren't really friends at all."

"You need to meet a nice girl. You have way too much time on your hands. Of course, it will depend on if you go to jail or not. But there are some nice girls in Blue Cove."

"Okay, sweetheart. He needs to rest. Did you say everything you needed to say?" Matt asked as he opened to door for her.

"He wouldn't have needed it at all if he hadn't been so stupid." She glanced at Dexter. "Pardon me, but you know it's true. I hope you feel better soon.

Remember, these guys aren't nice people to deal with and you'd be wise to get away from them."

"I'll remember, not that it will do me any good. They'll come after me again. I don't suppose you'd let me pretend to abduct you and take pictures."

"Don't go there." Matt said. "I'll be back."

"I'm sure you will." Hoffman laid his head back against the pillow.

"There's an officer outside your door in case you choose to run. You may be done, but the law is not done with you," Matt told him.

"I didn't think it would be." He turned his head on the pillow and his eyes flickered shut.

Matt closed the door to Dexter's room. "You constantly surprise me, Jess." He reached for her hand.

"Why, because I wasn't trying to kill him when you walked in? I can be nice you know. I was nicely telling him that there was no reason for him to be mad at me. He could be successful if he worked hard at it instead of blaming his failures on every woman he meets."

"You do understand that the person who shot him is still out there and is working for the guy who hired him." Matt pushed the down button on the elevator.

"Of course. That's easy enough to figure out, but I can't sit around and worry about it. You'll keep me safe. Isn't that what you always tell me?" She shrugged her shoulders.

"And you are accepting of that now?" His brows rose.

"Sure, why not. I can't do everything myself. I can use a bit of help once in a while. Since you love me, I figure it may as well be you." She glanced at him and grinned as the elevator started moving. "I'm convinced that I'm no different anyone else. At the end of the day people want to believe their lives matter, and someone cares whether they live or die. Women are often made to feel the opposite. I learned to make my voice be heard while working in a man's world. Remember me; I've existed, seems to be the cry of most hearts."

"That's true I guess." Matt stepped out of the elevator when the door opened to the lobby.

"Maybe not to you. You're a man and it's a man's world as they say. But I like to believe we make it kinder and gentler somehow." She got into the passenger side of the car.

"You make me see things differently." He started the car. "I'm a few steps above cave man thanks to you." He made eye contact with her. "I want to know how you handle it all. I mean, to see their ghosts is hard enough but to learn their stories and care enough to make sure they aren't forgotten is over the top. You do all this while sparking anger among those men who can't handle the strength they see in you."

"I'm not sure how well I'm doing yet. The jury is still out. I like my way and may be a tad selfish too. You know me—I like to believe I'm in control. That's a joke."

****

Peyton was at the store when Jessie returned. Of course, Jessie was bursting with news to tell her cousin about her time with Hoffman. "Before I knew what happened I was plumping his pillows and holding his drink for him." Jessie laughed. "I'm such a pushover sometimes. I'm surprised I was crying over him while I did it."

"More like you gave him what for." Peyton smiled. "I can imagine you standing there passively and smiling sweetly at the man who sent you those awful notes."

"You know me well. That's exactly what I did." Jessie checked out a customer who was ready to leave.

"How does he fit into your investigation, besides stalking you?" Peyton asked as soon as the woman left the store.

"He was hired by someone online to abduct me. It's the one that shot him that concerns me. Hoffman fails a lot at what he does. No follow through. The guy who shot him obviously knows that Hoffman didn't complete his task. I hope Jeremy cracks the money trail soon. Until he does, we all need to be on guard."

Jessie's afternoon picked up when a large group of tourists meandered into the coffee shop and then wandered into her store. Matt told her on the way back from the hospital that they were close to making several arrests but were waiting on evidence regarding suspects which meant he would be busy for the next several days. He loved this phase in a case, but she always missed their time together.

He did promise to come tonight and compare notes. Jessie glanced around her busy store with a sense of satisfaction. At least this part of her life, apart from the ghost hovering in the corner, made her day seem grounded and real.

****

Matt had spent the afternoon on the phone. Jaxon called him with the news he had hoped for regarding Johnson. Gary asked him to come to the tech room to show him what he and Jeremy had found. Matt was closer than ever to finding out who was feeding Zach

Johnson info and was changing files at the station. All he needed was the outside source the information was being directed through. If he found that, he would find Hoffman's shooter. Jess was right. He scratched his head. He had no idea how her mind could put these things together.

He ordered a pizza and texted Jess that dinner would be arriving soon. They needed to talk. His car knew its way to her place like a horse returning to the barn. Still, he would much rather she lived with him. He might have to work harder at convincing her.

Dylan waved at him as he got out of the car. "Nice evening. I'd ask you what you're doing here, but I know it's not to see me." Dylan laughed.

"You've got that right. No offense." Matt chuckled.

"None taken. Enjoy your evening. Katie is flying around the kitchen, and I came out here to stay out of her way. I guess I'd better go help the little woman." Dylan walked up the back steps of the inn.

"Heaven help you if she heard you. Katie is as independent as Jessie. You should have heard the lecture she gave Hoffman at the hospital. He was ready to crawl under the bed and hide." Matt started to walk the path toward Jessie's cottage.

"We sure know how to pick them," Dylan called after him.

"Affirmative. Jessie is a keeper." Matt heard the back door shut when Dylan walked into the inn.

Dylan was right about the evening. Spring was one of Matt's favorite times of the year. Summer meant not only hotter temperatures but more humidity. The winter he managed to survive. He wasn't a fan of the cold or the sticky heat but what was life if you couldn't complain occasionally.

She stood in the open door. He couldn't help himself. He pulled her into his arms and kissed her soundly. When she started to move away, he hugged her tighter and kissed her again. "Best greeting ever, sweetheart. I needed that." He kicked the door closed behind him. "Pizza will be here in a minute along with Jaxon and Peyton. We need to talk."

Matt and Jaxon did most of the talking. Matt wanted to impress upon the girls the next couple of days might get rough. The first arrests were happening tomorrow, and Matt knew that with them some rats would climb out of the sewer to vent their anger. He left the cousins with a warning, but his gut told him it wasn't enough.

Chapter Forty-One

Jessie's day started with her normal morning routine alongside of Matt's warning ringing in her ears. She spent the night thinking over every possible scenario, but no way could she account for a lone wolf who was bent on hurting her. Matt did his best to press home several things to watch for. Besides not remembering everything he said his handsome face was a major distraction. She would have to go with her instinct and hope that it worked. He often confused her with his logical approach to everything, and at some point she often quit listening. She didn't mean to but it was a bad habit she learned early in life.

Jessie waved at Reba in the coffee shop. "I'll be right there. I'm getting us a morning nosh and tea," Reba mouthed.

Jessie nodded. "See you in a few." She continued readying her store to open until Reba knocked on the doors and Molly followed her in when Jessie held them open. "You're here early. What's on your mind?"

"Plenty, but I also thought you could use some company this morning. I knew when my eyes opened this morning, dear, that this would be an eventful day. Drink your tea. Everything is better on a cup of tea in the morning."

"If only it was that simple." Jessie sipped her beverage looking over the cup at her friend. When she saw the ugly bruise on Reba's forehead, she got angry all over again. She would be ready next time.

"Of course, life isn't trouble free, but tea has a way of soothing the worries if only for a moment." Reba stirred her tea and carefully placed the spoon on the napkin beside her cup. "So, what's up?"

"Matt texted me earlier and they are making several arrests this morning and searching the premises of the training facility. He's concerned that as word gets out it will move up the timetable. I know he's right but I'm not sure what I can do about it. I'll do my best to be ready, and I don't want you around. The last time, you got hurt, and I don't want anything to happen to you again."

"I'll leave just as soon as we are finished with our tea and not a minute sooner." Reba lifted her cup to her mouth. "You were brought into this investigation for many reasons, my dear girl. The first being Sofia and to help her and the other girls. Kimama wanted you to find the missing and forgotten girls. You heard their killer's voice at some point, and you'll know when you hear the familiar voice again. That's why you were told to remember what you saw and heard."

"That's how I feel about it too. We are about to find out." Jessie finished her tea hoping to send Reba on her way. She couldn't be at her best if she were worried about Reba.

Reba stood to leave gathering her belongings. "You girls need to know that it's not simply a gift or even genetics that gives you the sight you have but rather that the gift is who you are. It's part of your genetic makeup yes, but you give the use your unique spin. Like mine is unique to me. I see many adventures in your future." She looked off in the distance.

"You mean like our trip to faraway places?" Jessie asked.

"Maybe. I see you in a lighthouse and few other out of the way places. You girls are a force to be reckoned with." She waved with a smile and walked out the door. "Tell Peyton what I told you."

"I will." Jessie opened the store. "I wonder what she meant by that," Jessie mused. To her way of thinking Reba's words sounded like they were about to become a target for the bizarre and anyone with something to prove. At least that was her modern spin on her words.

****

Timing was everything, the academy stressed during his training, and the element of surprise worked in their favor today. Waiting as their suspects were being processed, Matt couldn't believe how easy the morning had played out. Now if the computers told them the information they were looking for, he would count the day's work a great success.

—The morning went off without a hitch. I'll call you later, sweetheart.— Matt sent a quick text off to Jessie and motioned for Jaxon to enter when he knocked.

"What's up?"

"The tech department at the Agency was able to break around the security system. Do you know any of these names?" Jaxon handed him a list.

"We'll I'll be damned. This answers a lot of questions for me and leaves me with one or two more. At least I can see connections where I couldn't see them before." Matt ran his hand over the scruffy stubble on

325

his chin.

"I thought it might. Maxwell told me to work with you for the next few days until the final arrests are made. He's securing the warrants for the ones on our end. The names with the read marks beside them have been on our radar for a while." Jaxon sat in the chair in front of Matt's desk.

"Are they active agents?" Matt asked.

"One is but the other two are retired. Maxwell is thinking they might have worked with Zach all along and weren't suspected at the time of Johnson's formal accusation. Either way they're active now."

"There are thousands of good cops and agents who do their jobs every day and only a few bad apples that cast shadows on the rest of them. The politicians have always been a bit sketchy."

"What do you want me to do?" Jaxon stood. "You may as well put me to work while I'm here."

"Check on Gary down in tech and while you're walking around listen to any conversations and tell me if you hear anything suspicious. I'm closing in on the source for Johnson who is working here at the station. I hate to believe the possibility of an informant, but I refuse to be taken in again."

"When I worked in Arizona, we had the same issue. Someone was funneling info out of the department. It ended up being a plant. Maybe it isn't any one of your regulars. It could be a newbie planted for the purpose. Hell, it could be a woman. Johnson is a handsome, persuasive guy or, so I've been told." Jaxon chuckled.

"Who told you that?" Matt raised his brows with the question.

"Maxwell, or maybe Jessie. I can't remember which one said it."

Matt studied Jaxon's face. "You're trying to get a rise out of me. Jessie knows him and grasps what he is. She's not taken in by the pretty boy types. Believe me, he tried and never got anywhere with her. It took me a while to break through her defenses. Hell, I still am."

Jaxon stood. "I'll do some more snooping around."

Dylan knocked on the door. "Suspects are ready to be interviewed, and their lawyers are all present and are already talking bail."

"After their preliminary hearing. They know the protocol. We have charging documents." Matt stood.

"Hey, Jaxon. I'm beginning to think you work for us instead of Maxwell. You're here more than there," Dylan told him.

"I'm Tom's liaison when the agency has an invested interest in a case. Your department and the agency's investigations seem to intersect a lot. I'm cool with it. I'll let you know if I see or hear anything."

"First, I want you to sit in with me on these interviews. It was one of your agents that bungled this to begin with." Matt clapped him on the back.

"Works for me." He followed Matt into the first interview room.

The owners of the studio sat side by side with their high-priced lawyer. Matt couldn't help but notice how confident they both looked. He'd like to wipe the smirk off their faces. With the evidence his department had gathered and the strength of their case the cockiness he saw wouldn't be there long.

****

As soon as Peyton walked into the store, Jessie told

her what Reba said to her earlier. "What do you think?"

"It resonates with me. I know the gift is a part of who we are. I even understand why, but I don't know how to embrace the whole idea as a natural extension of my life. I'm sure with time we both will."

"You're probably right." Jessie scrolled through the messages on her phone.

"I've been thinking of the book we're reading. Every case we have been involved in is about bringing closure, giving a voice to those who had none, and telling a part of the world that their life mattered. It seems to me that is how we will embrace this in our life." Peyton reached for the stack of books that Jessie handed to her.

"They go on the shelves." Jessie picked up another stack and began placing them where they belonged. "I like when you come by."

"Cheap labor." Peyton laughed.

"Well, there is that, but you also help me make sense of everything. At least for a few minutes." Jessie got busy with a customer who walked in the door. Peyton picked up her phone to talk to Jaxon.

Jessie had finished placing the man's purchases in the bag when she noticed the two men that walked in from the coffee shop. She recognized Webster right away. The other man, who stood like a sentry guarding the doors, she had never seen before. Jessie had a bad feeling about their sudden appearance and tried to get Peyton's attention. Thankfully, she was watching her.

"May I help you?" Jessie plastered a smile on her face while her insides twisted in knots.

"Well now, little lady, that all depends," Sonny said with a heavy southern drawl and a sick smirk on his face.

The minute Jessie heard him call her little lady she knew who he was. She could play it safe and die or she could die trying to live. She decided the second option worked best for her. She noticed Peyton had slipped out of sight and had to be planning something. Taking a deep breath, she approached him. "I know who you are, and I've seen what you did." She pointed at Sonny. "You killed that beautiful girl, and several others."

"Didn't I tell you, Mack, she would be trouble? There's no way she saw me, I can assure you."

"Oh yes, I did. And I know how you got that nasty bruise you're trying to cover up with makeup. She hit you and got away." Jessie noticed the sweaty sheen on his face. The second man shifted his weight causing his jacket to fall open. Of course, there was a gun. There always had to be one.

"You see, sweet thing, that puts me in quandary. I don't want to hurt a pretty thing like you, but I'm going to have to. You know too much and I kind of like my life."

"Stop all the damn talking. Grab her and let's get out of here," Mack yelled reaching for his gun.

That's when Jessie saw Peyton, who had managed to go out the back into Joe's, kick the man in the side of the head and pin his arm behind his back. His curses filled the air. Several men in the coffee shop helped Peyton secure the man to a chair.

Jessie was free to deal with Sonny. "Did you want something?" She had pulled her gun from the drawer while he was distracted.

"No, can't say that I do," he said looking down at where the gun was pointed at him.

"Who's your friend? You may as well sit because you aren't going anywhere. I figure your welcoming committee should be here in a few minutes. My cousin was on the phone with her boyfriend. He's FBI in case you were wondering." Jessie smiled when Matt's car pulled up followed by several others. "Right on time, Parker," she said to Matt when he rushed in the door.

"We have another one in here," Peyton called out. "He's a bit tied up at the moment but I'm sure you'll want to meet our illustrious town treasurer."

Jaxon grinned when he saw her. "Don't tell me, let me guess. A nifty high kick took him out."

"She was amazing as usual." Jessie explained what had happened. "The Reservation Police will be interested in this guy. I knew the minute he started talking where I heard him before. I bet his house is filled with memorabilia of his awful handiwork."

"You've got nothing on me." Sonny cursed as the cuffs were put on him.

"At the very least, I have someone who can ID you trying to hit on her, but I've also linked you to a crime syndicate working in the area. Both you and your buddy Mack were on my list to interview. By threatening Ms. Reynolds, you made my job a whole lot easier." Matt glanced at Kip. "Take them away and book them."

"You're always right on time." Jessie smiled at him.

"We need to have a chat. It seems you hardly need me at all. I arrive after the fact. At least let me play the part of your hero once in a while." Matt pulled her into his side.

"I'm sorry. I wasn't thinking about your ego, only our survival." She stroked his cheek and whispered in his ear, "You'll always be my hero."

"Yeah, yeah, so you say." He kissed her and followed Jaxon out the door. "Later, sweetheart. We still need to have our chat."

Chapter Forty-Two

Jessie watched Matt leave as a sigh escaped from her lips. Sonny's sudden use of his fake accent gave him away. When he called her little lady, she recalled how he had said the same thing to a few of those beautiful girls. She hoped never to be called by that so-called endearment again. The twists and turns in this case were enough to leave her wondering how Matt would ever tie up all the loose ends. He would, of course.

After the excitement of the day and the police departed, Jessie had time to think. Matt was easy to love, so why was she so skittish? Life was short and she needed to make up her mind. The whole idea of marriage was a scary proposition to her. It seemed the institution tended to ruin a good relationship. In her heart she knew her thoughts weren't correct, but she hadn't anything to prove them wrong. Still, she loved Matt and couldn't imagine living the rest of her life without him.

Jessie wrestled out the issue the rest of the day. Taking out her pros and cons list she made several entries on the pro side. She made her decision hoping that her choice would prove to be the right one.

"You're quiet, cous." Peyton walked toward her after helping a customer.

"I'm thinking is all. Do you ever wonder if there

are any amazing love stories in our family? I'm obviously not talking about our parents."

"What do you mean by love story?" Peyton asked.

"Passion, you know. A strong love shared for a lifetime through all that life threw at them."

"Do you mean besides Max and Sadie? Their story is awesome if I remember correctly. I would love to find out if there were others. That would be quite a trip through time. One that I would dearly like to take." Peyton smiled at Jessie.

"You could count me in on that trip too." Jessie twisted one of her curls around her finger. "I may need to ask Grams to tell us their whole story and listen this time."

"What brought this on?" Peyton asked.

Jessie explained to her what her thoughts had been. They spent the rest of the day between customers talking about the great love stories in history that they had read. They continued their conversation as they went through the closing routine.

"Matt's my guy, but is it wrong to want us not only to be good together but great?" Jessie's brows furrowed.

"You're the one who must answer that question for yourself. Truthfully, I believe if you discover that special someone who sees you as their world, you're one lucky person. When you do, you have to hold on and enjoy the ride. Think about all those young girls that will never know the joy."

"You're right, of course. I am holding on but still I wonder if there is someone who has led the way in our ancestry. It would be fun to find out. Speaking of Matt, he will be at my house soon. I should get going."

****

Matt couldn't believe how fast the case moved once they unraveled the connections. Jessie was right as usual. To this point, their investigation had connected all but Ben Tso back to Zach Johnson and the prison syndicate he was operating with a few on the outside. Sonny Webster was fulfilling a sick fantasy and getting paid to do it. Thankfully, he didn't know the computer or phone well enough to hide his involvement. Matt watched as his team bagged up evidence and carried it out of Sonny's house and business office. Webster had kept a sick, twisted record of his crimes along with a photograph of each of his victims. All the details would make the investigators' jobs easier. They confiscated Sonny Webster's truck collection, mostly restorations, as well a new one he drove in town. Another team also searched Mack's and one of his employee's offices and homes. Webster was a surprise for him though. Matt had been in and out of the man's store many times during his remodel. *You think you know someone but do you really?*

He had a few more surprises to tell Jessie about when he saw her. Although he doubted he could ever surprise her when it came to a case. She seemed to always be one step ahead of him and more open to the strange than he was. He wondered how he ever got anything straight before she came into his life.

The afternoon had been tedious but profitable. Jaxon was at the prison with Maxwell having a chat with Zach Johnson who was about to be charged with another crime. Matt couldn't say he was sorry after reading his plan for Jessie. Johnson had a love-hate relationship when it came to her. Matt had stolen her out from under his nose which didn't sit well. Zach had been enamored with her, but her ability had put him behind bars. The longer he sat in prison seething the more vengeful he became.

Together, Jessie would help Matt straighten the story out. He liked when they collaborated together.

"I'm heading out." Dylan knocked on his door. "Here' s the search warrants you were waiting for. The judge said he would have the next one for you tomorrow." Dylan placed the warrants on his desk. "The charging documents are being prepared as we speak and will be ready for you in the morning too."

"Thanks, I appreciate your hard work," Matt said. "In the meantime, I want to know what your gut is telling you." Matt frowned as he fingered the warrants looking at the names on the documents.

"I'm not sure what to think other than you never really know people, I guess. I've talked to some of these guys every day as far back as I can remember. I never saw this side of them." Dylan leaned his hip against the wall. "It's one thing to arrest a creep like the doctor hurting those girls but it's another when it's your friend." Dylan pushed away from the wall. "I'll be in early, and we'll get the party started."

"Sounds good."

Matt knew how Dylan felt. He drove toward Jessie's with lot on his mind. It took a while to recognize that he was being followed. He radioed for backup when he saw the gun. Two police cars were sent racing toward his location. Matt made a quick U-turn racing back down Main Street. One of the cars pulled out of a side street in front of the pursing car and the other got behind them. Matt slammed on his brakes, drew his gun, and got out, kneeling behind his open door. The other police did the same. Instead of giving up peacefully the passenger began firing his gun and so did the officers. When the passenger was struck the driver threw out his gun.

"Don't shoot." He lay down on the ground with his hands behind his back.

Kip went to check on the injured man and call for an ambulance. "I've never seen these two around here before."

"They're coming out of the woodwork, and you can bet on them being part of this investigation somewhere. It looks like I'll be working late tonight." Matt sent a text off to Jess to let her know not to expect him anytime soon.

****

Jessie finished reading her book while she waited. "Oh, ye of little patience." She laughed and called to talk to her cousin who said Jaxon was still at work.

Thankfully, Peyton was as bored as she was. They compared their notes on what they got from the book. When Jessie hung up, she continued to think about the investigation, starting with the gym, Sofia Barton, and then the other girls betrayed by those in charge. The criminal indictment would keep the trainer and doctor in jail until their arraignment in court. The owners had already been turned over to their attorneys who paid their bail. She could only hope they didn't get off free seeing they did nothing to help the girls besides paying Anderson to make the scandal go away. They all were guilty on some level for Marcia's death.

She was working her way through her thoughts to the subject of Zach Johnson when Matt texted her that he was on his way. She knew Zach had a hand in covering the crimes of the doctor and trainer under Chief Anderson and he was still benefitting. How had Sonny Webster and Dexter Hoffman hooked up with him? She couldn't wait to hear what evidence Matt found, if any, to support her idea. Was it all cyber linked or was there more real skin in the game?

As far as she was concerned, there had to be more than a few involved in the cover up. How could she ever prove it? That was Matt's job, and she would leave it to him. All she knew was that Johnson was corrupt to the core. He was also once a real ladies' man, and his smile must have stolen a few hearts along the way. Would a few of them be willing to play a part in his organization now? He had come on to her during her first investigation with Matt. Next to Matt, Johnson was a pretty face with no substance.

Jessie rushed to the door when Matt arrived. She let him talk about his day and bounce ideas off her.

"It's late, Jess," he said pulling her into his lap after he sat down. "Man, am I beat."

"You could have gone straight home." She leaned her head on his chest toying with the collar of his shirt.

"I had to see my best girl and I wanted to ask you a question." He stroked his hand through her hair and took a deep breath. "I always relax when I'm with you."

"What's the question?" she asked after he was silent for a few minutes. She pulled her head up to glance at him and make sure he hadn't gone to sleep.

"What're your thoughts about Sonny Webster? How does he play into all this?"

"I'm glad you asked. Remember when I told you about the man with the patch coming into my store?"

She saw him nod. "It got me researching the pirate Blackbeard. At the time I was sure I got lost in one of my proverbial rabbit trails but now I'm not so sure."

"How so?" He perked up.

"Edward Teacher was a quiet, unassuming man, but he took on a sinister persona. Sonny is like Teacher, and he was living out some strange fantasy torturing and hurting young Indigenous women. He has two personalities. His store and charming personality were his cover. I should have put the two together the day he came into my store wearing that bandage and ridiculous patch to cover his black eye. I saw the girl who gave it to him."

"I can always count on you, babe. I'll make dinner tomorrow night and we'll talk."

"About the case?" She got off his lap so he could stand.

"That and our future." He lifted her chin. "Yep, we have some talking to do." He pulled her into his arms resting his chin on her head. "I love you, Jess," He gave her a quick kiss and was gone.

****

Another night that he didn't want to leave her. Matt frowned as the door closed behind him. He started on the path to the car and when he turned to look back at her cottage, he noticed someone run around the side of her house. Reaching for his gun, he stealthily moved toward Jessie's place and hid behind a tree waiting. The motion detector on the front of the house came on and he slowly made his way in that direction. He was sick of this nonsense for one day. He came up behind the guy and pointed his gun at him.

"I hope you have a good reason for being here at

this time of night. Turn around, slowly." When the man turned to face him, Matt was taken aback. "Aren't you supposed to be in prison? I can't wait to hear this one." Matt cuffed the man and took him to the station. And he thought nothing could surprise him anymore.

Chapter Forty-Three

Matt and Jaxon drove home together in the early morning hours after a long night. The story they heard during their last interview was enough to give them both pause.

"I can truthfully say I didn't see that coming." Matt pulled into the garage at home.

"We were just beginning to see the possibility of their scheme but hadn't put the whole picture together and never saw that twist coming. To think Zach Johnson had an identical twin working on the outside. It's mind bending and one for the record books, though it explains a lot." Jaxon opened the car door. "We'd better get a bit of sleep in because we'll be back at it in a few hours."

"You've got that right." Matt dragged in behind Jaxon and made a beeline for his bed. He had planned a special surprise for Jessie, his ultimate charm maneuver that he hoped would be a win for both of them. He smiled and closed his eyes thinking he might just have pulled it off without her getting wind of his plan, which wasn't easy. Damn, he was tired.

****

Jessie awakened with a start. She knew what the missing piece was now. All she had to do was to find out if any of it was real. It seemed liked a fabrication in her mind and yet her heart told she was headed down the right path. Like the crazy day the man with the eye patch and the limp came into her store. As bizarre as it seemed, his appearance pointed her in the right direction. She sent a text to Matt to read in the morning telling him her working theory. When she awakened later, she read his text and laughed.

—We'll discuss this later but damn, how did you come up with that?—

Jessie was excited to find out if her theory was right. Matt didn't call her all day and she went home after closing the store. She still hadn't heard from him. Nothing about this case seemed normal, but then again none of theirs had been since the beginning.

Jessie sent a text back to him.

—Come for dinner. I know you said you would make me dinner but let me make you something instead. I'll keep it warm.—

With her store hopping most of the day she barely had a spare moment to plan a special meal for her tired guy. Thankfully, Molly came to her rescue with several wonderful ideas she could add her own flare to. The aroma whiffing through her kitchen proved the merit of Molly's suggestions and added to the ambience of her small, cozy kitchen. When Matt called to say he was on way anticipation built within her. She glanced in the mirror and knew she was ready. "It's now or never, Jessie. Don't mess this up."

****

Matt had seen many odd events in a case, but he hadn't seen this one coming. Jaxon was taken back too. Waving at Dylan, he walked out the station door to his car. Secretly, he was happy to not have to worry about going anywhere but to see Jess. He had no idea what she was making for dinner but at this point even one of her salads would be great because he didn't have to make it.

He went over the proceedings of the past few days and placed them in order to tell Jessie. He didn't want to spend hours going over each incident. Other more interesting thoughts were more to his liking. He wondered about all the times he had driven this route, parked in the spot next to her car, and walked the same path to her cottage. It might be fun to hazard a guess. He smiled when he knocked on her door.

Damn, she's beautiful. Matt pulled her into his arms. "Hey, sweetheart. Something smells good in here."

"Dinner is served." She smiled and led him into the kitchen. "I hope you like chicken parmesan."

"If it tastes as good as it smells I'm sure I will." Matt forked a bite of the chicken and closed his eyes mimicking the look Jessie made when she liked something.

"Okay, I get what you're doing." She laughed. "Does that mean you like it?"

"I do." He filled his plate with more spaghetti and another piece of chicken. "What more could a man ask for, sweetheart? You have brains, beauty, and can cook too. Ours is a match made in heaven."

Jessie laughed. "Even with all the ghosts? Think long and hard, my love. Ours could be a crowded and complicated relationship."

"I'm up to the challenge." He flexed his muscles. "I hope those brownies are dessert. Add a bit of decaf and I would call this a feast."

"Choose your favorite and we can go in the living

and get comfortable. I want all the details." She handed him the brownie he wanted on a plate.

"You already know most of them." He went over the details of the past few days. He added a few that she hadn't heard before.

"Why didn't you tell me you were shot at?" she asked.

"It was a part of a long string of events, and I didn't want you to worry about it."

"You mean no harm no foul? That wouldn't fly with you. Care goes both ways." She frowned and playfully slapped his arm.

"You're right. I should have told you." He took a sip of his coffee.

"What about the owners of the gym? Will they get off with a slap on the wrist?" She took a bite of her turtle brownie.

"Not this time. They are out on bail but face charges and civil lawsuits that will bankrupt their business. Their days of operating a prestigious business are over,"

"I can't say I feel sorry for them, or for Ben Tso for that matter. Jeremy told me he had been on a few of the chat rooms spouting anti-women rhetoric."

"True, but his main problem is alcohol and he'll need help to stay clean. I hope he finds it. He'll be in prison with time on his hands to consider what he's done." Matt licked the chocolate frosting off his lips.

"What about Sonny Webster?" Jessie asked.

"Remember when Reba told you Sonny's brother owned the store, and he supposedly had a heart attack and died? Truth is Sonny needed a cover for his life and he chose his brother's business. It afforded him time to travel and still keep his face in the community. His brother and his wife were collateral damage. He buried them in his backyard when they came for a visit and took over their lives here. Plus, he loved restoring old trucks; he had a few. That's why Winnie described his truck as a new looking old one."

"He murdered his own brother and his wife. That's sick." Jessie shook her head.

"That brings me to the place where I get to ask you a question. Your text this morning was spot on. How did you figure it out?" Matt asked.

"I wasn't sure. I got to thinking about the case we did that had twins involved. Their DNA had similar markers and were different too. It made me wonder if the way Zach could continue to do business was if he had someone on the outside who looked just like him."

"He did. I caught him sneaking around outside of your place the other night. Imagine my shock when he turned around. Zach hid the secret of his twin brother well. The twin cleaned up for him on the outside. He's the one who shot Hoffman and hired the two goons who came after me. He also charmed his way with Carry, one of our new data entry employees, to give him access to the storage room and keep him informed of what was going on at the station. She would send our man out on some false errand promising to keep watch in records and open the door for Zach's twin. It's been an eye-opening few days. I am glad, though, that it wasn't any of our long-term staff helping Johnson." He leaned his head back against the chair and closed his eyes.

Chapter Forty-Four

Jessie had no idea how long she watched Matt sleep not wanting to wake him, and yet desiring to at the same time. In her heart she knew she had made the right decision. Love was a strange emotion. The passion of her feelings for the man reached up and grabbed her by the throat until she could scarcely contain herself. She wanted to wake him and tell him, but she waited.

"Jess, I'm sorry. I didn't mean to fall asleep on you." Matt rubbed his eyes. "You're a beautiful sight to wake up to, though."

"Do you want to go home?" she asked hoping he would say no.

"Not yet. When I'm with you I feel like I am home." He glanced at her. "Being here is where I want to be." He slipped over to the couch where she sat.

"Matt, you know I love you, don't you?" She saw him nod. "In fact, if I remember correctly, I'm the one who asked you to marry me first." She smiled at his facial expression. "And you did promise me to be fair, continue to work cases with me, and not to tell me what to do without asking first." She leaned her head on his shoulder.

"True, but I asked you in front of all our friends and family making it official when I slipped this ring on your finger." He touched the ring on her hand. "And I did accept all of your conditions, didn't I?"

"Yes, you did." She caressed his cheek. "You've been perfect, and I love you even more today if that's possible."

He reached for her hand. "Jess, sweetheart, if you keep this up, we won't do any more talking."

"Sorry—it's just when it comes to you I get a bit carried away." She fluttered her lashes at him.

"That's nice to hear." He held her face between his hands. "Now it's my turn. You know I love you, sweetheart." He leaned close and kissed her. "With that said, I'm not as sweet as you. I'm not above the use of bribery to get what I want." He waggled his eyebrows at her and reached for something inside his jacket. "I have a gift for you."

"For me?" Jessie tried to guess what was in the large envelope. Her hand shook as she opened it and pulled out the contents. She jumped up and squealed. "Oh, Matt. Tickets to Ireland." In her excitement she hugged him tight. "How did you know?"

"A little birdie told me you had a dream. I've been keeping it a secret, which isn't easy when it comes to you. They're for you, Sadie, and Peyton. I told you I'm willing to stoop to bribery. As for an exotic location, you'll only do that with me. You see, I'm hoping that you'll miss me so much that when you get back you'll set a wedding day." He paused and started to say something more.

Jessie put her fingers to his lips. "Not yet. I can't imagine a more wonderful gift. But in all fairness, I need to tell you that I've been thinking about the perfect date for our wedding for many days now. I'm ready to marry you. But I've been wondering about something."

"What, sweetheart?" He looked intently at her.

"What's going on in that pretty little head of yours?"

"Will ours be one of the great love stories? You know, passion until death parts us." She gazed into his incredible blue eyes. At the moment they were a smoldering azure and she saw the answer she needed to see.

"Go search, my love. You know you want to, and then come home to marry me, Jess. Name the date and time and you'll see how passionate our love can be." He ran kisses down her cheeks until he captured her lips in one long, delicious kiss.

Jessie sighed, leaning her head back against his shoulder breathing in his scent. She could live with his answer and with this romantic man for a lifetime.

A word about the author…

I am a multi-published, award winning Amazon best-selling author who writes romantic suspense with a touch of the paranormal. I enjoy writing fiction. The character development, their stories, and the twists and turns in the plot intrigue me. Once I let the characters loose, I can't wait to see where they take me. I'm hooked from the first words on the paper, and I have to keep writing to see how the story ends. Layer by layer I build it until I come to the happy conclusion.

I live in Colorado with my husband and family. I am a member of the RMFWPAL (Rocky Mountain Fiction Writers Published Authors League) and have enjoyed becoming involved in my community as one of the many authors living in Colorado. I invite you to read one of my Blue Cove Mysteries and see for yourself why Blue Cove is a special and unusual place. http://www.ionamorrison.com

Thank you for purchasing
this publication of The Wild Rose Press, Inc.

For questions or more information
contact us at
info@thewildrosepress.com.

The Wild Rose Press, Inc.
www.thewildrosepress.com

www.ingramcontent.com/pod-product-compliance
Lightning Source LLC
Chambersburg PA
CBHW072314020726
47501CB00002B/502